A Candy Shop Mystery

Peppermint Twisted

Sammi Carter

BERKLEY PRIME CRIME, NEW YORK

THE BERKLEY PUBLISHING GROUP
Published by the Penguin Group
Penguin Group (USA) Inc.
375 Hudson Street, New York, New York 10014, USA
Penguin Group (Canada), 90 Eglinton Avenue East, Suite 700, Toronto, Ontario M4P 2Y3, Canada
(a division of Pearson Penguin Canada Inc.)
Penguin Books Ltd., 80 Strand, London WC2R 0RL, England
Penguin Group Ireland, 25 St. Stephen's Green, Dublin 2, Ireland (a division of Penguin Books Ltd.)
Penguin Group (Australia), 250 Camberwell Road, Camberwell, Victoria 3124, Australia
(a division of Pearson Australia Group Pty. Ltd.)
Penguin Books India Pvt. Ltd., 11 Community Centre, Panchsheel Park, New Delhi—110 017, India
Penguin Group (NZ), 67 Apollo Drive, Rosedale, North Shore 0632, New Zealand
(a division of Pearson New Zealand Ltd.)
Penguin Books (South Africa) (Pty.) Ltd., 24 Sturdee Avenue, Rosebank, Johannesburg 2196,
South Africa

Penguin Books Ltd., Registered Offices: 80 Strand, London WC2R 0RL, England

This is a work of fiction. Names, characters, places, and incidents either are the product of the author's imagination or are used fictitiously, and any resemblance to actual persons, living or dead, business establishments, events, or locales is entirely coincidental. The publisher does not have any control over and does not assume any responsibility for author or third-party websites or their content.

PUBLISHER'S NOTE: The recipes contained in this book are to be followed exactly as written. The publisher is not responsible for your specific health or allergy needs that may require medical supervision. The publisher is not responsible for any adverse reactions to the recipes contained in this book.

PEPPERMINT TWISTED

A Berkley Prime Crime Book / published by arrangement with the author

PRINTING HISTORY
Berkley Prime Crime mass-market edition / December 2007

Copyright © 2007 by The Berkley Publishing Group.
Cover art by Jeff Crosby.
Cover design by Steve Ferlauto.
Interior text design by Kristin del Rosario.

ISBN: 978-0-425-21227-1

BERKLEY® PRIME CRIME
Berkley Prime Crime Books are published by The Berkley Publishing Group,
a division of Penguin Group (USA) Inc.,
375 Hudson Street, New York, New York 10014.
The name BERKLEY PRIME CRIME and the BERKLEY PRIME CRIME design are trademarks of Penguin Group (USA) Inc.

PRINTED IN THE UNITED STATES OF AMERICA

10 9 8 7 6 5 4 3 2 1

For my Dad,
who filled my life with wonderful memories.
I miss you.

Chapter 1

"Thank God you're there, Abby," Rachel Summers shrilled into the phone. "I need you at the artists' guild right away."

"Now? Are you kidding?" I was up to my elbows in melted chocolate, peanuts, marshmallow, and raisins, trying desperately to finish the second of three batches of Rocky Road Drops I needed to make that morning. Any minute, my brother and his friends would show up to work on the repairs to the second floor of the old building that housed my candy shop, Divinity, on the first floor and my tiny apartment on the third.

"I'm serious," Rachel insisted. "The committee is falling apart right in front of my eyes."

She was talking about the arts festival committee, which we'd both been serving on for the past six months. Under the direction of Meena Driggs, the committee ran like clockwork, and so far, planning had gone as smoothly as anyone could have asked. So smoothly, in fact, that in a moment of weakness I'd agreed to become

Meena's second-in-command—a decision I was beginning to rethink now that we were gearing up for the real work.

I didn't let Rachel's panic worry me. Emotions had been simmering for days all over town and boiling over into arguments between members of the guild over the smallest things. Keeping folks calm and smoothing ruffled feathers had become my domain.

"I really can't come right now," I said. "Just tell me who's done what, and why."

"All hell's broken loose, that's what. The whole arts festival is ruined. You have to do something *right now*, before somebody gets hurt."

I rolled my eyes at Rachel's over-the-top reaction. At that precise moment, a saw buzzed to life on the second floor, proof that Wyatt and his friends had arrived. Plugging one ear, I did my best to tune out the noise overhead. "Give me details," I said. "I can't fix what I don't know about. So tell me, who's on the hot seat this time?"

"Felicity Asbury and that idiot Jeb Ireland."

Felicity was one of the wealthiest (and most thoroughly unlikable) people in Paradise, and Mayor Ireland would probably break his own neck to make her happy. We didn't need either of them sticking their fingers in the pot at this stage of the planning.

"What have they done?"

"You're not going to believe this," Rachel warned. "Jeb showed up about an hour ago and told Meena she was out. Just like that."

I didn't know whether to be more disappointed or outraged. Meena Driggs is one of the most organized people I know, which made her the obvious choice to head the festival planning committee. She'd put heart and soul into the work she'd been doing, and without her, some of us would have given up long ago.

The scales tipped toward outrage. "Jeb can't do that."

"Wait," Rachel said, cutting me off. "It gets worse. Guess who he put in Meena's place."

Something sour churned in my stomach. "Felicity?"

"Bingo."

Felicity had a history of taking over where she wasn't wanted. Back when I was a kid and Felicity was still married to her first husband, she'd stirred up a fuss over the judging of a talent show at the local junior high school. My mother had been President of the PTA that year, and I'd overheard enough to know that Felicity didn't hesitate to play dirty. Just the thought of working with her made my mouth pucker.

"The minute Jeb left, she started giving orders," Rachel went on. "She's already made such a mess, I don't think we'll ever get things straightened out. She told Nicolette to refund Rasheed Vanderkamp's registration because people might 'feel uncomfortable' if he's around. She gave Shellee Marshall a dress code because she says Shellee dresses too provocatively, and she told Kirby North that she wants final approval of every piece he intends to exhibit so she can make sure he doesn't put out anything that's politically inflammatory. Meena's furious, and half of the artists are threatening to walk out on the festival."

Rachel was right. We had a disaster on our hands. "Where is Meena now?"

"I have no idea. She stormed out of here about twenty minutes ago. I'm telling you, Abby, this place is pure chaos, and word is spreading like a forest fire. People are threatening to pull out of the festival left and right."

Somebody upstairs started hammering, and a sharp pain shot through my head just above my eye. "Who's talking about pulling out?"

"Ask me who isn't," Rachel said. "The list will be a whole lot shorter. Every one of them is demanding a refund. Tonight."

We both knew that wasn't going to happen. There had been a Paradise Arts Festival every year for the past fifteen, but it had always been a weekend event held in early April on the edge of town. This year, after a long, protracted battle, the city council had voted to expand the festival to four days and move the whole thing to late May in the center of town. The changes meant that we'd had to buy new banners, new booths . . . new everything. We'd already spent every penny we'd received in registration fees, and a run on the bank now would kill the festival for this year and probably next.

Something heavy hit the floor above, and the windows in the kitchen rattled. Praying for patience, I closed my eyes and kneaded my forehead. "I don't know what I can do that Meena couldn't," I said after a minute. "This has to be the worst decision Jeb Ireland has ever made."

"No kidding." Rachel took a deep breath and tried again. "I need your help, Abby. I can't handle this myself."

Wyatt and his buddies chose that moment to blurt out a Joe Nichols song at the top of their lungs—and suddenly the idea of leaving for an hour or two didn't seem like such a bad idea after all. Plugging my free ear again, I carried the cordless phone to the kitchen door where the sunshine and blue sky made the afternoon look warmer than it actually was.

My brother had backed his truck up to the outside stairs leading to my third-floor apartment. His toolbox lay open in the truck bed, and half a dozen tools were scattered around it. His carelessness made me crazy at times, but all my warnings had fallen on deaf ears.

"I don't know what I can do," I repeated, crossing to the truck to close the toolbox. "Felicity's not likely to listen to me, especially if she has backing from the mayor."

"Maybe not, but you have to try. Please, Abby? I need your help. I can't handle this on my own."

Back in the kitchen, I checked to see what my cousin Karen, Divinity's newly promoted assistant manager, was doing. Two or three customers browsed the aisles while she rang up a sale. We had business, but it wasn't overwhelming.

I covered the phone and caught Karen's eye. "Rachel's got a problem with the festival. Will you be okay here alone if I leave for a little while?"

Karen shook a few more butter mints into the sample dish and lifted one rail-thin shoulder. She's one of those people who can eat anything and never gain an ounce—a trait I think is unnatural, especially in a candymaker. She nodded and said, "Sure. Just keep your cell phone on so I can call if I need you."

"Will do." Wondering, as I frequently do, how I'd ever get by without Karen, I promised Rachel that I'd be there as soon as possible and disconnected.

Divinity would be fine without me for a little while, but I couldn't say the same about the arts festival. I had no idea what I could do to change Mayor Ireland's mind or keep Felicity under control, but if Meena had skipped out, even for a little while, I couldn't just ignore the trouble brewing at the artists' guild. Thirty minutes now might save us hours of stress later.

It took me fifteen minutes to leave the shop, and another ten to drive to the building that houses the Silver Strike Arts and Crafts Guild—a long stretch of office space on the second floor of a strip mall on the north end of town. Like many of the buildings in Paradise, the outside walls were covered in cedar shake siding to make the building look rustic.

Inside the guild offices, there's space for about twenty artists to work on site. The remaining members work in shops or home studios. I'd never considered myself an artist before, but my great-aunt Grace had been a charter member of the guild, so I'd joined when I inherited Divinity after she died. It just seemed like the thing to do.

I pulled my '95 Jetta into the only space left in the parking lot—a narrow spot too close to a concrete pillar. Eileen Nuttall stood in the window of the Spinning Wheel, hands on hips, a deep scowl on her long face. I waggled my fingers in a friendly wave. Eileen gave me a grudging nod in response, which made me suspect that she'd already heard about the trouble upstairs.

Steeling myself for the task ahead, I climbed the stairs and followed the sound of angry voices to the guild office. That was my first clue that Rachel might not have been exaggerating. The second came when I looked into the guild office and saw a sea of bodies packed together.

I wasn't sure the room could hold one more, but I squeezed inside anyway.

"Just be patient," I heard Rachel shout from somewhere in the back. "We're doing our best to fix this."

Voices rose in protest. I couldn't make out what anyone said, but by that time I was pretty sure I didn't want to.

"Please wait," Rachel shouted again. "If we work together, we can get ourselves back on track."

So many bodies packed into one space took the edge off the spring chill. By the time I'd searched three rooms, sweat trickled down my back and matted the hair on my head. I finally found Rachel standing on a desk in the back office, her face flushed, her eyes a little wild.

Rachel owns Candlewyck, a shop just a few doors down from Divinity, but her life's ambition is to become a plus-size model. Usually she dresses to be seen, just in case, but today her short brown hair lay flat on her head, an oversized T-shirt fell shapelessly from her shoulders, and dark circles of makeup were smudged under her eyes.

"That's not going to be a problem," she shouted to someone standing near the window. "We're going to work out a solution. Felicity Asbury will *not* be taking over. Abby Shaw and I are going to make sure of that."

I sucked in a breath at Rachel's rash promise, and a few nearby heads swiveled in my direction. I resisted the urge to stuff a sock in Rachel's mouth and tried to look like a person who had matters under control.

It wasn't easy.

I'd been a corporate attorney while I lived in Sacramento, and that had put me in plenty of uncomfortable situations, but this was the first time I'd faced an angry mob. I had no real hope that we could keep the promise Rachel had just made, and I wasn't eager to find out what our colleagues would do to us when we failed.

The people nearest to me shifted to look at me, and I realized that Kirby North—all six feet of him—stood just a few feet away. A thick black beard shadowed his face, leaving only a pair of unsettling blue eyes visible. The expression in them wiped out any questions I might have had about his reaction to Felicity's decision to approve his pieces for the festival.

He turned toward me, the muscles of his arms straining beneath his plaid flannel shirt. Kirby has lived in Paradise all his life, and he's a member of the festival committee, but I still don't know him well. He's always been something of a recluse, and he was a rabid environmentalist since long before caring about the world became popular. His parents have been dead for years, he has no brothers or sisters, and if he has any close friends, I don't know who they are.

"You can get Felicity to step down?" His voice rumbled like thunder in a summer storm.

Under normal circumstances, Kirby doesn't intimidate me, but I backed away from his concentrated gaze before I realized what I was doing. I thought about just flat-out admitting my doubts, but people were listening, and I didn't want to add to the hysteria. I whipped up a brave smile and said, "I can try."

"How?"

If I'd known the answer to that, I wouldn't have been so nervous. "I think the first step is to find out why Mayor Ireland decided to make the change he did. I'm sure he had some reason—"

"Yeah," Shellee Marshall shouted. "Felicity rattled her bank account at him."

I ignored the comment, hoping I could cool tempers, not inflame them. "It might also be a good idea to make sure Jeb was following policy when he removed Meena from the committee. Once we have the answer to that, we'll be able to decide on our next step."

Kirby's thick black brows drew together over his nose. "And if he *didn't* follow policy?"

"Then we'll talk to an attorney. Maybe file for an injunction to keep Felicity from taking any action until the matter is settled by the court."

"I thought *you* were an attorney," someone behind me said. "Can't you just do it for us?"

I shook my head. "I haven't practiced law since I came home, and I was never licensed to practice in Colorado. We'll have to hire someone if it comes to that."

Kirby raked me over with that penetrating stare of his. "Fair enough, I guess. But what if Jeb leaves Felicity in charge? What are you going to do about the censorship?"

"We'll cross that bridge if we have to."

Shellee Marshall pushed to the front of the crowd and turned to face the others. "Going to court will cost money. Who's going to pay for it?"

Good question. "We'll all have to stand together," I said. "Just like we always do."

"We've already paid enough," someone else protested. "I'm not paying another dime. I want my money back."

Shouts of approval rose to the rafters. I held up both hands, hoping to quiet the mob, and raised my voice to make myself heard. "I'm on your side," I assured them. "This affects all of us. But if we start pulling out of the festival, we won't hurt Felicity. We'll only hurt ourselves and the rest of the town."

Garrett Roth, a photographer whose nature shots had won an impressive array of awards, leaned into the conversation. "Waiting for courts and attorneys and all that takes time. Time we don't have. I think somebody ought to just go to the mayor and Felicity and lay the cards on the table. Tell them we want her gone or *we're* gone."

"I'd rather talk to Meena first," I began.

"Meena's not here," Kirby snarled. "I'm not waiting for her to finish nursing her tender feelings and get back to work."

I'd never thought of Meena as the type to pout before, but I couldn't deny that it looked like she'd abandoned ship after the first volley. "Look, I know you're upset that she left this afternoon, but she has been in charge of the festival since we started working last year. She may already be on top of the situation."

Shellee laughed through her nose. "Yeah. I'll just bet she is."

Rachel scrambled off the table and came to stand beside me, the exhaustion on her face so heavy I could feel it dragging at me. "I've tried calling Meena's cell phone at least a hundred times," she said, her voice low so it wouldn't carry. "I don't know what's going on with her, but I really think we're on our own here."

I shook my head firmly. "Meena wouldn't do that. She's too responsible."

"And if she's not?"

I refused to even consider the possibility that Meena might have bailed out and left me to deal with the mayor and Felicity. "Maybe the battery on her phone is dead," I suggested. "Or maybe she left the phone somewhere and doesn't have it with her. There could be half a dozen explanations for why she isn't answering."

Rachel glanced at the crowd around us, and I knew she was seeing the same mixture of anger, frustration, curiosity, and expectations that I saw. "I hope you're right," she said under her breath.

So did I. So did I.

Chapter 2

It was after five when I finally left the guild. My head hurt, my eyes burned, and my throat ached from trying to make myself heard over the crowd of angry artists. Rachel and I had managed to ward off the immediate threat of a walkout, and I was feeling pretty good about what we'd accomplished . . . until I took my first full breath of fresh air.

That's when reason returned, and the enormity of the challenge I'd taken on finally hit me. I'd left Karen alone at Divinity for hours already. I just hoped she'd be okay if I left her a little while longer.

The city offices closed at five, but I drove over there on the remote chance that I'd be able to catch Jeb before he left work for the day. By the time I arrived, however, the office building was deserted and locked up tight.

Paradise is a small town, and I'd known Jeb since we were in school together. I considered calling him at home to ask what he was thinking, but I didn't want to approach this problem the wrong way and create more animosity. I'd just have to try to catch him early in the morning.

As I drove along Prospector Street toward home, I ran through a list of questions I wanted answered. First, why had Meena walked out on the committee? Quitting was completely out of character for her. No matter what the others said, I couldn't believe she'd walked away from a fight. Jeb must have presented her with a compelling reason to leave, and I'll admit to more than a little curiosity about what that reason might be.

Even more puzzling, why had Felicity agreed to take over the committee? She'd always considered herself a patron of the arts, but her involvement in the local artists' community was limited. Her tastes were very particular, and she snubbed local artists more often than she supported them. So why was she suddenly all gung ho about the festival and determined to be involved? It didn't make sense.

Since I couldn't see the mayor until morning, I decided to talk with Meena before I did anything else. If Meena wasn't answering her phone for Rachel, she probably wouldn't answer for me, either. Besides, I wanted to talk to her face-to-face. Some conversations are just better that way.

With a silent apology to Karen, I drove past the shop and turned south on Ski Jump. I didn't want to take advantage of my cousin, but I couldn't go back to work as if nothing had happened while festival preparations spiraled out of control.

Fifteen minutes later, I pulled into the driveway of Meena's modest post–World War II home in the foothills known as the "east bench." Her car was parked in front of the garage, and the car's hood felt cool to the touch as I passed by. Apparently, she'd been home for a while, so why wasn't she answering her phone?

She didn't answer the door right away either. I rang the bell twice and knocked once before she finally dragged the door open and peered at me through the opening. Meena's a small woman with a no-nonsense face and a cap of short brown hair, and she didn't look happy to see me. "Abby? What are you doing here?"

"We need to talk. Can I come in?"

Meena shook her head. "This isn't a good time."

"I just came from the guild. It's a madhouse over there. Why did you leave?"

"I thought you would have heard by now. I've been replaced."

"I heard. I'm here to ask why."

Meena's gaze drifted to her hands. "It's a long story."

"I've got time."

With obvious reluctance, she met my gaze. Her dark eyes were dull and lifeless on the surface, but there was something lurking behind them, too. Something I couldn't quite identify. "I had to leave," she said. "Believe me, it was the best thing for everyone."

"I find that hard to believe. What happened? Did the mayor threaten you with something?"

Meena cut a sharp glance at me. "Why would you ask that?"

"Because I know how you feel about the festival, and I don't think you'd leave without a very good reason. So what happened when Jeb and Felicity showed up today?"

"I don't want to get into it."

"Are you kidding? The guild is in chaos. Half of the artists are convinced you're not coming back, and they're demanding refunds of their booth fees. We need you there, Meena. If you'll just tell me what's going on, maybe I can help."

Meena shook her head slowly. "I'm sorry, but it's not something I want to talk about. Not now, not ever."

My head throbbed with frustration, but there wasn't much more I could say, so I decided to stop pushing—at least for now. "Well, whatever's going on, we need to stop it before Felicity really stirs up trouble."

A bitter smile tugged at the corners of Meena's mouth. "Have you ever tried to stop Felicity Asbury when she makes her mind up to do something? She's impossible, Abby. Nobody tells her no."

My mother had, but the fallout had been horrendous. "I know Felicity's a big deal in Paradise, but we can't just sit back and let her take over the festival. Not after all the work you've done to pull it together."

Meena gave a listless shrug. "It doesn't really matter. The artists will complain for a day or two, but they'll accept the change eventually."

I looked deep into her eyes and tried to read what was going on inside them, but all I could see was a lethargy that overshadowed everything else. "Are you feeling all right?"

"I'm feeling fine. Why?"

"*Why?* Because this isn't you, Meena. Why are you letting Felicity take over like this?"

She lifted her chin stubbornly. "I don't have a choice, do I? This is what the mayor wants, so this is what the mayor will get. He thinks Felicity can do a better job with the festival than I can, and now she gets her chance to prove it."

"And you're just going to sit back and let her do it?"

"Would it do me any good to fight her?"

"You won't know the answer to that unless you try."

Meena shook her head and backed a step away from the door. "In some towns you can't fight city hall. In Paradise you can't fight Felicity Asbury. You might as well just accept it. You'll save yourself a lot of trouble." And before I could work up a response to that, she shut the door in my face.

The conversation with Meena left me with a splitting headache. The last thing I wanted to do was talk with Felicity, but I was afraid that if I put off the conversation, I'd lose the support of the artists.

I drove back to Divinity so I could check on Max, the Doberman pinscher I'd inherited a few months earlier. I changed into jeans and a sweatshirt, exchanged the flat black shoes I'd worn to work for sneakers, and clipped Max to his leash.

I wasn't sure whether I was taking Max to the Asbury house because he loves riding in the car or because having him nearby would give me confidence. Either way, listening to Max playing "wind tunnel" as he leaned out the open window and let air rush through his mouth made the drive a lot more pleasant.

The sun was low on the horizon when I pulled up in front of the gate that protected Felicity and her family from the common folk. Fully expecting someone inside to give me the third degree, I buzzed for entry. To my surprise, nobody challenged me, and the gate swung slowly open on mechanical arms.

From the road, I could see part of the rooftop at the crest of the hill. The rest of the house was hidden from view by thick stands of aspen, pine, and spruce. Where the sun could get through the trees, the undergrowth was thick and lush. In other places, only dry needles and dead branches covered the soil. Wondering what Felicity would do when she found out I'd been granted access, I put the Jetta in gear and drove along the deeply shaded drive.

The Drake Mansion, originally the home of Felicity's father, Andrew Drake, had been built of stone cut from local quarries. Though I'd never been close to it before, I'd heard stories about it all my life. But even with all the rumors I'd heard, I wasn't prepared for my first full view of the rambling multistory building that Felicity Asbury called home. The house crowned the top of the hill like a castle. I counted at least four chimneys, a handful of turrets, and twice as many balconies. Huge windows looked out on the scenery from every angle, and I suspected that the view included most of Paradise in the valley below.

A few cars—all newer and more expensive than my Jetta—lined the circular drive in front of the house. A few others had been parked in front of a fence at the bottom of a short hill. I knew Felicity would think it presumptuous of me to park in the drive, but I didn't want to approach the conversation feeling inferior. I pulled in behind a Mercedes, rolled the windows down partway to give Max some air, and set the brake.

Andrew Drake had been a land developer who saw potential in Paradise long before anyone else did. He'd burst on the scene in the early sixties, offering cash for property nobody else considered valuable. He'd made a killing.

Four decades ago this hillside had belonged to Clyde Nixon, a good old boy who'd been smart enough at what he did but naive when it came to the ways of the world. Clyde had believed that the hills around Paradise weren't good for much besides grazing cattle, hunting, and mining. Since he was getting too old to do any of those, he sold out to Felicity's father just two short weeks after Andrew came to town.

Turns out, Clyde's lack of foresight cost his family a fortune. For almost five years, Clyde held on to the belief that he'd taken Andrew Drake for one helluva ride, and he'd said as much to anyone who would listen to him. But eventually, reality caught up with him. From the minute he realized that Andrew had seen what he couldn't, Clyde's attitude toward life had grown more bitter by the day. Every dollar Andrew added to his bank account had been like a knife in old Clyde's heart.

Clyde passed on a few years ago, but his son Lloyd lives on the floor of the valley in a tiny house deep in the shadow of the Drake Mansion. I could see Lloyd's rooftop from where I stood. In the way of small towns everywhere, folks around Paradise stood behind Clyde. Instead of considering him a shortsighted fool, people said he was simply too trusting. Instead of acknowledging that Andrew was farsighted, they blamed him for being greedy and taking advantage of Clyde's trusting nature.

That might explain something about the way Felicity felt toward the people of Paradise, and how we all felt toward her. The truth is, most of us would probably have sold a prime piece of real estate dirt cheap under the same circumstances, and we all knew that we could have too easily ended up in Clyde's shoes. No one liked that one bit.

As I turned away from the view and took a deep breath to prepare for the fight ahead, the roar of an engine cut the silence. A second later, a gray Ford pickup with one blue door shot out from behind the garage, its tires spitting gravel as they battled for traction. When the tires finally caught, I heard the grinding of gears, and the truck raced past, leaving me in a cloud of dust as it disappeared into the trees. The truck looked vaguely familiar, but Paradise is full of old pickups, and since Felicity's second husband, Oliver Birch, was up to his neck in construction of a new restaurant, I didn't give it another thought. Instead, I wondered why Felicity continued to use her first husband's name now that she was married to Oliver. It probably had something to do with business. After all, she'd been an Asbury for a long time and most of her business contacts knew her by that name. Still, I couldn't help wondering if Oliver minded.

I climbed the steps, punched the doorbell, and listened to it echoing inside the massive house. After a while, the door opened, and I found myself looking into the disapproving face of Ursula Drake, Felicity's younger sister.

I hadn't seen Ursula since I left Paradise more than twenty years ago, and the changes in her shocked me. Her once-dark hair was now more salt than pepper, and the years had etched wrinkles into her narrow face. Thanks to a few bad decisions when she was younger, Ursula's share of her father's money had disappeared a long time ago. Now she earned her keep by working as Felicity's assistant.

Her build was sturdier than Felicity's, and each of her features somehow harder, less refined. She kept her hair short, and I swore her face would crack if she ever smiled. It's understandable, though. She'd spent the past thirty years living on her sister's charity. Frankly, living with Felicity under any circumstances would make me ornery.

Ursula gave me a once-over dripping with distaste. If she didn't curl her lip when she spoke, it wasn't because she didn't want to. "Yes?"

I'd spent too many years married to a man who looked down on my family, so Ursula's attitude didn't sit well with me. Money and social class aren't everything. They're not even close to everything.

"Abby Shaw," I said, meeting Ursula's glare head-on. "I'm here to see Felicity."

"Do you have an appointment?"

Since she's the one I would have made the appointment with, she knew damn well I didn't have one. "No, but it's concerning the arts festival, and it's important that I see her right away."

Ursula's spine was already rigid, but somehow she managed to stiffen it a bit more. "I'm afraid that's impossible. If you need to discuss something with her, call and schedule time on her calendar." As if that was that, Ursula stepped back so she could shut the door.

I'd already had one door shut in my face that day, and I wasn't interested in repeating the experience. I planted myself in the open doorway a split second before the door hit. Pain shot up my thigh, but I tried not to let it show. "Why don't you let Felicity know I'm here before you shut the door?"

"That won't be necessary," Ursula snarled. "I know her schedule, and I know she doesn't have time to see you."

Maybe I should have walked away, but I didn't. I didn't want to be here at all, but since I was, I was going to see this through to the end. "Look," I said, refusing to budge, "maybe Felicity doesn't realize it, but she's about to have a mutiny on her hands. If she doesn't talk to me right now, there won't *be* an arts festival."

"I'm sure Felicity can handle whatever it is without you."

"And I'm sure you'd be wrong. You can either tell her that I'm here, or you can refuse, and I'll go away, but if I leave here without a solution, what happens next will be on your hands, not mine."

She had the good sense to back down, but her lips pursed so tightly I knew it must have hurt to do it. "You can wait in the library," she said, yanking open the door so that I nearly fell into the flagstone foyer. Waving one hand toward a large, open doorway on the left, she turned away. "I'll let Felicity know you're here."

With her pointed chin held high, she marched up an ornately carved staircase that looked as if it had been crafted in another century, then stopped on the landing and looked back at me to make sure I was obeying instructions.

What I could see of the house was exquisite, and I would have given almost anything to look around on my own for a minute, but I'd probably pushed hard enough for the time being. With my hands in my pockets, I crossed the foyer and stepped into a richly paneled room filled with so many books I had something close to a religious experience just walking through the door.

Row upon row of leather-bound books drew me into the room as if I'd suddenly slipped into a trance. I trailed my fingers along the spines of old favorites and unfamiliar titles, and took a deep breath, trying to capture that unmistakable scent that brought back memories of the Paradise Library and the bookmobile.

"Ms. Shaw?"

I dropped my hand guiltily and whipped around to face Felicity Asbury. Unlike Ursula, she hadn't changed much at all. Her chin-length hair was still dark, her skin smooth and unlined, but her wide mouth had that unnaturally stretched look that made me suspect that she'd used some of her inheritance to buy that youthful appearance.

Wearing an obviously expensive linen pantsuit, she swept into the library and motioned me toward one of the leather wing chairs flanking the fireplace. Keeping perfectly straight posture my mother would have loved, she sank into a chair and crossed her feet at the ankles. "Ursula tells me there's some kind of trouble with the arts festival?"

"That's right." I sat, feeling large and clunky next to her. "I understand that you paid a visit to the guild this afternoon and started making changes to the work we've done."

She inclined her head—barely—and her mouth turned up at the far edges. "That's true."

"Would you mind telling me why?"

The minuscule amount of warmth there had been in her expression disappeared. "Does it matter?"

"The members of the arts and crafts guild are upset over the changes you're making. They're loyal to Meena Driggs, and they're not interested in having anyone else step in and take over at this late date."

"Is that so?"

"They asked me to talk with you about it."

Felicity waved a hand in the air between us, as if the concerns of the artists meant nothing. "There's no need for anyone to be upset. The changes I intend to make will only make the festival better."

"In your opinion, maybe."

Her lips thinned. "I think that's the point. Tell me, Ms. Shaw, what are you doing here?"

"I'm assistant chair on the committee," I told her. "I want to know why you're doing this when we're just three weeks from the festival."

"I think you've been misinformed. I'm not doing anything except helping the mayor with a difficult situation."

"Really? And what situation is that?"

"If that were any of your business, you wouldn't have to ask me."

"But it *is* my business," I said. "I'm supposed to know what's going on with the committee, but the mayor has made a huge change without saying a word to me. I'm trying to figure out where to go next."

A smile played along the edges of her mouth. "I'm sure someone will be glad to tell you. All you need to know is that the mayor is concerned about the festival, and has been for some time. It became obvious that someone needed to take charge and keep the city from being embarrassed."

I fought the urge to wipe the smile off her face. "If that's true, why hasn't he said anything to us?"

Felicity shook her head. "I can't speak to the mayor's reasons. You'd have to ask him. He mentioned his concerns to me, I offered to help, and he accepted my offer. Beyond that, I don't know anything, and I certainly didn't think it was my place to question him."

I wasn't buying the demure act, but calling her on it would only make her more determined to win. "That may be," I said, "but the members of the guild are unhappy about the change. Already they're talking about boycotting the festival."

A tinkle of laughter that sounded surprisingly girlish escaped Felicity's stretched-out lips. "People always make big threats when they don't get their own way, but nobody will follow through. They wouldn't dare."

Her self-assurance chipped away at my patience. "I wouldn't be so sure if I were you. I've been sent to tell you that if you don't step aside, they'll all pull out."

Felicity's smile faded ever so slightly. "Really, Abby, think about this rationally for a minute. These people struggle all year long to get a little exposure to the public. If they refuse to exhibit at the festival, they'll only be hurting themselves." She relaxed her posture, and her expression grew more self-satisfied. "They certainly won't be hurting me."

"I don't think the members of the guild care if they're hurt by this," I said, sparing her a brittle smile of my own. "They're standing on principle."

Felicity laughed again, and she relaxed enough that her back actually brushed against the chair. "Principle is a nice word and a pretty dream, but when push comes to shove, people don't actually sacrifice for principle. It's all about the bottom line, Abby. You'll do well to remember that. And for the record, I have no intention of stepping aside just to placate a handful of artists with 'principle.'"

"And if they make good on their threat to boycott the festival?"

"They won't." She stood abruptly.

Apparently, the conversation was over. "Meena has friends in Paradise," I said, standing to face her. "The members of the guild are loyal to her. Unless she's done something wrong, I'm afraid things might get ugly."

Felicity's eyes grew hard. "Are you threatening me?"

I let out a harsh laugh. "Don't be melodramatic. I'm just warning you that in spite of what you believe, some people might actually feel strongly enough about this to take a stand."

"I see." All expression left her too-smooth face. "Well, why don't you let everyone at the guild know that I have no intention of making anyone do anything that's distasteful to them. If people feel that strongly about me stepping aside, they needn't feel obligated to have a booth at the festival. Just let me know who these principled people are, and I'll solve the problem by removing them right now."

"You can't do that!" The protest escaped my lips before I could stop it. "They've paid good money for their booth space."

Felicity's gaze bored into mine. "I most certainly can do

it. Booth space is allocated by the committee, and as of this afternoon, I *am* the committee. If their principles are so precious, they won't care about a few measly dollars, now will they?"

She was an awful woman. Worse even than I'd imagined. No wonder the guild members were up in arms over her involvement. "You're making a huge mistake," I warned. "The town won't stand for this."

"Well, we'll see, won't we? But I'll tell you what. Since you so obviously feel strongly about this whole thing, why don't you and I prove how serious I am? I know that your little shop has booth space reserved at the festival. Why don't we just scratch your name off the list right now and show the rest of your friends how it's done?"

Chapter 3

Felicity's threat knocked the air out of my lungs. It hung in the air between us while I fought to start breathing again. "You can't do that," I croaked. "Divinity has had a booth in the arts festival every year since the festival began."

Felicity turned away, but I glimpsed the gleam of satisfaction in her eyes before she did. "Yes, I know. It's too bad that you decided to change that, isn't it?"

Seething, I grabbed her arm and jerked her around to face me. "You can't kick Divinity out of the festival just because I said something you don't like. There are rules. Laws."

Felicity looked pointedly at my fingers on her sleeve. "Take your hand off me, Ms. Shaw."

"Not until you change your mind."

One perfectly arched eyebrow rose. "And just how do you intend to make me do that?"

I had no idea, but I wasn't going to tell her that. Besides, it's not a good idea to show your opponent the cards in your hand. "You're being completely unreasonable."

"I'm not the one resorting to physical assault."

I don't often feel like hitting someone, but I had to force myself to pull my hand from her arm. She was crazy, but she also had a lot of clout, and I didn't need her filing a lawsuit against me. "You haven't heard the last from me," I said, struggling to keep my voice level. "I'll see you in court."

Her eyes glittered hard and cold. "That's fine. We'll see whose money runs out the fastest. I believe you can find your way out?" Without waiting for an answer, she swept from the room.

Steaming, I pushed out into the foyer. I barely registered the sound of tires on the drive outside, but I started paying attention when footsteps thundered up the front steps. A second later, the front door banged open, and Felicity's daughter, Jacqueline, stood framed in the sunlight. Even from a distance I could tell she was almost as furious as I was. I was surprised to see her there. As far as I knew, she and Felicity hadn't been on speaking terms since Jacqueline got pregnant her sophomore year of high school.

If I hadn't known they were related, I never would have guessed that Jacqueline Asbury was Felicity's daughter. Jacqueline is a couple years younger than me, overweight, broad-faced, and coarsely featured. When Jacqueline and I were kids, Felicity tried everything to turn her daughter's mousy brown curls into something sleek and sophisticated, but nothing had ever seemed to work.

Her hair still corkscrewed away from her face in uncontrolled curls, but she'd dyed the unremarkable brown a new shade of auburn, rich and dark and almost pretty. But it was hard to tell if it suited her at the moment. Her chest heaved, and her round face was mottled, either from emotion or the effort of climbing the stairs.

The door hit the wall with a crash, and Felicity turned on the stairs with a glare of disapproval. "Really, Jacqueline. A little decorum, please."

"The hell with decorum," Jacqueline said as she lunged across the foyer. "I swear, Mother, you've crossed the line this time. I could kill you for what you've done."

"Jacqueline, please. We have a guest." Felicity turned a pointed gaze in my direction, and Jacqueline seemed to see me for the first time.

She didn't say a word, but color flooded her cheeks, and she moved aside to let me leave. I'd have given anything to watch somebody topple Queen Felicity, but I had no excuse for staying, so I stepped past her into the cool mountain air.

The only coherent thought I had as I hurried down the steps toward my car was that if Jacqueline wanted to kill her mother, she'd have to stand in line to get her chance.

I drove back into town with the windows down, hoping the breeze would help clear my mind. It didn't. I pulled into the driveway beside Divinity just as my brother clambered down the steps at the end of his workday. He stood beside his truck, stroking his mustache and watching as I parked.

Wyatt is five years older than me and, frankly, looks every minute of it. Must be all the time he spends out in the sun. Or the years he spent smoking before his wife convinced him to quit. Or the fact that he's too damn cantankerous for his own good.

His cocoa brown eyes were barely visible amid the smile lines, and the thick swags of his handlebar mustache drooped over his mouth. We'd never been particularly close as kids, but our relationship took a direct hit when I left home for college. It's not that Wyatt was jealous. School never was his strong suit. He just resented the fact that I left Paradise, got married while I was away at school, and came home only sporadically after that. I'd spent the whole time resenting Wyatt's resentment, and the walls between us had grown a little stronger with every passing season.

Since coming home after my divorce, I've stopped even trying to pretend that I'd been right. My marriage had been unhealthy on nearly every level, and though I'd love to blame Roger for the entire mess my familial relationships were in now, I have to shoulder responsibility for my part in it. Since our parents had moved to Denver to be near bus lines and doctor's offices, Wyatt and I were pretty much on our own to figure things out between us.

My brother gave me a chin lift in greeting as I got out of the car. "Where've you been?"

"Don't ask." Max tugged toward the patch of flowers that separate Divinity from Picture Perfect, the shop next door. I relaxed the death grip I had on the leash, and he got to work sniffing out a perfect spot to take care of business.

I stood beside Wyatt and saw that in the time I'd been gone, he'd once again littered his truck bed with tools. "You ought to be more careful," I said, just as I always did. "Anybody could walk off with your stuff when you're not looking."

Wyatt rolled his eyes, just as he always did. "This is Paradise, sis. Things like that don't happen."

"They happen everywhere."

"Look, Abby. I've been living this way for forty-five years, and I'm not going to change just because you think I should."

"It's just a friendly warning," I said with a shrug. "No skin off my nose."

Wyatt dropped the tools he was holding into the metal box. "What's eating at you tonight?"

I'm not in the habit of confiding in Wyatt because, like so many men, he thinks he needs to fix all my problems. That always causes trouble, because I'm no good at taking advice. But I was so frustrated, words tumbled out of my mouth before I could stop them. "Nothing, really. Or everything. I just got back from seeing Felicity Asbury."

Wyatt looked at me as if I'd lost my mind. "What in the hell did you do that for?"

I hitched myself onto the tailgate of his truck. "Jeb

Ireland kicked Meena off the festival planning committee this afternoon and dropped Felicity into her spot. Meena's thrown up her hands and walked away, and everybody else is threatening to pull out of the festival unless Felicity steps down. They talked me into delivering the ultimatum."

"And you agreed?"

"Long story." I didn't feel like explaining my reasons. I didn't think Wyatt could appreciate the emotional complexity involved. "And before you ask, no, it didn't do any good. Not only did she refuse to step aside, she threatened to yank Divinity out of the festival completely."

Wyatt cocked a sidelong glance at me. "She can't do that, can she?"

"Not legally, but she'll try. I told her I'd see her in court, and that's exactly what I should do, but I don't have the time or the money for a court battle."

"Just as well," Wyatt said, leaning against the bumper of his truck and scratching his forehead with a thumb. "If you took that old battle-ax to court, you'd lose."

"Why? Just because she's the richest woman in town?"

Wyatt slanted a look at me. "Because she's the richest and most influential person in Paradise, and she always gets what she goes after."

I gaped at my brother, who'd said all of that with a straight face. "So I should just step back and let her do whatever she wants? Didn't you hear me? She wants to kick Divinity out of the festival just because I offended her." Max finished inspecting flowers and decided to investigate Wyatt's bumper. "We've already paid for the booth and planned what we're going to sell, but that's not what upsets me. The cost of the booth space was minimal, and I haven't ordered the supplies yet. The point is, Divinity's had a booth every year since the festival started, and now, as soon as I take over, Felicity threatens to kick us out. If the family finds out about this, they'll string me up."

The family I was referring to included all the cousins who resented me for inheriting Divinity. In spite of her hurt feelings, Karen had pitched in to help, but the others hadn't been nearly so obliging. At least half of them were just waiting for me to fall flat on my face.

Wyatt conceded my point with a dip of his head. "I never said you should back off and let her do whatever she wants. But if you take her on in a straight-up fight, she'll mow you down. She's made too many contributions to too many campaign funds over the years."

"So you're saying that she's got people in her pocket?"

"Oh, not officially. At least I don't think so. But she's had her finger in half the buildings that have gone up around here lately. Practically ruined the town, if you ask me, but Jeb Ireland thinks the sun rises and sets on her."

I pulled my knees up under my chin. "So then how do I fight her?"

"Carefully."

I made a face at him. "Gee, that's helpful."

Wyatt grinned. "You want me to beat her up for you?"

I chuckled at the offer. "Oh, yeah. That'd fix everything." My smile faded, and I shook my head. "Thanks, but this is my battle, not yours."

"So what are you going to do about it?"

That was the million dollar question. I was just surprised that Wyatt had asked it instead of telling me what to do. "I don't know, but I'll think of something."

"I'm sure you will."

Max jumped onto the tailgate to sit beside me. I scratched his head and studied the building that now held my entire life inside. Thanks to Aunt Grace's notorious flair, I now own a graceful old building that dates back to the early days in Paradise history. It was originally the territorial jail, so the building is filled with plenty of cubbyholes, nooks, and crannies. The store and kitchen take up the first floor, and I live on the third. Storage rooms and a large, airy meeting room—a courtroom during much of the nineteenth century—occupy the second level.

"How's the remodeling going?" I asked when I realized Wyatt was waiting for me to say something.

He shrugged. "Slow but sure, I guess. We ran into a nasty nest of old wiring this afternoon. You're going to need an electrician to check it out for you."

"I can't afford an electrician," I reminded him. "That's why you're working for me, remember?"

He slapped the side of the truck with one palm, then moved to the back, ready to close the tailgate. "If you need help with Felicity, let me know."

"I'll do that," I promised as Max and I scrambled down, but I think we both knew that wasn't going to happen. I had to create my own space in Paradise, and there was only one way to do that. Hiding behind my big brother wasn't it.

My alarm went off at six the next morning, jerking me out of a troubled sleep long before I was ready. Determined to sleep at least ten minutes longer, I hit Snooze and snuggled down into my pillow.

I'd stayed up for a while trying to come up with a way out of my predicament. I'd finally crashed around midnight, still without any solutions. Taking Felicity to court would be the best way to punch a hole in her sails, but Wyatt was probably right about my chances of winning. Besides, I had no way to pay an attorney to represent me. I could have gone to court without an attorney, but I'd still have to come up with the money for filing fees and other court costs. I couldn't spare the cash or the time a lawsuit would take away from the store.

Face it, Felicity had us all over a barrel. This morning I'd have to tell the members of the guild that I'd failed them. I wasn't looking forward to doing it, but I couldn't leave them clinging to false hope.

I might have gotten that extra ten minutes of sleep if

Max hadn't started whining that he needed to go out, but time and dogs wait for no man. Still too groggy to think, I stumbled into the kitchen and started coffee. Once it was gurgling contentedly, I headed back to my bedroom, where I tugged on sweatpants and a sweatshirt and ran my fingers through my hair.

By the time I was dressed, Max was at the front door trying to dig his way out. I left the coffee brewing, stuffed a couple of plastic bags into my pocket, and slipped my feet into an old pair of loafers. Clipping Max to his leash, I led him outside.

I stood for a minute on the porch, letting Max sniff the air while I yawned, stretched, and let my eyes adjust to the brilliant spring sunshine. I'd left my dark glasses inside, so I didn't see the Mercedes in my parking lot until I was halfway down the staircase. I could see the shadow of someone sitting behind the steering wheel, staring straight ahead, but the windows were tinted too dark for me to see who it was. Probably a customer waiting for Dooley Jorgensen to open Picture Perfect, Divinity's neighbor on the uphill side of the street.

Curious, Max tugged me toward the car. I wasn't in the mood to make small talk with anyone, so I tugged back on the leash and kept him walking straight. At the sidewalk, we turned uphill. Max lowered his nose to the ground to begin his search for a good spot to take care of business. I tried to decide the best way to present the bad news to the guild. Could I talk them into using the court system to fight this battle, or would they ignore me and walk away from the festival? I wanted to think I could make them listen to reason, but I was afraid we'd lose too many artists to make the event a success.

Preoccupied by my thoughts, I didn't pay close attention to my surroundings until Max dragged me around the corner of Forest Street. Too late, I realized that someone was standing directly in front of me. I tried to swerve, but I ran straight into a man standing just outside Bonner's

Bakery. He stood a foot taller than me, and his broad shoulders and sturdy build left me feeling as if I'd run into a brick wall.

I let out an embarrassed laugh and backed away. The man danced sideways to avoid Max, then put a steadying hand on my shoulder. "Good morning, Abby. You're in an awful hurry aren't you?"

As soon as he spoke, I recognized Oliver Birch, Felicity's most recent husband. His silver hair ruffled in the light breeze, and a smile stretched across his open, friendly face. He was so different from Felicity, so different from her first husband, I've never been sure what brought the two of them together. The story floating around Paradise was that they'd met at a party hosted by one of Felicity's society friends in Denver. Oliver had been dabbling in construction, and Felicity's position as head of Drake Development had given them a common interest. The cynic in me thinks Oliver is probably just attracted to Felicity's bank balance, but even after my divorce, I have a small romantic streak that doesn't want to believe that.

Oliver has been a customer at Divinity a few times, but I was surprised that he knew my name. On the other hand, I had found him sitting with Wyatt and his crew talking construction once or twice in the past few weeks, so maybe I shouldn't be.

"Sorry," I said, backing away quickly while Max gave Oliver's khaki-clad leg a sniff. "I wasn't paying attention."

"No harm done. Are you all right? You look like a woman with a lot on her mind."

"I guess I am a little preoccupied," I admitted. I wondered if he knew what his wife had been up to in the past twenty-four hours. If he did, how did he feel about it? I was dying to ask, but years of training at my mother's knee made me stifle my curiosity and ask, "You're out and about early, aren't you?"

Oliver jerked his chin toward the building under construction across the street. "Have you forgotten that I'm a working man? Gotta ride herd on those construction crews, or they'll do nothing but sit around all day. You probably don't run into that problem with your guys, do you?"

I laughed and shook my head. "If they want to sit around, I'm not exactly in a position to be upset about it. So you're here every morning to keep an eye on them?"

"Just about."

I wondered how his crew felt about that.

As if he could read my mind, he said, "It's not as bad as it sounds. I'm usually doing two or three things at once. This morning, I'm meeting with my new chef to talk about the menu for the restaurant."

"You've found a chef, then?" Last I heard, he'd still been trying to woo one.

"Indeed I have. His name is Henri Guischard. Do you know of him?"

"No," I admitted, "but I don't run in gourmet circles."

"Well, if you don't know of him now, you soon will. He trained in France, and he's spent the past ten years at one of the top restaurants in New York."

"Impressive. How did you find him?"

"With a lot of work. You'll like what he does, I'm sure. He's creative and talented, and his presentations are breathtaking. But enough about me. What has you so pre-occupied this beautiful morning?"

I debated for a second over whether to tell him, but he'd been married to Felicity long enough to know what she was like. Besides, maybe he could offer a suggestion or two. "It's the arts festival," I said. "Things have been hectic since yesterday."

"Oh? What happened yesterday?"

"You don't know?"

Oliver gave his head a shake. "Should I?"

"I thought Felicity might have told you. The mayor put her in charge, and that's upset a lot of people."

"In charge of the arts festival?" Oliver smiled slowly. "I shouldn't be surprised, I guess. Every time I turn around, she's involved in something new."

"Yes. Well. The festival is just three weeks away, and the artists don't want Felicity coming in and making changes at this late date."

"I'm sure they'll appreciate what Felicity has in mind once they see the whole picture."

He had more faith in everyone concerned than I did. "I don't think they'll give it that long," I told him. "The artists are already threatening to pull their exhibits out of the festival if she refuses to step down."

Oliver scratched his chin thoughtfully. "I see. Does Felicity know that?"

I nodded. "I talked to her last night."

"Judging from your expression, I take it the conversation didn't go well?"

"That's putting it mildly."

To my surprise, Oliver laughed. The sound echoed in the street around us. "Sounds like Felicity was in one of her moods. She's my wife and I love her, but I know how she can be. She means well, but she can come on a little strong at times. You wouldn't be the first person around here to get upset with her."

That was a *major* understatement. "Well, she's upset a bunch of people this time," I told him. "If I can't convince her to give up on this idea, we may not have an arts festival this year."

Oliver slid a look at me from the corner of his eye and started walking slowly away from the restaurant and back toward Divinity. "So you want to change her mind, do you? I wouldn't get my hopes up if I were you. Felicity doesn't change her mind easily."

"I know. She's not going to change her mind for me, but she might listen to someone else."

It took a second or two for my meaning to sink in.

When it did, Oliver pulled back sharply. "Are you asking *me* to talk to her?"

"I wouldn't ask if it weren't important, but I can't let the festival fizzle out without trying everything."

Scowling thoughtfully, Oliver slipped his hands into his pockets. "I'd like to oblige, Abby, but Felicity and I have an agreement. I stay out of her business, and she stays out of mine."

He hadn't left me much room to argue, but I felt uncomfortable with the silence. As we reached the corner of Prospector Street, I said the first thing that came to mind. "I hope I'm not taking you away from your work."

Oliver shook his head. "I told Henri I'd meet him for breakfast at Martine. You want my advice? Just give Felicity a few days. She'll probably listen to you once she has a chance to calm down."

"Thanks, but I doubt that. Can you think of someone Felicity might be willing to listen to? I'm willing to try anything."

"Felicity isn't easily influenced."

"What about Ursula?"

He fell silent for a few steps. "That's not a good idea. Ursula's the last person Felicity would take advice from."

So there were hard feelings between sisters. Imagine that. "There has to be *someone* who can make Felicity listen to reason."

Oliver touched my shoulder gently. "Really, Abby, I wish I could help, but I don't know what to suggest." All at once, his step faltered, and his expression changed. He nodded at something behind me and said, "Maybe she's changed her mind already."

I turned to look and realized that he was gesturing toward the car that had been sitting in the parking lot when I left my apartment a few minutes earlier. My heart dropped, and the hair rose on the back of my neck. "That's Felicity's car?"

Oliver nodded. "Shall we see what she wants?"

Now that Oliver had identified her, I could tell it was Felicity behind the wheel, but I could also tell by the way her head lolled against the backrest that something was wrong.

Oliver must have sensed trouble, too, because he almost ran toward the car. Whining impatiently, Max tugged on his leash and dragged me forward, so I was just a step behind Oliver when he let out an anguished cry. "Felicity? Oh my God. My God."

Against my better judgment I craned my neck to see what he'd seen, but he was clawing at the car, trying feverishly to pull the car door open. "Call for help," he shouted.

"Is she—?"

"Call 911!" Oliver shouted, his face red and his expression wild. He shifted just enough to let me view the inside of the car, and my stomach lurched into my throat. Time stopped as I gazed at Felicity Asbury, covered in blood, her eyes open wide and staring at the roof of her Mercedes. Her skin had already grown pasty, which probably meant that she'd been dead a while.

"She might still be alive," Oliver insisted. "Call 911. *Now!*"

In spite of the urgency in his voice, I couldn't make myself move for what felt like minutes. Maybe I was in shock. Or maybe I knew on some instinctive level that the awl buried up to its hilt in her chest had already done its work, and Felicity Asbury was dead.

Chapter 4

It seemed to take forever for the police to arrive. While we waited, I put Max inside the apartment and did my best to keep Oliver from contaminating the crime scene. At least, that's what I think I did. The whole thing, from the minute Oliver let out the first cry until I sat at my kitchen table looking at Pine Jawarski—a friend who also happens to be a detective with the Paradise Police Department—felt like a bad dream.

I don't know how Jawarski got his first name, but it suits him. He's tall and solid. The kind of guy you can count on in the tough times—like when you find a dead body or need someone to share a pizza with.

This wasn't the first murder victim I'd ever seen, but the way I reacted, it might as well have been. My hands trembled, and the whole time the uniformed officers had been asking their questions, my stomach had remained lodged in my throat. The image of Felicity's wide eyes and gaping mouth kept rising up to fill my mind, and I knew I'd never forget the sight or the sickening smell of all that blood.

By the time Jawarski arrived, I was ready to think about anything but Felicity Asbury's death. I'd have given just about anything to curl up in bed and bury my head under the covers for the rest of the day.

Instead, I sat at the kitchen table in my apartment while Jawarski talked to someone on his cell phone. I knew he was worried about me. He kept one piercing blue eye on me through his entire conversation.

Jawarski's in his early forties, and his short, dark hair is flecked with gray, but his broad shoulders and narrow waist make him look at least ten years younger. Like I said, we're friends. We've dated a few times, so some people might even say we're more than friends. Frankly, I'm not sure what we are.

We never talk about all the reasons why we don't call what we have a relationship, but it's obvious that neither of us is ready to take that step. My divorce was little more than a year old, and his hadn't been on the books much longer. Plus, he has kids. If we ever came up against the need to make a commitment, we'd probably both turn tail and run.

Trying to focus on details to keep me feeling rational, I spooned chocolate into a cup of coffee and slowly stirred. I didn't want the chocolate—didn't even want the coffee—but holding the cup gave me something to do. Jawarski had his cop face on, but I'd had enough of cops. I needed a friend.

After a few minutes, he disconnected his call and slipped his cell phone into his pocket. "You okay, slugger?"

I worked up a thin smile. "Yeah. As okay as I can be under the circumstances, anyway. Are you guys through with me?"

Jawarski shook his head. "Not quite. You feel up to answering a few more questions?"

"Now?" I groaned and sank down on my tailbone.

"Can't I come down to the station and talk to you later? I'm exhausted."

"I may need you to do that, too," Jawarski said. "I promise this won't take long."

"I'll give you five minutes," I told him. "Then I'm taking a shower."

His top lip twitched slightly beneath his regulation police mustache. "It's a deal."

"Good. Neither of the officers I talked to would tell me anything," I said before he could get started. "Was she killed here?"

The smile that had been playing with his lip disappeared. "I don't know."

Maybe not for certain, but I was fairly sure he had a pretty good idea. "How long has she been dead?"

"It's hard to say at this stage. Judging from the condition of the blood, I'd say a few hours at least." He leaned back in his seat and hooked one ankle across a knee. "You didn't hear anything unusual last night?"

It was bad enough knowing that I'd walked right past her body earlier, but thinking that someone had killed her just a few feet from where I'd slept freaked me out. I shook my head and focused on the warmth on my hands from the cup. "I didn't hear a thing, and that's what's bugging me. I like to think that if somebody was outside my apartment killing Felicity or planting her body in the parking lot, Max would have barked or something."

"He didn't?"

"No. If he sensed anything unusual, he was awfully quiet about it."

Jawarski gave that a moment's thought. "What time did you go to bed last night?"

"Around midnight. I took Max for his walk at about ten thirty, but I don't remember looking outside again after that." I sipped coffee, but my stomach gave a violent lurch, so I pushed the cup aside. "I've answered these questions twice already, Jawarski. Can't you just talk to the guys who were first on the scene?"

"Afraid not." He tried to look sorry, but he failed miserably.

"Do you have any idea who killed her?"

He sat back and linked his hands over his stomach. "I was just about to ask you the same question."

"I have no idea. But she wasn't what you'd call a well-liked member of the community, you know."

Jawarski nodded. "So I've heard." He wrote something in his notebook and glanced up at me. "Tell me about what happened at the artists' guild yesterday."

"I don't know much," I told him. "I wasn't there when the whole thing started. The first I heard about it was when Rachel called to tell me that the mayor had put Felicity in charge of the arts festival, and Meena had walked out."

"Why did Rachel call you?"

"Because I was Meena's second-in-command, and Rachel thought I ought to know what was happening."

"That's all? She just wanted to tell you what was going on?"

I shook my head. "She said that all hell was breaking loose and asked me to come to the guild. When I got there, she was promising everyone that she and I would make everything all right."

Jawarski looked confused. "How did she think you were going to do that?"

"Good question." I rolled my head on my neck to work out the kinks. "I don't think Rachel actually had a plan. I wanted to file an injunction with the court, but the others wanted me to talk to Felicity and convince her to back off."

Jawarski's brows drew together over the bridge of his nose, and his eyes darkened to a stormy blue gray. "Tell me you didn't."

"Well, of course I did. It seemed reasonable to at least talk before taking legal action. How was I supposed to know somebody was going to kill her?"

Jawarski let out an exasperated breath. "What happened when you saw her?"

"I drove out to the house and asked Felicity to back off and let Meena finish the job."

"And?"

"She refused." I broke off and gave serious thought to what I said next. Lying to the police during a homicide investigation was a very bad idea, but I didn't want him to know that I'd been furious with Felicity a few short hours before she turned up dead in my parking lot.

"I tried to reason with her," I said, hoping I looked like someone who was being open and honest. "She didn't want to hear a thing I had to say."

Jawarski glanced up from the page. "What happened then?"

"I knew I wouldn't get anywhere with her, so I gave up and came home."

"That's it?"

"That's it."

"How long were you there?"

"Ten minutes. Maybe fifteen."

Jawarski studied me for a long time before asking, "Was anyone else at the house while you were there?"

"Felicity's sister, Ursula. She answered the door when I got there. And Jacqueline—Felicity's daughter—showed up as I was leaving. You might want to talk with her. She was pretty upset about something."

"Any idea what?"

"I didn't stick around to find out."

Jawarski made another note and switched tracks. "You and Oliver Birch found the body together?"

"Yes."

"How did that happen?"

"I ran into him while I was taking Max for his morning walk. He was coming out of Bonner's Bakery."

"Pretty early for him to be in town, wasn't it?"

"He was here for a meeting with his new chef."

"How did you end up back here together?"

"He was on his way to Martine for breakfast. I asked for his help changing Felicity's mind about the festival."

"What did he say?"

I stifled a yawn. "He said they had a strict rule about staying out of each others' business."

"And that was that?"

"Pretty much."

Jawarski craned to look into the living room. "Did you use your front door when you went outside, or did you go out through the shop?"

"I used the front door."

"So you saw Felicity's car in the parking lot. Didn't you think that was strange?"

"I didn't know it was Felicity's car. I thought it was someone waiting for Picture Perfect to open."

"So you just walked on by."

Exhaustion made me edgy. "Yes, I did, and you would have, too. I had no idea there was a dead woman inside." I stood abruptly, and my chair teetered on two legs before landing on all four with a thump. "It's been more than five minutes, Jawarski. Time's up."

His eyes clouded. "I know you're tired, Abby, but I'm trying to figure out what happened."

"What happened," I said evenly, "is that somebody plunged an awl into Felicity Asbury's chest, and they did it in my parking lot. I've already gone over all of this several times. Why aren't you out trying to find whoever did this?"

Jawarski closed his notebook and slipped his pen into his pocket. "You found the body, Abby. Your statement is important. Do you have any idea why Felicity was in your parking lot?"

"None," I admitted.

"She wasn't here to see you?"

"If she was, I didn't know she was coming," I said, making a show of checking my watch. "Tell you what, Jawarski. If I've forgotten anything, I'll call you the minute I remember."

"You'd better." His gaze softened slightly. "You'd also better stay as far away from this case as possible. No poking around on your own."

I was already in a bad mood, and his warning only annoyed me more. Sure, I was curious to know who'd killed Felicity. Who wouldn't be, especially under the circumstances? But I'm also a reasonably intelligent woman. I've been involved in a couple of investigations before, and I know how dangerous they can be. I had no desire to repeat the experience.

I gathered my cup and spoon and carried them to the sink. "Don't worry. I have no intention of 'poking' into anything."

Jawarski came to stand behind me, so close I could smell the spicy scent of his aftershave and the mint of his toothpaste. "That's it? You're not even going to argue with me?"

I rinsed the cup and turned back to face him. "Why would I argue with you?"

"Because it's what you do."

In spite of my frayed nerves, I laughed. "Look, Jawarski, I know I've gotten involved in a couple of things in the past, but it was never by choice. I'm perfectly content to let you do your job."

"You're serious?"

"Absolutely." I met his gaze steadily, determined to show him just how serious I was. "I have way too much on my plate with the festival. Besides," I patted his shoulder and moved past him into the living room, "you're good at your job. You don't need my help to figure out who killed Felicity."

I could hear his footsteps on the vinyl floor of the kitchen, and I knew the moment he stepped onto the old, faded area rug that covers the scarred hardwood floor of the living room. "You're not even slightly curious."

"Well, of course I am, but Meena's still off the committee, and Felicity's still dead. Somebody has to make sure preparations stay on track until the mayor comes to his senses and puts Meena back in charge." I plucked a piece of homemade Almond Roca from my stash on the coffee table and popped it into my mouth. The chocolate melted on my tongue, and the rich, buttery taste of the toffee helped relax me.

"Let somebody else take over the festival," Jawarski said.

"Absolutely not. This whole can of worms opened in the first place because somebody else tried to take over. I'm not going to make things worse by turning my back on the group."

A deep frown creased Jawarski's face. He perched on the arm of my beat-up old couch, and I was surprised to find that he looked good sitting there. Kind of natural and like he belonged. "There's a good chance Mrs. Asbury's murder is connected to that festival of yours."

My little flash of sentimentality disappeared quickly. Jawarski wasn't here as a friend. I should remember that. "There's an equally good chance that it's not connected at all."

"Yeah, and until we figure out which, I want you well away from it." Jawarski's eyes roamed my face, and his eyes darkened to a deep blue. Just when I thought I'd pulled myself together, there he was, looking like he wanted to do something masculine and protective, like pulling me into his arms.

His sudden intensity freaked me out a little. My head wasn't sure I liked that look on his face, but my heart gave a flip and raced a little faster. "I've told you that I won't get involved in the murder investigation, but I won't turn my back on the festival. Please don't ask me to again."

Jawarski stood, towering over me. "Don't be a hero, Abby. It's just a stupid arts festival. You can get involved with it next year."

"No."

"Abby—"

I cut him off before he could say more. "I'm not doing it, and that's final. Not unless you can show me tangible proof that I'm in some kind of danger."

"You don't consider a dead body in your parking lot tangible proof?"

"It's proof that Felicity should have been worried. It has nothing to do with me."

He looked me square in the eye for a long time, then let out a heavy breath. "Fine. Do what you want. But if you see or hear anything out of the ordinary, I want you to call me immediately."

I tossed him a smile. "Well, of course I will. I'm not stupid."

"No investigating on your own. No asking questions about the murder."

"Cross my heart," I told him. And I meant it.

But plans sometimes have a way of changing.

Chapter 5

"This is absolutely unbelievable," Nicolette Wilkes said a few hours later. She's a regular customer and a member of the Paradise Pageturners, a book club whose monthly meetings are held at Divinity. She sat inside Divinity at one of the wrought-iron tables, nursing a Coke and watching the police, who still clogged the crime scene in my parking lot and out onto Prospector Street, blocking traffic. We hadn't had a single other paying customer all day, and Karen had left a few minutes earlier for her lunch break.

I'd been so busy all morning, my planned conversation with Mayor Ireland had fallen right off my radar screen. Jawarski finally gave me permission to open the shop a few minutes before noon, but even then, my thoughts jumped from subject to subject like water in a hot skillet. Who had hated Felicity enough to murder her so brutally? And why had they done it here?

I stood at the stove, stirring sugar and cream into caramel, waiting for it to hit the firm ball stage, and trying not to think about the horror of finding Felicity's body. Over the half wall that separates the candy kitchen from the store, I watched Nicolette draw her gaze away from the window and run one acrylic-tipped finger down the side of her cup. She's thirty or so, a tall blonde with legs a mile long. I'm not sure where she gets her money, but she always seems to have plenty, even though I've never seen her work. She's also beautiful, a combination that routinely throws men off stride. The fact that she never seems to notice the effect she has on them is what allows me to be friends with her.

"I can't believe somebody murdered Felicity right outside your door," she said. "It must be like a nightmare for you."

"That's putting it mildly," I agreed. "I keep hoping they'll get everything cleaned up soon, and then I feel guilty for feeling that way. A woman's dead, but all I want is for her death not to inconvenience me."

Nicolette's carefully painted lips curved slightly. "I think that's a perfectly normal reaction. Anybody would feel that way." In the next breath, her smile evaporated like the steam rising from my copper kettle. "Was it horrible? Finding her, I mean."

I shuddered at the memory and switched the spoon to my other hand to relieve my cramped muscles. "Yeah, it was. I'm trying not to think about it."

Nicolette crossed her long legs and shook her head slowly. "I just can't imagine. I don't know how you can stand there making candy as if nothing happened."

"It's not easy," I admitted, "but I have too much to do. I can't afford to take time off."

"Well, you're a stronger woman than I am. If I'd been the one who found her, I'm sure I'd be curled up in the fetal position right now." She flipped a lock of blonde hair over her shoulder and glanced out the window again. "So who do you think killed her?"

"I have no idea, but I'm sure the police will figure it out soon."

Nicolette's serene expression puckered into a frown. "Isn't the husband usually the first suspect?"

"I guess so." Oliver had seemed genuinely upset about finding Felicity, but I couldn't rule him out as a suspect. If, you know, I was thinking about suspects. Which I wasn't. Just ask Jawarski.

Nicolette let one shoe dangle from her toes and jiggled her foot. "Do you think he did it?"

"I don't know. It's up to the police to figure that out."

"Oh come on," she teased. "You aren't seriously trying to tell me that you're not going to get involved."

The sugar mixture on the stove began to boil. I hooked the candy thermometer onto the side of the pan and kept stirring. "I'm not getting involved. I'm going to focus on getting the arts festival under control."

Nicolette uncrossed her legs and gaped at me. "But she died right here. What if somebody thinks you did it?"

I laughed. "Don't be ridiculous. I didn't have any reason to kill her."

"But she was killed what? Five feet from your door?"

"Maybe. The police don't even know that much yet."

"I'm just saying that you ought to be careful. You did go to see her last night."

"Because the guild members asked me to."

"And then she turns up dead in the parking lot outside," Nicolette went on as if I hadn't spoken. She started jiggling her foot again. "I'm just saying you should look out for yourself, that's all."

Steam rose from the kettle, and a trickle of sweat inched down my back. "What are you getting at, Nicolette? Has somebody been talking?"

She shrugged and watched a couple of people stroll slowly past the front window. "Not yet."

"But you think they will?"

"What I think is, it's no coincidence that she was found here. I think somebody set it up that way."

"To frame me?"

She lifted an eyebrow as if to say, *What else?*

I laughed again, but I felt a faint twinge of uneasiness. "That's crazy. Why would anybody do that?"

"Oh, I don't know. Maybe so they could get away with murder?"

I checked the candy thermometer and repeated my question. "Who's been talking, and what are they saying?"

Nicolette left the table and came to stand in the doorway. "Just that you went to see Felicity last night—"

"Because the members of the guild asked me to," I said again. It seemed like an important point to me, even if nobody else appeared to think so.

"Right." Nicolette glanced at the street again, then back at me. "Look, I'm sure you have nothing to worry about. I just don't want you to be surprised if you hear rumors flying around town."

"In Paradise?" I tried to grin, but my mouth felt stiff. "I'm never surprised to hear rumors around here." I wondered what folks would say if they found out Felicity had kicked Divinity out of the festival.

Just thinking about that possibility made my stomach cramp. I didn't think anyone had overheard our conversation, but how could I know that for sure? Ursula could have been lurking somewhere nearby. I wouldn't put it past her.

I wanted to trust Jawarski and give the police a chance to find the murderer, and that's exactly what I should do. But Nicolette had a point. If rumors did spring up on the town grapevine, I might have to take steps to cut them down.

I sighed heavily. "All I want is a normal life. Is that too much to ask?"

"Face it, honey," Nicolette said with a soft laugh, "the

richest woman in Paradise has been killed right next to Divinity. Life isn't going to feel normal for a long, long time."

The candy thermometer finally reached 245 degrees, so I stopped stirring and carried the pot toward the buttered pans I'd set out on the long counter beneath the window. I couldn't see Nicolette any longer. "I don't even know how I got into this mess. Why did Felicity suddenly care about the festival? It's not as if she would have made money from it."

"No." Nicolette came further into the kitchen. "And it's not as if being in charge would have enhanced her reputation."

"So what *did* she want?"

"I don't know." Nicolette leaned against the supply cupboard. "I called Meena last night, but she refused to talk about it. Maybe we'll never know."

"She wouldn't talk to me, either," I admitted as I poured hot caramel into one pan and moved to the next. "The mayor must have had some reason for making such a big change. I hope he'll tell me when I talk to him."

"Yeah, well, good luck with that." Nicolette watched me pour another pan in silence. "Hey," she said as I checked the hot caramel for air bubbles, "what about her sister? Ursula?"

"What about her?"

"Maybe she did it. I'll bet she can't wait to get her hands on Daddy's money."

"There's enough of it, that's for sure. But do you think she wants control of Drake Development enough to get her sister out of the way?"

"I don't know. She might not even get the company. It might go to Jacqueline."

I shook my head firmly. "I'll bet Felicity made sure a long time ago that Jacqueline wouldn't get a thing."

"Okay, then, Oliver. Unless old Andrew tied the business up in some kind of trust to keep it in the family. Knowing how he felt about outsiders, I wouldn't be a bit surprised."

"Yeah, well, nobody's going to know that except Felicity's attorney. He'd be able to tell us if anyone in the family had a motive for murder."

"The murder you're not going to investigate."

I glanced over my shoulder. "That's the one." At least for now. If people started crossing the street to avoid me, I might have to rethink my decision.

Nicolette laughed and started to turn away, but something outside the kitchen window caught her attention. She stood on tiptoe to get a better look. "What's going on out there now?"

I followed her gaze and saw a large delivery truck stopped in the middle of the street a few doors uphill. Its driver tried in vain to get past the police with a handcart filled with boxes. When they stopped him, he gestured broadly, first at Divinity, then toward the back of his truck, where it looked like three more stacks of boxes waited to be unloaded, every one of which bore the logo of my largest supplier.

I thought I'd received everything from my last order, but I'd been too busy to reconcile all my paperwork lately, so it was possible that I had an outstanding shipment. "I can't leave this caramel right now," I said over my shoulder to Nicolette. "Would you mind seeing what that's all about?"

Nodding, Nicolette let herself out the back door. She was back in two minutes holding an invoice. "It's for you," she said, holding out the invoice so I could see it. "Seven gallons of peppermint extract and twenty cases of peppermint disks."

A drop of still-hot caramel hit my finger, and I nearly lost my grip on the pan. I swore and lunged for the sink. "That's a mistake," I said as I flushed the burn with cold

water. "I never ordered any of that. Would you tell the
driver I refuse shipment?"

Nicolette glanced out the window with a frown. "Too
late. He's already gone. I didn't realize—" She broke off,
looking sheepish.

"You signed for it?"

"I thought you wanted it."

A dull ache started in my forehead and pulsed with
every heartbeat. "It would take me years to use that much
peppermint," I said, trying not to overreact. "But don't
worry about it. It's not your fault. I'll work it out with the
supplier."

"Are you sure? I feel horrible."

"Of course I'm sure." I sent her a reassuring smile and
finished pouring the caramel. But this camel's back was already starting to ache. I wasn't sure how many more straws
I could take without breaking.

When Karen came back from lunch twenty minutes
later, she stopped cold at the sight of the boxes piled in the
kitchen. "What in the hell is all this?"

Since we still hadn't had any customers, I'd been cleaning out the old refrigerator we keep for personal stuff. I
tossed an unidentifiable something into the trash can at my
side. "Don't ask."

"Did you order this?"

"Nope." I straightened with an old jar of mayonnaise in
one hand and an empty mustard bottle in the other. "I'm
guessing from your reaction that you didn't, either."

"No, of course not. What is it?"

"Twenty-seven cases of assorted peppermint." I nodded
toward the counter near the half wall. "The invoice is over
there."

Scowling in confusion, Karen crossed the room. "If you
didn't order it, why did you accept it?"

"I didn't. Nicolette signed for it." I tossed the jars into

the garbage and cut off her next question with, "Long story. I'll explain everything later."

Karen picked up the invoice and let out an audible gasp. "Did you see the total amount due? This is nuts!"

"Tell me about it. As soon as I'm finished with this, I'll call Sweet Dreams and straighten the whole thing out."

"Call now."

"I'm almost finished. Only a few more containers I have no intention of opening."

"If you wait much longer, they'll be closed for the day," Karen said, wagging the invoice under my nose. "If you wait until tomorrow, they'll use that to argue we should keep it. We need to straighten this out now."

She had a point, so I closed the refrigerator and headed into the cramped room that serves as Divinity's office. While Karen hovered in the doorway, I punched the supplier's number into the phone and began the arduous task of working my way through the automated answering system.

Of the dozen or so choices the computer-generated system gave me, none included speaking to a live person. Frustrated, I punched 0 and paced back and forth inside the cluttered office while I listened to an instrumental rendition of "Light My Fire." After what seemed like an eternity, I heard a series of beeps, a couple of clicks, and—finally—a live voice. "Customer Service, this is Penny."

Penny spoke with a Southern accent so thick she pronounced her name with three syllables instead of two.

"Hi, Penny," I said, trying to sound cooperative and friendly. No sense starting the conversation on the wrong foot. "This is Abby Shaw from Divinity in Paradise, Colorado. I just received a shipment from you, but I think there must be some mistake."

"I'm sorry about that," Penny chirped. "Are you missing items?"

"Actually, no. You sent me twenty-seven cases of peppermint I never ordered."

"We did?" Penny's drawl lost some of its lilt. "I can't imagine how we made a mistake like that. Hold on while I check the invoice. If there's been a mistake, you can send the merchandise back with the driver, and we'll credit your account as soon as we receive it."

"Tell them we don't want it," Karen prompted.

I nodded and perched on one corner of my desk. "There *has* been a mistake," I told Penny, "but the driver has already gone."

"He left without a signature?"

"Well, no, but the person who signed for the shipment wasn't authorized to accept it. Technically speaking."

The warmth in Penny's voice evaporated completely. "I'm not sure I understand. The driver left our shipment at the wrong place?"

Letting the driver take the blame might have been the easiest way to get a refund, but it wouldn't have been fair, and my conscience wouldn't let me do it. "Not exactly. He couldn't get to our store because . . ." I didn't want to tell her there had been a murder in our parking lot, so I skirted the issue and finished with, ". . . it's complicated."

"I see. So who signed for the delivery?"

"Tell them we don't want it," Karen urged again.

I waved a hand to let her know I had the conversation under control, but that only earned me a disapproving scowl.

"A friend who happened to be here when the delivery arrived signed for it," I told Penny. "I didn't even realize what was happening until she brought the invoice to me. If I had, believe me, I would have refused delivery."

"It was a mistake to send her out there," Karen mumbled, as if I hadn't figured that out for myself.

"I see," Penny said again, her voice flat. The sound of fingers clicking on a keyboard filled the silence for a moment before Penny said, "You say you never placed this order?"

"No, I didn't. So, really, the question of who signed for it is beside the point."

"But I have record here of an order for seven gallons of peppermint extract and twenty cases of peppermint disks. Is that what you received?"

Stunned into silence, I studied the invoice for a minute. At over three hundred dollars a gallon, payment on the extract alone would send Divinity to bankruptcy court. "Yes, that's what I received, but I didn't place that order."

"The order was placed on April fifteenth."

"Not by me," I insisted. I covered the receiver with one hand and whispered to Karen, "She says we placed that order on the fifteenth of April."

"She's wrong," Karen said firmly. "Neither of us would have done something that ridiculous."

"This whole thing is a mistake," I told Penny, speaking slowly and clearly so she couldn't possibly misunderstand. "I want you to send someone to pick up everything the driver left here today."

"I'm afraid I can't do that, Ms. Shaw. These items were part of a clearance sale. There are no returns and no refunds."

"But I didn't order it. None of it. Not even *one* gallon. You can't force me to take product I didn't order, even if it is on clearance."

"But you *did* place the order," Penny said, her voice infuriatingly calm. "Or at least someone from your store did. Sweet Dreams would never send you product you hadn't asked for."

"Well, you did this time."

"I have a purchase order number," Penny said, "if that would help you figure out what happened."

"I know what happened," I snarled. "Someone has made a huge mistake. Someone at *your* end."

"I'm sorry you feel that way." Penny seemed to grow more calm by the second, while I was just the opposite. "The number I have here is BN-415. Maybe that will help you track down what happened."

I was clenching my jaw so tightly, the muscles in my face ached. "It doesn't help at all. We don't use purchase orders here."

"But I have one on the order. BN-415."

"So you said, but we're a small shop. Just two people and sometimes three, and I'm the only person authorized—" A thought hit me then and stopped me midsentence. My stomach churned the way it had after I'd spent an entire afternoon grazing on Aunt Grace's candy the summer I turned eight.

BN-415. Beatrice Neville, April 15. It would be just like my cousin Bea, who resented me for inheriting Divinity, to place an order like this. Bea, who never turned down an opportunity to take over, change what I'd done, or show me where she thought I'd gone wrong. Bea, who was convinced that I was going to run Divinity into the ground if she didn't prevent me from doing so.

I closed my eyes and took a couple of deep breaths. Maybe Bea wasn't responsible, I told myself. Maybe it was just an odd coincidence. "I'll uh . . . I'll do a little research at this end," I said.

Eyes wild, Karen flew into the room. "Don't let them push you around. This is *not* our fault." When I disconnected the call, she looked at me as if I'd suddenly sprouted a third and fourth head. "Are you *crazy*? They're never going to take the shipment back now."

I sank into the chair behind the desk. "Take a look at the purchase order number."

"We don't use purchase orders."

"Just look at it. BN, Beatrice Neville, 415. Didn't she work that afternoon while I finished the taxes?"

The fire left Karen's eyes, and her knees seemed to give

out on her. "Oh, but surely—I mean, she wouldn't dare . . . Would she?"

"We're talking about Bea," I reminded her.

"But we can't afford this."

"Tell me about it."

Karen sank into a chair and closed her eyes in despair. "You have to talk to her. You have to convince her to fix this."

"Oh, I'll talk to her," I promised. "I don't know what she can say. The entire shipment was on clearance, and Sweet Dreams isn't going to take it back, but I'll definitely talk to her."

Could things get any worse? Scratch that. I knew they could, and I didn't want to tempt fate.

Now that Felicity was dead and I was acting chair of the arts festival committee, I could put Divinity's booth back in the lineup, but why bother if everything I had to sell was peppermint flavored? Peppermint overload might be a hit in December, but not in May.

But why was I worried? Unless the police solved Felicity's murder quickly, we might not have a festival. In that case, what I offered for sale in Divinity's booth wouldn't be an issue.

Chapter 6

Karen and I kept the store open until seven that evening—not that it mattered. A few people came through the doors that afternoon, but only to satisfy their curiosity about the yellow crime scene tape stretched across the parking lot. Sales on the cash register when we rang out for the evening hit an all-time low.

I had only an hour before a meeting of the festival committee, but if I waited until the next day to talk with Bea, I probably wouldn't get any sleep that night. I loaded Max into my Jetta and aimed the car across town toward Bea's house. I could have called her on the phone, but this conversation was too important. I had to look her in the eye when I asked her about the order, and I needed her to see that I meant business when I told her to stay away from Divinity from here on out.

Bea lives with her husband in a small home on the east bench of Paradise. It's one of the oldest houses in town, a two-bedroom number that I'd swear has been in a perpetual state of renovation since Bea and Kenny bought it more than thirty years ago. I'm not sure whether that's because Kenny is a major procrastinator or because Bea is never satisfied. Maybe it's just a sad combination of both.

Just as the sun dropped behind the western mountains, I pulled up in front of the house and let Max out of the car. A light breeze ruffled the new leaves on the trees, filling the air with the soft *shhhh* of quivering aspen. Kenny came to the door when I rang the bell, and the rich smell of simmering pot roast floated out into the cool, evening air.

Bea's husband is in his midfifties, a tall man who has bulked up a bit over the years but still looks pretty good for a man his age. His hair might have been streaked with silver, but the wheat-blond made it hard to tell. He grinned when he saw me, propped the screen door open with one hand, and bent to scratch Max with the other.

"What brings you two here?" he asked when he straightened again.

"I need to talk to Bea. Is she around?"

He jerked his head toward the back of the house. "Cooking supper. We're running late tonight. Go on back. You're welcome to stay if you haven't eaten already."

"Thanks," I said, "but I can only stay a minute." If I was right about the peppermint overdose sitting inside Divinity, Bea wouldn't want me sticking around anyway.

She looked up as I came through the kitchen door, and I could tell by the sour-patch expression on her face that she'd heard me arrive. "We're about to eat," she said pointedly. "Whatever you want, can it wait?"

Bea can be intimidating, but I was too angry to let her get the best of me. "I won't stay long, but I need to ask you about a shipment I received today from Sweet Dreams. Seven gallons of peppermint oil and twenty cases of peppermint disks. Do you know anything about it?"

Bea bent to pull a cast-iron pot from the oven. "You had to drive all the way over here to ask that?"

"I was out taking care of some other things," I said, the

lie rolling off my tongue easily. "I was close, so I decided to just drop by. I called Sweet Dreams today when the order arrived. They told me someone from the store had ordered it."

Bea set the pot on an empty burner and tossed her oven mitts into a corner. "What if I did?"

Confronting my relatives isn't easy for me to do. I'm carrying around twenty years of guilt for leaving town and turning my back on them, and they know it. Some try to relieve that guilt. Some don't. Bea falls into the latter category.

"If you did," I said, "then we have a problem. For one thing, Divinity can't afford to pay for the order. For another, you've made it impossible for me to place the order I had planned for next week."

Bea shot me with a laser-beam glare. "Two years ago, it wouldn't have been a problem. Are you saying that you've dragged the store into some kind of financial trouble?"

"The store has been struggling since Aunt Grace died," I admitted. "But that has nothing to do with me. In fact, I think I'm doing pretty well, considering." I didn't mention the money Grace had divided between the rest of the cousins in her will. I didn't want Bea to think I begrudged them their inheritance. But as a result, the store's cash reserves had already been low when I got there.

One of Bea's eyebrows arched pointedly. "*Do* you?"

"Yes, I do, but that's beside the point. Who authorized you to order those supplies, Bea? I know I didn't."

"You left me in charge of the store while you were doing your taxes. I became aware of a spectacular sale on supplies that I knew the store would need in the winter."

"Seven gallons of flavor oil? *One* flavor?"

"It was a great price."

The smug look on her pinched face made me want to shake her, but I tightened my hands into fists and held them at my sides. "If you think that, then you should pay for the shipment. I can't afford it."

She reached into a cupboard and pulled out plates and glasses. "Don't be ridiculous. I don't have that kind of money."

"All the more reason for you to have checked with me before you placed the order. The arts festival is just three weeks away, and now I can't afford to get the supplies I need. Thanks to you, I'll be stuck selling nothing but peppermint. Why are you so determined to make sure I fail?"

Bea rolled her eyes and pushed past me into the square dining area that looked out over a postage-stamp-sized backyard. "That's nonsense. Why would I want you to fail?"

"Maybe because you resent the fact that Aunt Grace left the store to me. We both know you think you could have done the job better."

Very slowly, Bea straightened and turned to look at me. Her eyes glittered with some emotion I couldn't name, but it made me distinctly uncomfortable. "I could have done the job better," she said stiffly. "I think we both know that. This latest mess you've brought on the family *should* be the straw that broke the camel's back. But you're my cousin, and while there are times I don't like you very much, you *are* family. I would never do anything to purposely make you fail."

I didn't know whether anger or embarrassment was stronger. Bea has that effect on me sometimes. But anger is easier for me to deal with, so I went with that. "I didn't bring any mess on the family," I snarled. "And you have no right ordering supplies for the store unless I ask you to. From now on, please remember that."

She drew herself up to her full height and skimmed a look down her nose meant to crush me. If I hadn't been so angry, it probably would have. "Don't worry, Abby. If you really believe that of me, when all I've tried to do is help, there won't be a next time. I won't darken your door again."

"Yeah? Well, you've promised that before, and look what happened."

A look of hurt flashed across her face, but it disappeared so quickly I wasn't sure I'd actually seen it. Whether real or imagined, it ignited a spark of guilt inside me.

"I don't know what happened to you out there in California," Bea snarled. "You didn't used to be so selfish."

That's all I needed to extinguish that annoying guilt. "Don't try to make this about me," I warned. "You're the one who has put Divinity in this position, not me."

"Divinity should be in a position to take advantage of a great opportunity when one comes along."

"Twenty-seven cases of assorted peppermint? Come on, Bea. You and I both know that's not a great opportunity for an operation our size. It's overkill."

Bea slammed a cupboard door and glared at me across the counter. "Fine. Now, if there's nothing else you want to berate me over, I would like to serve dinner to my family."

I was as eager as she was to end the conversation. I pivoted away. "No, that's it."

I heard another cupboard slam shut as I plowed through the house and grabbed Max's leash. It wasn't my fault, I told myself again. I didn't *want* to alienate Bea, but she was so damn stubborn, I didn't know how else to get her to back off. Divinity wasn't hers, and the sooner she accepted that, the better off we'd all be.

I was halfway down the walk when I heard someone call my name. Turning, I saw Iris Quinn waving at me from her yard across the street. Iris is a small woman of about sixty, with a wide smile, teeth too large for her face, and graying hair that hangs to the middle of her back. She runs Once Upon a Crime, a mystery bookstore downtown, and no matter the weather, she's always wearing a cardigan.

She's a nice woman, but she likes to talk. After my argument with Bea, I wasn't in the mood to socialize.

I waved back and pulled my keys from my pocket, but before I could get into the car, Iris abandoned her gardening and called, "Abby? Do you have a minute?"

I came *this close* to saying no, but none of this was Iris's fault. I took a couple of calming breaths and shoved my argument with Bea to the back of my mind before leading Max across the street. Iris met us at the end of her driveway. She wore a pair of khaki pants with dirt stains on the knees and a faded purple T-shirt that had seen better days under a plain gray sweater. Smudges of soil dotted her cheeks and nose, but I don't think she realized it was there.

"I heard about Felicity," she said when I drew up beside her. "It's horrible, isn't it?"

I was tired of thinking about the murder, but Iris knew people and heard things. If she knew something that could help, didn't I have a civic duty to listen? "Yes," I said, trying to drum up a little enthusiasm, "it is."

"Was she really killed at Divinity?"

That was a rumor I wanted to squelch right away. "Not at all. Her body was in a car in the parking lot."

"And you found her. Did I hear that right?"

The curiosity sparkling in Iris's eyes made me cautious. "I was there when she was found. Oliver Birch and I both were."

Those curious eyes narrowed. "You were with Oliver? I didn't realize the two of you were friends."

"We're not. I ran into him on the street a few minutes before that. We were discussing how to get Meena back to work on the festival planning committee."

"I heard about that." Iris lowered her voice as if she worried about being overheard. "Why did the mayor remove her?"

"I don't know. She's not talking about it. I was going to talk to him about it today, but I got a little sidetracked."

That earned me a sympathetic smile. "I'm sure you did. Do you think Felicity's murder has anything to do with all of that?"

"With the festival?" I shook my head. "There's no reason for anyone to kill her just because she stepped in as committee chair. It's not *that* big a deal."

She gave that some thought. "I suppose not, but it's an odd coincidence, isn't it?"

"Yeah, it is. The murderer is probably counting on everyone thinking that."

I couldn't tell if Iris agreed with that or not. She moved away from the idea before I could find out. "Did Oliver have any ideas about how to get Meena back on the committee?"

"I'm afraid not. I thought maybe he could convince Felicity to step down—for the good of the festival and all that—but he wouldn't."

Scowling slightly, Iris brushed a twig from the sleeve of her cardigan. "Nobody could ever convince Felicity to do anything, not even Oliver."

"Yeah. Well. I never got the chance to find out. She was already dead before we had the conversation."

"It's such a shame," Iris said. "So senseless, but murder always is. Do the police know what time she was killed?"

"It had to be sometime after midnight and before six."

Iris gazed up the street as if she was looking toward town, but the sun had slipped so far behind the mountains we could barely see to the corner. "I know Felicity wasn't well-liked, but I really can't imagine why anyone would want to kill her."

"Well, somebody had a motive," I said with a thin smile. "I'm sure the police will figure it all out soon enough. But it does make you wonder, doesn't it? The big question is, who's going to benefit from her death?"

Frowning thoughtfully, Iris bent to scratch Max between the ears. "I'm sure Oliver will. And Ursula." She glanced up sheepishly. "Not that I'm accusing either one of them. Oliver's such a gentle man, and he was so devoted to her. And Ursula . . . well, she comes into the store sometimes. I don't know her well, but I can't imagine her murdering her own sister."

I could, but I didn't say so. "There were no bad feelings between Felicity and Ursula?"

"Well, I don't know for sure. The Drakes have always kept to themselves. Ursula never said anything about Felicity. And why would she hurt her sister after Felicity gave her a place to live all these years? Felicity didn't have to take Ursula in after she lost all her own money, you know."

"You don't think Ursula resented the fact that Felicity treated her as little more than an employee?"

"I've never had that impression, but Carma knows her much better than I do." Carma is Iris's longtime friend and roommate. Almost everyone in town accepts that they're more than just friends, but neither Iris nor Carma has ever admitted it aloud. Iris stopped scratching Max and sobered. "Actually, Ursula is the reason I wanted to talk to you."

"Oh?"

"Carma delivered a shipment of books to her this afternoon, and apparently she said some things . . ." She broke off with an uncomfortable laugh. "I'm sure it's just the grief of the moment, but I thought you should know that Ursula thinks you . . . That you . . . Well, I might as well come right out with it. She's saying that you pushed your way into Felicity's house last night and that you had an argument with her."

The hair on the back of my neck stood up. "I didn't push my way in," I assured her. "Ursula let me in." I didn't add that she'd needed some convincing. It seemed like an unnecessary detail.

"Ursula told Carma that you threatened Felicity. Is that true?"

My heart turned to stone in my chest, and Ursula dropped several spots on my list of favorite people. "No, it's not true. I asked Felicity to leave the festival committee so Meena could finish what she started. She refused, and that was that."

Iris put a hand on my arm and looked deep into my eyes. "I'm not for one minute suggesting that I think you killed her, Abby. But you need to know that Ursula is talking, and some people are getting concerned."

I held back a bitter laugh. I'd worked my tail off over the past eighteen months to carve out a new place for myself in Paradise. Now, thanks to Felicity Asbury and her sister, I stood to lose everything I'd gained. "Well, you can tell those people to relax," I told Iris. "I didn't kill her."

"Why was she in your parking lot? Was she there to see you?"

"If she was, I didn't know about it."

"So she just showed up for no reason?"

"I'm sure she had a reason," I said cautiously. "I just don't know what it was."

Iris's plain face puckered into a deep scowl, but she patted my arm gently. "Well, of course you don't. It's just such an unfortunate situation, with Ursula telling people that you threatened Felicity and then her turning up dead right on your doorstep."

"She *wasn't* on my doorstep." Yeah, I know. Close enough. But I thought the distinction was important. "And I didn't threaten her, but apparently Ursula has some reason for wanting people to think I did."

Iris's eyes widened with shock. "Oh, I can't imagine Ursula—I mean, I know she's reserved and difficult to get to know, but I just can't imagine her being capable of something so mean-spirited. Why would she try to make you look guilty?"

"Maybe she murdered Felicity herself. If Felicity pushed her far enough, I'm sure even Ursula would protect herself."

Iris's glance flashed to meet mine. "But Ursula is such a gentle soul."

"So gentle she's trying to make me look guilty of her sister's murder?"

"Oh, I don't think she's trying to do that. She's just trying to help the police figure out who killed Felicity, that's all. You *did* go out there last night. You said so yourself."

It's true. I had said so. All at once it seemed like a good idea to stop talking before I said anything else. I glanced at my watch and tried to look surprised by the passing of time. "I'm sorry, Iris. I have a meeting in town in ten minutes, and I'll be lucky to make it if I leave now."

She drew her hand away from my arm, but even in the twilight I could see questions still flashing in her eyes. "Of course. I didn't mean to keep you. I just thought you should know."

I mumbled a thank-you and led Max across the street. I won't deny that I breathed a little easier once I was in the Jetta and driving away. Iris was only one person, but how many others had heard Ursula's story? And how many believed it?

Chapter 7

I smelled trouble the minute I walked into the guild hall a few minutes later. The other committee members were already there, gathered around the oval table in the community dining area and wearing long faces.

Rachel met my gaze as I came through the door. She was back to her usual dressed-to-kill self in a caramel silk blouse and pants the color of tempered chocolate. Her hair had that casually tousled look that takes hours to perfect, I think. I've never actually accomplished it. Unfortunately, the expression on her face sent a chill skittering up my spine.

Sliding into the empty chair at Rachel's side, I asked, "Am I late? I thought the meeting started at eight."

"It does," Rachel assured me. "Apparently the rest of the committee decided to have a premeeting meeting."

I glanced from face to face around the table, but none of the others would look at me. "Anything I should know about?"

Charmaine Frye, a slender woman with thin, flyaway

hair, spoke up before Rachel could. "As a matter of fact, there is. We've been talking about Felicity's murder and the impact it's going to have on the festival."

"I see. And what did you decide?"

Marisol Delgado, a softly curved woman with short, dark hair and expressive brown eyes, glanced up from the notebook in front of her. "There's no question that it will have an impact." Her gaze settled at about cheek level, not quite making it to my eyes. "I think we all know that, don't we?"

Rachel snorted a laugh. "We don't *know* anything. We're speculating, that's all. Making any decisions based on nothing more substantial than what we think might happen is dangerous."

Kirby North huffed with irritation. "Climb down off your soapbox, Rachel. We're talking about using common sense, that's all. Doing what's best for the majority. There's nothing wrong with that, so stop trying to make us feel guilty."

Charmaine turned a smile on me that was so brittle, I expected her face to crack. "Of course you know it's nothing personal, Abby. It's just that the festival has already taken a couple of direct hits. We don't need any more bad publicity."

A few murmurs of agreement floated up from the table, but nobody else made eye contact. "I guess I'm supposed to read between the lines here," I said, "but I'm not sure what you're trying so hard not to say."

Yvette Owens looked up for the first time. "We think you should leave the committee."

Was she serious? Apparently so. I swallowed my irritation and asked, "Do you all feel that way?"

"Absolutely not," Rachel snapped. "I have no intention of turning my back on you."

I flashed a grateful smile. I'd been without close friends for a long time, and it felt good to know that someone had my back. "But the rest of you want me to leave?"

Kirby North sucked something from a tooth and shrugged. "I'm not going to say one way or the other."

"Because you have no opinion, or because you don't want to make waves?"

His gaze met mine for a full tenth of a second. "Because I don't think it matters. Whether or not you're on the committee, the damage is already done."

Shellee Marshall let out a heavy sigh and leaned so far onto the table, her breasts nearly spilled out of her low-cut blouse. "Of course it matters. Abby, like Charmaine said, it's nothing personal, but Felicity *was* found dead right outside your door. People are going to be freaked out enough about the murder. The more we can do to separate the murder from the festival, the better."

Rachel huffed disapproval. "And I still say that it's ridiculous to make Abby pay for something that wasn't her fault."

Kirby cut her off with a wave of one massive hand. "Shellee has a good point, and you know it. We should be doing everything we can to insulate the festival at this point."

"Felicity was found dead in the parking lot near my shop," I said for what felt like the hundredth time in the past fourteen hours. "That doesn't mean I killed her."

"Nobody said you did," Marisol assured me. "But you're connected to the murder in people's minds."

"She went to see Felicity last night because we asked her to," Rachel reminded them.

"Whoever killed Felicity must have known that," I said. "I think someone must have seen it as a good opportunity to cast suspicion away from themself and onto someone else."

A couple of people mumbled under their breaths, but I couldn't hear what they said well enough to guess whether they agreed with me or not. "I understand why you're concerned," I assured them, "but if I walk away now, that will make it seem as if I'm admitting I'm guilty. There's no way I'm going to do that."

Yvette Owens shook her head briskly and set the long bands of silver dangling from her ears jingling. "I don't think that's true at all. You'd just be doing what's best for the rest of us. For the group as a whole."

Yeah. Well. Call me selfish, but I was a little more concerned about me as an individual.

"The committee has already lost its chair," Rachel pointed out needlessly. "Two chairs, if you want to get technical. If Abby leaves, too, there won't be anybody left who knows what's going on."

Shellee looked thoughtful. "She has a point," she said to the others.

Charmaine nodded and glanced around the table to see what the others thought.

"I suppose as long as there's no *direct* connection between Divinity and the murder," Marisol said.

Kirby drummed his beefy fingers on the tabletop. "I guess we could watch and see what happens over the next few days."

Their enthusiasm was underwhelming, but I wasn't in a position to complain.

"Nobody really wants you to leave," Marisol assured me. "We're trying to make sure the festival doesn't suffer, but it's nothing personal."

Easy for her to say. It sure felt personal to me. I'd promised Jawarski that I wouldn't get involved in the investigation, but that was before I found out I was already involved—the wrong way.

I hit the sack the minute I got home that night and slept surprisingly hard all night. By the time I woke up the next morning, the building was already shaking with the sounds of hammers, saws, country music, and whatever else the guys were playing around with down on the second floor.

Knowing that Wyatt's buddies, Charlie Stackhouse and Toby Yager, were in the house, I slipped into an old T-shirt and sweatpants before I scuffed into the kitchen to start coffee. They'd been hard at work for two weeks already, and I still couldn't see any discernable progress.

Because they were working on their own time, Wyatt was beginning to take exception to my unnatural and ungrateful hurry. I was beginning to take exception to Wyatt in general—especially after the past few days. If it hadn't been for those two nasty citations from the health department, I would have marched downstairs and sent them all packing.

The citations weren't critical, thank God. Aunt Grace had been meticulous about keeping the building up to code. But pipes, wiring, and other things invariably got old, and that meant I had to make a handful of changes before the end of the month if I wanted to keep the store open. Which, of course, I did.

If I wanted free labor—the only kind of labor I could afford after spending my savings on lumber, tools, and other construction material—I had to take advantage of Wyatt's offer to spend his vacation working for me. Someone dropped something heavy downstairs, and dust seeped under the door into the apartment's tiny kitchen. Normally, it wouldn't have bothered me—at least not a lot—but the past couple of days had left me feeling as if every nerve in my body was on fire.

I watched the dust rise up to coat the table and counter, debating whether to scream or pull my hair out. Before I could decide, my tone-deaf brother chose to add his voice to a Tim McGraw/Faith Hill duet. I tossed a towel over the coffeemaker, hoping to keep the dust out, and headed back to the bedroom to get dressed, but before I got even halfway down the hall, a loud boom rocked the building.

Swearing under my breath, I pushed through the veils of Visqueen between my apartment and the building's second floor. Max trotted behind me, his little stub of tail wagging with anticipation over the adventure.

When I realized that billowing dust filled the entire second floor, I pulled the neck of my T-shirt over my mouth and nose and told myself not to panic. The guys knew what they were doing . . . at least I hoped they did.

As the dust began to clear, I spotted Wyatt, Toby, and Charlie in the middle of the room, all staring at a pile of debris. Each of them wore that blank, slightly surprised look a cat gets when it knocks something onto the floor.

Wyatt and I have been mending our relationship since I came back to Paradise, but there will probably always be a little wedge between us. You just can't undo what's been done, no matter how much you might want to. Anyway, the hope that we could undo most of it kept me from yelling at him.

When Max saw Wyatt, his little stub of tail began to move faster. I don't know why the dog likes hanging out with the guys while they're working, but he's much happier amid all the bedlam than upstairs alone. I have to be honest and admit that I'm happier when he's not chewing up my stuff. He's calmed down a lot since he first came to live with me, but I still find the occasional ravaged shoe or gnawed tube of lip gloss when I climb the stairs after work.

Charlie saw me coming and rolled his eyes at the others as if to say, *here it comes.* Sometimes Charlie really annoys me. He's been Wyatt's best friend since they were kids, and there are times when I think he holds a bigger grudge against me for leaving Paradise than Wyatt does.

I ignored Charlie and asked Wyatt, "What happened?"

Toby ran a nervous hand across his freshly shaved head and shifted his weight from side to side almost as if he didn't trust my veneer of calm.

He didn't need to worry. Not really. The Shaws are a passionate family. We're ruled by emotion, every one of us. But years of living with my ex-husband, Roger, and pursuing a career in the law had taught me how to maintain my cool under most circumstances.

The portable stereo in the corner switched to a Toby Keith song. I leaned in close and shouted, "Can you turn that off for a minute so I can hear?"

Wyatt's mouth twitched beneath his mustache and he shared a look with Charlie. "Whatever you say, boss."

It wasn't *what* he said, but how he said it that stuck in my craw. Deep down, Wyatt's a good guy. It's just that his best qualities are buried under forty-five years of macho bullshit, which sometimes makes them difficult to find.

"Can the sarcasm, okay? Whatever that was, it nearly brought the building down around my ears." So I exaggerated. I had a point to make, and subtleties are lost on my brother. "All I asked was what happened. I don't think I'm being overly demanding to want an answer."

Wrinkles appeared around Wyatt's eyes. "We're working."

"You knocked down a wall?"

"Had to. You need that wiring fixed, don't you?"

The pressure of the past couple of days made my head ache. "Yes, I do," I snapped, "but I thought it might be possible to replace a few wires without razing the building."

Wyatt's expression went cold, and he held the hammer toward me. "You know so much more than I do? Go ahead and take over. I don't mind spending the rest of my vacation in front of the television."

Toby snorted. Charlie moved a few feet away and poured coffee from a thermos.

"I don't want you to quit," I assured my brother. "I appreciate what you're doing for me."

"Then let me do it."

"It's just that I didn't realize you'd be knocking down entire walls. I thought you said this would be a minor renovation, not a major remodel."

Wyatt shared a long-suffering look with his buddies.

"This is an old building, Abby. It's in worse shape than any of us could have guessed."

Oh goody! More bad news. I groaned and rubbed my temples. "How bad?"

"The wood in this wall was nearly rotted through. It had to come down."

"Fine. How much will it cost to rebuild it?"

Wyatt shrugged. "I don't know yet. Charlie thinks we're going to have to replace the windows overlooking the street, and the floor over on the west side is bad. Looks like water damage."

I perched on a nearby sawhorse and made myself ask, "From what?"

Another shrug and a glance at the ceiling. "Leak in the upstairs bathroom, maybe. Or could just be from those windows. Looks like the seal's been bad for a while."

I could almost see my bank balance swirling down the aforementioned toilet. "Is that all that's wrong?"

"So far."

I rubbed a little harder at my temples and wondered if there was anyone out there willing to extend me credit. I hadn't checked my credit rating lately, but it hadn't been really healthy since the divorce. Roger and I had lived well, but not because of our annual incomes. It had been Roger's family money that allowed us to live in an upscale condo with a view of Sacramento.

After the divorce, the senior partners at the law firm where Roger and I worked had decided he was more valuable to the firm than I was, and they'd showed me the door. The shock of losing my job had been minor compared to the shock of finding Roger and his little playmate copulating on my bedroom floor, but the two things combined had sent me into a tailspin.

In just a few months, I'd run through my meager savings. I don't like admitting it, but poverty had been the catalyst that drove me home to Paradise. That and the need to have a roof over my head while I figured out which direction I wanted my life to go. I'd never dreamed that I'd land here for good.

The point is, I didn't exactly have deep pockets. Not deep enough to embark on a major construction project, anyway. Not that I had a choice. The building was falling apart, so I had to do something.

While I contemplated my options in the middle of the war zone that had once been the second-floor meeting room, sawdust and dirt coated my hair and settled in creases I didn't even know I had. "Is there any of this that can wait until business picks up again for the summer?"

Toby held back a belch. Classy. "You think it will pick up? I mean, what about the dead lady in the parking lot? People don't like shopping where somebody has died. Freaks 'em out or something."

"Felicity's death has nothing to do with Divinity," I said, but even I could hear the lack of conviction in my voice. I was starting to think I might be the only person in Paradise who believed that.

Toby lifted one shoulder and turned away.

I told myself to stay focused on the crisis du jour. "Can we forget about the murder and talk about the renovations?"

Wyatt shrugged to show he didn't mind.

Charlie took a moment longer to make the shift. "Trouble is," he said after a while, "you've got some pretty serious structural damage here. We could put a patch on it, but it's just gonna get worse. You wait, you could find yourself with some real trouble."

"This doesn't qualify as real?" I didn't want to ask how much worse it could get. He might tell me. "What kind of money are we looking at to fix everything now?"

"I don't know yet," Wyatt said. I thought I spotted a gleam of sympathy in his dark eyes, but that only made me feel worse. "I can talk to a few people. Come up with an estimate."

Somehow I managed to squeeze "Thanks," around the lump in my throat. The catch in my voice embarrassed me, and I turned away so they wouldn't see me cry.

Too late. Wyatt got all mushy on me. He cleared his throat and came to stand in front of me, embarking on a thorough study of the toe of his boot. "Look, Abby, if you need a loan, Lizzie and I might be able to help out a little."

His offer surprised and touched me. I didn't let myself say no, but I wasn't seriously considering saying yes, either. So I didn't say anything at all. Wyatt and his wife Elizabeth had reconciled only a couple of months earlier, and they were still walking on eggshells around each other. I didn't want to add stress on their marriage.

Even so, as I stood there surrounded by chaos, I had the strangest impulse to hug my brother. Wyatt and I aren't the touchy-feely type, though, so I settled for putting a hand on his shoulder. "Let's find out how bad it is," I said. "Then I can figure out what to do."

"Sure. But you know . . ." He cleared his throat again, and his gaze flickered to my face for half a second. I guess he felt just about as uncomfortable as I did.

"Yeah," I said. "I know." And I did. It was getting harder and harder to stay positive, but at least I wasn't going through this alone.

Chapter 8

Trying to keep a firm grip on my emotions, I stood under the spray of a hot shower until the water started to run cold. When I couldn't take it any longer, I climbed out, toweled myself dry, and threw on a pair of jeans and a sweatshirt. I let Max drag me around the block for a while, then left him with Wyatt while I went downstairs to work.

I found Karen in the kitchen, surrounded by gallon jugs and stacks of boxes, a deep scowl on her face. The sharp scent of peppermint overpowered even the heady aroma of chocolate. She ran a quick glance over me as I came through the kitchen door. "Any ideas about what we're going to do with all of this?"

Shaking my head, I dug a coffee filter out of the cupboard and set to work making my second pot of the day. I didn't know how to tell her that we were in danger of being voted out of the arts festival. Maybe it wasn't fair to keep her in the dark, but she's been fighting clinical depression for the past few years, and I'm never sure how much to tell her about anything. Some days she's on. Some days she's not. I still have a hard time telling the difference. With any luck, I'd find the real killer in time to save our spot in the festival, and she'd never need to know.

The rising sun spilling in through the window turned Karen's auburn hair to flame. There are times when I envy that hair. My own is dull by comparison, and I've never had the patience to grow it longer than my chin.

"If you ask me," Karen grumbled, "Bea ought to pay for it, but that'll never happen. I've been thinking, though. Laid awake most of last night, in fact. I think I've come up with an idea."

I pulled two mugs from the cupboard. "Really? What?"

Karen put sugar and creamer on the table and held up a cautionary hand. "I don't have all the details worked out yet."

"You've still got more than I do. So tell me, what have you come up with?"

"We both agree that all of this peppermint is outrageous, right?"

"To say the least."

"So what if we did something outrageous with it for the festival? Let's invite people to talk about the peppermint instead of treating it like it's a huge mistake."

Intrigued, I poured coffee into two mugs and joined Karen at the table. "And how would we do that?"

"I don't know exactly," Karen admitted. "I was thinking about making a bunch of huge peppermint lollipops—big enough so that all the kids would want one. Maybe we could make one really big one and have a drawing for it. We could make peppermint the theme and have that old Chubby Checker song playing from the booth . . ." She broke off with an uncertain smile. "I don't know if it would work, but when life hands you peppermint—"

I laughed and finished for her. "Make lollipops?"

"Something like that."

Again, I considered telling her about the festival, but even if we didn't have the booth, we might still get plenty of walk-in customers during the festival. The booth would double our exposure, but we might survive without it.

As her smile slowly faded, she sat back in her chair and picked up a spoon. For a long, uncomfortable moment she focused on her coffee as if she'd never seen anything like it before. "Have you heard from any of the other cousins?"

I immediately grew wary. "No. Am I going to?"

Karen lifted one shoulder in a casual shrug. "I don't know. You might."

My heart dropped. Bea had worked her way through the family a few months earlier, stirring up trouble with complaints about the way I handled the store. It had taken way more time than I wanted to spend soothing ruffled feathers and setting boundaries. Unfortunately, my family is no good at respecting boundaries, and I had to be constantly on the alert for a sneak attack. "Why?" I asked. "Has Bea been on the phone with them again?"

Karen's gaze flickered to my face for an instant. "I don't know if Bea started it this time or if someone else did." She sipped slowly, but she still didn't make eye contact. "Apparently one of them heard that we'd been kicked out of the festival."

My face grew warm, and I mentally cursed Paradise's overactive grapevine. There were good things about being back home, but I wondered if I'd ever get used to the whole town knowing my business almost before I did. "Where did they hear that?"

"I don't know. Is it true?"

There didn't seem to be much point in hiding the truth from her now. "Some people think that I'll damage the festival's reputation if I'm there," I admitted. "They think people might stay away to avoid me. I convinced them to give me some time, but there's a possibility they may ask us to leave."

She looked at me hard. "And just when were you going to tell me about this?"

I felt about an inch tall. "I don't know. I was hoping I wouldn't have to."

She gave me a look that could have withered mountains. "Really? How kind of you to protect me."

Call me cynical, but she didn't sound like she meant it.

"Seems to me," she went on, "you don't want me having any *real* say in what goes on around here. Making me assistant manager was all just a smokescreen, wasn't it?"

I *so* didn't want to have this conversation right then, but I'm smart enough to know that putting her off wouldn't be a good idea. "It only happened last night. I haven't seen you until now."

"My phone works."

"It was late. I didn't want to wake you up."

Karen laughed harshly. "At least tell the truth, Abby. You didn't call because it never occurred to you that I should know. Or worse, you thought I was too emotional to know." She folded her arms across her chest and glared at me. "I realize that Aunt Grace left Divinity to you, but it would be nice if you'd acknowledge my contribution once in a while."

"I *do* acknowledge your contribution," I assured her. "I couldn't do this without you."

"But you still act as if what goes on around here is none of my business."

"I don't mean to. That's not how I feel. I'm just worried about you, and I don't want to upset you."

The frown on Karen's face deepened, and her eyes turned an opaque chocolate brown. "I'm not fragile, Abby. You don't have to protect me."

"I wasn't trying to protect you," I said. "I was trying to protect me."

Karen's eyes flew wide. "From what? Me?"

"From everything. From failing again in the family's

eyes. From letting you down. I thought that if I could prove that I didn't have anything to do with Felicity's death, I could get Divinity back into the festival before anyone found out what happened."

Karen barked a reluctant laugh. "You're in Paradise now, remember? You can't keep anything secret around here."

"Yeah. How could I forget?" I sipped coffee, but it had already grown lukewarm. I pushed the mug away and rested my chin in my hand. "Let's hope you're right when it comes to the murder. Somebody hated Felicity enough to kill her. You can't hide that kind of hatred for long."

"Finding someone who hated Felicity isn't going to be your problem," Karen said thoughtfully. "That list probably goes on forever."

"Yeah, but the person we're looking for is gutsy. He plunged an awl right through her heart, so he got right in her face and killed her, and he did it right in the middle of town, where anyone might have seen him."

"Or her."

"Or her." I put my feet up on an empty chair and locked eyes with Karen. "So which *her* are you thinking about? Ursula?"

"I think it's possible. She had plenty of reason to hate Felicity."

"What about Jacqueline?"

"I wouldn't cross her off the list, but Felicity could have been murdered by just about anybody. According to you and Rachel, all the members of the guild were ready to kill her the night she took over the festival."

"And Jacqueline looked mad enough to take the house apart when I was up there the other night."

Karen nodded slowly. "You never did tell me what she was mad about."

"That's because I don't know. I didn't stick around long enough to find out."

"If you ask me, Jacqueline had plenty to be mad about,"

Karen said. "So she got pregnant with Brenda while she was young. So what? That's no reason for Felicity to treat her granddaughter like a second-class citizen."

"I'm sure Felicity thought it was plenty of reason, and she figured the baby's father gave her even more reason."

"The way Felicity treated Jacqueline was positively shameful," Karen insisted, "and the way she acted toward Brenda was even worse."

I grinned. "I don't know if you've noticed, but I'm not arguing with you."

With a roll of her eyes, Karen tore open a bag of peppermint drops and popped one into her mouth. "I've always wondered which upset Felicity more: the fact that her daughter was a teenage unwed mother or the fact that the baby's father was the gardener's son."

Neither of us bothered mentioning specifically that the gardener in question had been of Chinese descent, but we were both thinking it. Felicity's bigotry was the stuff legends are made of, and Jacqueline had practically guaranteed her mother's lifelong anger when she fell in love with Galen Chen. Getting pregnant by him at sixteen and then actually having the baby had made everything worse.

Karen nudged the package of peppermint toward me. "Can you imagine how that must have upset Felicity? She was probably relieved when Galen disappeared."

The whole drama had played out the year before I left Paradise for college. It was the last really juicy bit of gossip I'd heard in years, and the details were surprisingly fresh. "I'm sure you're right, but I wonder how Jacqueline felt about it."

"She was devastated. She thought Galen was going to marry her."

"Well *that* was naive," I said, fishing out a peppermint drop for myself. "I wonder how many girls in the course of history have given it up for that 'Come on, baby. I'll marry you when you're eighteen' shtick."

"Don't try to count," Karen said with a smile. "It'll make your head hurt." After a moment she grew thoughtful again. "Still, I really thought she and Galen were in love. I would have bet money that he really cared about her."

"Felicity's reaction was cruel," I agreed, "but I doubt Jacqueline just flew into a rage after more than twenty years and chased her mother through town so she could kill her."

Karen glanced at the clock and pulled her work apron from its hook, "No, but there was bad blood between the two of them for years. It probably wouldn't have taken much to push Jacqueline over the edge."

"And all I have to do is find out what set her off. Piece of cake."

Karen slipped the apron over her head. "Don't complain. It's a place to start. That's more than you had five minutes ago. Talk to Felicity's family, but be careful. I'll bet one of them can even tell you why Felicity was sitting in the parking lot."

She might be right about that, but even if one of them knew what had brought Felicity out that night, would they tell me? Like most of Paradise, they might fight among themselves, but they would probably close ranks against an outside assault. And where would that leave me?

Since we had no customers, Karen kept herself busy dusting and cleaning fingerprints from glass surfaces. I decided to take advantage of the slow morning to start asking questions. I didn't expect to learn that anyone from the neighboring shops on Prospector Street had been around in the middle of the night while Felicity was being killed, but I thought it might be a good idea to make sure.

I pulled two Cokes from the old refrigerator we keep for personal items and carried them across the parking lot to Picture Perfect. Dooley Jorgensen has been a close friend since I came back to Paradise. When Aunt Grace was still alive, Dooley had made it a daily habit to check on her and make sure her world was spinning smoothly. After her death, he took me under his wing as well. I found myself appreciating his concern a little more all the time.

He grinned broadly when he saw me coming through the door—or maybe he was just happy to see the Coke. It was hard to tell. I browsed through photographic supplies while Maris Corwin, my seventh-grade English teacher, hemmed and hawed over whether to get two or three copies of the pictures on her roll of film.

After finally deciding on two copies of each print, she sidled a few feet away and left me free to approach the counter. I handed one of the Cokes to Dooley. He gave me a fatherly smile and cracked it open. "Heard about the excitement you had over at your place. I tried to come over there yesterday, but the police wouldn't let me get close. How are you holding up?"

"They wouldn't let you?" I gave a weary laugh. "Well, that might help explain why we hardly had a single customer all day. And I thought people were just avoiding me."

Dooley knew how to sympathize without pity. That's one of the things I liked about him. "I doubt that. Things going a little better today?"

"It's too early to tell."

"Well, I'll keep my fingers crossed. What brings you out and about this morning? Anything special I can do for you?"

I glanced over my shoulder at Mrs. Corwin. I didn't want to discuss the murder in front of her, but it didn't look as if she'd be leaving anytime soon, and I couldn't wait indefinitely. "I'm trying to figure out what happened when Felicity was murdered," I told Dooley. "I'm looking for anyone who might have been downtown between midnight and six thirty on Tuesday morning. I don't suppose you were hanging around then, were you?"

Dooley wagged his head back and forth. "Sorry, pumpkin. Wish I had been. Only person I know who gets up that early is Jessie McGraw from over at Bonner's Bakery."

"Thanks. I hadn't thought about Jessie. I'll stop by and talk to her."

"Leave it to the police," Dooley said, sobering. "Let them figure out who killed her."

"I wish I could, but too many people are imagining some kind of connection between Felicity and me just because she was found outside in our parking lot. I have no idea what she was doing there . . . unless she was a customer of yours?"

"She came in a few times a year," Dooley said. "But I wouldn't call her a regular or anything. Her sister's in and out quite a lot, though. And her husband has been in a time or two. Maybe one of them knows why she was here, but they've always been a tight-lipped bunch."

I made a face and chugged some caffeine as Mrs. Corwin finally wandered out the door and left us alone. As soon as the door shut behind her I asked, "What was your opinion of Felicity?"

Dooley shrugged. "She was demanding. Pushy. Curt. As far as I know, that's how she was with everyone."

"That's probably true. So who do you think killed her?"

His expression grew thoughtful. "That's hard to say. You could probably find somebody who resented her almost anywhere you look."

"I don't think there's any question about that," I said with a grin. "I want to know if you suspect anybody in particular."

"How should I know?"

"Oh come on, Dooley. When something like this happens, everybody has an opinion. I'm not asking you to accuse anybody. I want to know, just between the two of us, who you think had the most reason to want Felicity dead."

Dooley chuckled and turned away to pull something from a shelf behind him. "Well, I'm *not* accusing anybody, but those Greentree people have been trying to shut down

Felicity's latest construction project for months. There's been a fair amount of trouble on the job site, too."

This was the first I'd heard of it. Or maybe just the first time I'd paid attention. When you live in a wilderness area, it's hard to keep track of who's fighting who over what. The Greentree people were a group of radical conservationists who made their battles more interesting by striking in the dark and remaining anonymous. "Do you know anybody who's in Greentree?"

"Can't help you there, pumpkin. Nobody knows who's in Greentree. I've heard rumors that the leader is some guy who used to live down in Greeley, but I don't know if it's true, and I can't remember his name anyway."

"I guess that means they don't keep an office around here, huh?"

Dooley gave me a look. "They're a hit-and-run outfit, Abby. They deal in sabotage, and they never step out into the sunlight. I'll tell you who might know, though. That sculptor . . . what's his name? Kirby something."

My head shot up as if Dooley had jerked it with a chain. "Kirby North?"

"That's the one."

"He's a member of Greentree?"

"I can't say for sure, but he's a member of every other conservation group around. He gets so worked up about it, a fella can't even step on a bug if he's around."

Well, well, well. Slowly, like thick caramel, a grin spread across my face. "Thanks, Dooley. You're the best."

"I'm not saying he *is* a member of Greentree," Dooley said again. "Just that he *might* know something about it."

"Right. Got it."

"And don't go doing anything dangerous."

I was already halfway to the door, so I waved a hand over my head and kept going. I appreciated his concern, but nobody else was going to look out for me. I'd have to do the job myself.

Chapter 9

Feeling better than I had in two days, I hurried back across the parking lot. I didn't know who to talk with first. I didn't expect Felicity's family to tell me much. Like Dooley said, they were a close-mouthed bunch. If Kirby was involved in Greentree, he'd be too busy trying to protect himself to tell me anything helpful, but Jessie McGraw had nothing to hide. At least, I didn't think she did. At this point, I couldn't be certain of anything.

I still hadn't talked to Mayor Jeb Ireland, and I needed to do that just to find out where the committee stood. Would he bring Meena back, or would he put someone else in charge? I hoped he was planning on the former, because bringing anyone else up to speed would be too time-consuming, and the only other alternative was to put me in that spot. With everything else I had to worry about, I wanted to make sure Jeb didn't get any bright ideas.

Just as I was about to let myself into the kitchen, I caught movement from the corner of my eye—a car pulling into the lot. Hoping we finally had a customer, I turned to see who it was. And instantly regretted it.

A black-and-white Paradise Police cruiser came to a stop, straddling two painted lines. My stomach sank at the sight of it and turned over when Nate Svboda, official good old boy, climbed out from behind the wheel.

Nate's a sometime friend of Wyatt's. I've known him since I was a kid, but for all the warmth he's shown since I came back to Paradise, I might have been a complete stranger.

Nate stands a good half foot taller than me, and he probably weighs in at two fifty or more. Back in the eighties he had one of the best mullets around. These days, he shaves off what's left of his hair. He raked a gaze across me as he closed the car door, his dark eyes opaque and almost black. "Abby."

"Nate."

"I was just coming to see you. You got a minute?"

I wanted to say no, but I knew being uncooperative wouldn't earn me any brownie points. I spooned a little sugar into my smile and hoped I looked accommodating. "Sure. What can I do for you?"

He pulled a notebook from his pocket and flipped it open. "I'm working on the Felicity Asbury murder. I need to ask you a few questions."

"Anything to help, but I've already told Detective Jawarski everything I know."

"Jawarski's not on the case. I am."

Jawarski was off the case, and he hadn't told me? I felt a little jab of betrayal but told myself not to let it get to me. Jawarski didn't have to report to me. "Okay," I said to Nate. "We can talk in my apartment." The suggestion wasn't as cooperative as it might seem. If by chance a customer or two wandered into the store, I didn't want them to see me being questioned by the police.

After a moment's hesitation, Nate nodded, and I led him

up the wooden stairs to my third-floor apartment. It took a few minutes to convince Max that Nate wasn't a threat, which only reinforced my suspicion that Nate didn't think of me as a friend.

Inside, our noses filled with the tang of peppermint and sawdust. Nate gave an appreciative sniff and made himself comfortable on my old plaid couch. I took the most uncomfortable chair in the world, a hand-me-down from my parents, circa 1972.

"I know you've already talked to Detective Jawarski," Nate said, a catlike smile playing with the edges of his thin lips, "but I'm sure you understand why the chief wants someone else to talk with you."

Not really; Chief Daly has known my parents since before I was born, but maybe that's why he was being especially careful. The Asburys could make a lot of trouble if they thought he'd overlooked evidence because of friendship. "Of course," I said. "What do you want to know?"

"I'd like to know what you were doing between midnight and six a.m. on Tuesday—when Felicity Asbury was being murdered."

"I was here, sleeping."

"Alone?"

"With Max. He sleeps curled up by my feet every night."

Nate's eyes narrowed almost imperceptibly, and the smile slid from his round face. "I won't bother asking the dog to verify your alibi. What time did you go to bed?"

"Around midnight. I took Max out for a walk at ten thirty, watched Letterman, and then turned in."

"Did you see anything unusual in your parking lot when you went out?"

There's something about Nate Svboda that rubs me the wrong way. Always has been. It's hard not to turn into a smart-ass when he's around. "Like Felicity Asbury with an awl sticking out of her chest? No. She wasn't there at the time."

Nate's gaze locked on mine. "Anything else?"

"No."

"What time did Felicity arrive?"

"I have no idea. It must have been sometime after I went to bed."

"You didn't hear her pull in?"

I shook my head. "I didn't hear a thing. Not Felicity arriving, not somebody else joining her, no arguments, no murder. Nothing."

He shot a glance at the dog, who sat at my feet with ears pricked. While we both watched, Max's ears twitched at some faraway sound. "The dog didn't hear anything either?"

"If he did, he didn't mention it to me." Nate's scowl deepened, and I reminded myself of all the reasons I needed to sound like a friendly witness. "I know it's hard to believe, but it's the truth. Maybe he saw the whole thing happen, but he didn't bark, and I didn't wake up, so I don't know."

"Mmm-hmm." Nate scribbled something in his notebook before lifting his gaze to mine again. "What was Felicity doing here?"

"I don't know."

"She wasn't here to see you?"

"Not that I'm aware of."

"You didn't call her?"

"No."

Air whistled in his nose as he pulled in a deep breath and leaned back in his seat. "According to her sister, she received a call from a woman at a few minutes before eleven. If it came from you, it will be easy enough to prove."

Ursula lost a few more points for casting more suspicion my way. "I'm not worried. It didn't come from me."

Nate made another note, shifted his position, and crossed an ankle over his knee. "Tell me what you did earlier that evening."

"I worked here until Rachel Summers called and asked for my help at the guild. I went over there and learned about the trouble with the arts festival. Since I was Meena's assistant, people asked me to go talk to Felicity and convince her to step aside. They were threatening to walk out on the festival, so I agreed."

"So you went to the Asbury house. What time was that?"

"About seven thirty."

"You saw Felicity?"

"For a few minutes."

"Witnesses say you argued with her. What was that about?"

"We talked about the arts festival," I said, desperately clinging to my patience. I really shouldn't be annoyed with Nate. After all he was just doing his job. "I wouldn't call it an argument, though. It was more of a disagreement."

Nate looked up with a scowl. "Really? Then maybe you can explain why you were overheard threatening Mrs. Asbury."

Ursula had certainly been busy. "Threatening? Admittedly, I was upset when I left, but I'm sure I didn't threaten her. I'd remember if I had."

"You didn't say that you'd do whatever it took to make her change her mind?"

The air left my lungs in a whoosh. "No, of course not. Come on, Nate. You've known me since I was a kid. You know I couldn't kill anybody."

Again, those opaque brown eyes locked on mine. "I knew you *when* you were a kid, Abby. You've been gone from here a long time, and people change, so I really have no idea what you're capable of."

Gee, Nate, why don't you say what you really think? I took a couple of calming breaths and said the same thing I'd been saying for two days. "I didn't kill her."

"Why did you threaten her?"

"I didn't. I wanted her to leave the festival to those of us who've been working on it for the past six months, but I would have taken care of that through legal channels. I wouldn't have murdered her."

"What time did you leave Mrs. Asbury's house?"

I couldn't tell whether he believed me or not, and that made me edgy. "About eight o'clock, I guess. I was leaving just as Jacqueline got there—Felicity's daughter. If you ask me, that's who you should be interrogating. She *did* threaten to kill her mother."

One eyebrow arched. "Oh?"

"She told Felicity she could kill her for what she'd done."

"And what was that?"

I shook my head. "I have no idea. I didn't hear much more than that, except I can tell you that Felicity wasn't happy to see her there."

Nate made a note and glanced at me briefly. "Anything else?"

While talking to Jawarski about the murder I'd forgotten all about the truck I passed as I was pulling in, but I remembered it now, so I told Nate. "There was someone else there when I arrived. I don't know who it was. He passed me on his way out, but whoever it was drove an old pickup."

"What year?"

"I don't know."

"Color?"

I searched my memory for the forgotten details, but I'd already lost them. "I don't remember. Gray maybe. I think it had a blue door, but it was kicking up a lot of dust, and I was thinking about the conversation I was about to have with Felicity, so I didn't really pay attention to detail."

"What about the make? Ford? Dodge? Chevy?"

"Ford, I think. It seemed vaguely familiar at the time, but I couldn't say where I've seen it before."

Nate laughed and closed his notebook. "An old gray

Ford pickup. That narrows the field down. Hell, Abby, you can't turn a corner around here without running into half a dozen trucks or more."

"I realize that, Nate, but I thought you should know."

"And I appreciate that." He stood, smoothing his pants along his legs as he straightened. "You're going to stick around town for the next couple of weeks, aren't you?"

"Of course. I'm not going anywhere."

"Good. That'll be smart." He reached for the doorknob but stopped before turning it. "I don't know what happened here Tuesday morning, but I'm going to find out. You might be Wyatt's baby sister, but that's not going to get you any special treatment, so don't ask."

I held up both hands in a gesture of surrender. "Wouldn't think of it."

And then he was gone. Max stood at the window watching him negotiate the stairs to the parking lot. I stood with my back against the door and wondered when Jawarski would get around to telling me he wasn't working on the murder any longer. He'd been noticeably absent the past couple of days, but I'd chalked that up to the case. I didn't know which bothered me more: the fact that Jawarski wasn't coming around or the fact that I cared.

After Nate drove away, I went back to the shop and found it swarming with customers. Karen looked so relieved to see me, I didn't have the heart to leave her alone, even though people seemed more interested in the murder than our inventory. For the rest of the afternoon, I answered questions and tried to interest people in spending a little money.

Whenever there was a break in customers, I worked on creating stacks of ant sticks: pretzel logs dipped in chocolate and rolled in sprinkles. Karen had assured me they were a kid favorite at the arts festival every year, and apparently the adult versions were even more popular.

People don't always believe this, but adults eat 65 percent of the candy produced in the United States each year. We just like to blame it on kids. With that in mind, I planned to fill our inventory with milk and dark chocolate–dipped pretzels drizzled with white chocolate, and white chocolate drizzled with milk or dark chocolate. We also offered milk, dark, and white chocolate rolled in chopped walnuts, almonds, or macadamia nuts, and those were only a few of the varieties. If it could be chopped, diced, or grated, we'd roll a chocolate-covered pretzel in it. Today, I'd decided to experiment with crushed peppermint.

Ant sticks aren't difficult to make, and they don't require a lot of thought, which made them the perfect job for the day. I doubted I could corral my scattered thoughts enough to tackle anything more complicated. But my choice of tasks left me with plenty of time to think about the murder, and unfortunately, the more I thought, the less I knew. Nate said that a woman had called Felicity and lured her to Divinity. But who? And why had she chosen *my* store as the scene of the crime?

In between nonpaying customers and dipping pretzels, I fielded half a dozen distress calls from members of the guild and sorted out a problem with the soft drink vendor we'd contracted.

With no time to call our own during the day, Karen and I both worked late that night, making plans for our spring Christmas at the arts festival booth. Over the next two weeks, I'd be making peppermint fondant and peppermint lollipops, peppermint fudge, bark, petits fours, and twists—and that was just the start of the list. Whether or not we could get festivalgoers excited about all that peppermint was anyone's guess, but we had to try.

Next morning, I was waiting when the doors to the city building were unlocked, but Mayor Ireland was scheduled to be out of the office all day, and his executive assistant had taken the day off. The temp worker at the reception desk looked blank when I asked if I could leave a message. I scrawled my name and phone number on a message slip anyway, but I didn't hold out much hope that she'd figure out what to do with it.

The shop saw a steady stream of customers all day, but once again actual sales were low. The only bright spots in the day were brief visits from Rachel and Nicolette, both of whom slipped in to make sure Karen and I were holding up.

I knew it wouldn't be pleasant, but I'd decided that I needed to go back to the Drake Mansion and talk to Ursula before she spread more nasty rumors about me. That evening, I closed up at seven on the dot. Leaving dozens of ant sticks cooling on trays in the kitchen, I locked the doors and ran upstairs. I waved to Wyatt on my way past and changed into jeans and a sweatshirt before leading Max downstairs on his leash.

I was also curious to know what Jessie might have to say, but she arrived at the bakery every morning at four, and I had no idea how early she went to bed. Before I talked to Kirby, I wanted to find out a bit more about Felicity's feud with Greentree, and once again, it was too late to catch the mayor in his office. I was still reluctant to phone him at home, so I put meeting with him on hold and instead drove out of town toward the Drake Mansion.

Ursula answered the door almost immediately, and her face set into hard, cold lines when she saw me standing there. "What are you doing here?"

Was she Felicity's killer? I couldn't see any guilt in her eyes, but I couldn't see any grief, either. Just the usual irritation with the world in general and me in particular. "I need to ask you a couple of questions," I said.

"I have nothing to say to you."

"Well, I have a few things to ask you. You told the police that a woman called Felicity the night she died. I need to know about that phone call."

Ursula gave me a look that could have turned marshmallow to stone. "If you're still here in two minutes, I'm calling the police."

"I know you're upset. You have every right to be. I don't want to intrude on your grief, but I didn't kill Felicity, and I need to find a way to prove that."

Ursula's mouth puckered as if she'd just sucked on a lemon. "I heard what you said when you left here the night before Felicity died, and I heard her arranging later to meet you at the candy shop."

"I don't know what you heard, but I didn't threaten Felicity, and I didn't make that phone call. Once the police check the phone records, they'll know I didn't. Just tell me, did you answer the phone when the call came in?"

Ursula kept her eyes locked on mine. "Felicity answered it herself."

"Then why did you tell the police it was me?"

"She went to your place. Who else could it have been?"

She was making my head hurt. "Are you kidding? It could have been *anyone*. If you didn't answer the phone, why did you tell the police that a woman called?"

Her mouth pinched so tightly, fine lines radiated out from her lips. "Felicity said it was a woman who called. And she didn't end up dead in just *anyone's* parking lot."

"Could she have been lying about the caller?"

Ursula gave her head an angry shake. "Why would she do that?"

I was sure I could think of a reason or two but talking to her was like arguing with a sour ball. I decided to give up and move on. "Did Felicity often answer the phone herself?"

"Not often, but she did occasionally. Now, if you'll please leave, I have things to attend to."

Not a chance. I still had too many unanswered questions. "Jacqueline came in just as I was leaving. She was furious with her mother. What was that about?"

Ursula dragged in a deep breath, and her nostrils flared slightly. "Even if I knew, I wouldn't tell you."

"Was it about the problems with Greentree?"

Ursula snorted. "Jacqueline has nothing to do with Felicity's business concerns."

"Then it must have been about family. Was it Brenda?"

"That is none of your concern."

I switched gears again, hoping to keep her off balance enough to get a few answers. "What did Felicity say when she left the house that evening?"

Ursula shook her head stiffly. "Felicity didn't confide in me, and she didn't answer to me. She went where she wanted, when she wanted."

"You weren't concerned when she didn't come back?"

"I wasn't in the habit of keeping track."

"What about when Felicity was killed? Where were you then?"

Her expression grew even more foreboding. "Are you asking me for an alibi?"

"If you have one."

"I was here. Asleep."

"Alone?"

She looked down her nose at me and sniffed. "Yes. Alone."

"So there's no one who can vouch for you that night. I'm curious. What will happen to all of this now? Will it be yours?"

Ursula's eyes flashed. "How *dare* you suggest that I killed my sister for money."

Obviously, I'd touched a hot button. "I'm not suggesting anything."

"Well, you can wipe that idea right out of your head, because it won't be mine. Oliver Birch gets everything."

Now, that was interesting. "Does he know that?"

Ursula smirked. "Of course he does. Felicity made sure we both knew exactly what she intended to do with the money. She told us when she changed her will six months ago. It only took Oliver eighteen months to convince her to leave it all to him. I expected her to be stronger than that."

"You think Oliver was behind the change?"

"Of course he was. You don't think he married Felicity for her sense of humor, do you?"

My mind clicked into high gear, concocting motives and wondering about opportunity. "What did Oliver do when Felicity didn't come home on Monday night?"

"Nothing. He wasn't here."

I wasn't expecting that. "Do you know where he was?"

Ursula shook her head. "You'll have to ask him. But just remember, Oliver had everything to gain from Felicity's death, and I had everything to lose."

Chapter 10

All the way back down the mountain, I thought about what Ursula had told me. A deep twilight had settled over the valley, and lights blinked on across town as I rolled downhill. Old downtown Paradise nestled in the deep V created by two steep granite mountains, but as the town grew, it spread out into a broader valley ringed by peaks of varying height. I'd been back for eighteen months, and slowly but surely it was beginning to feel like home again.

Even so, the stab of affection I felt for the sprinkle of twinkling lights surprised me. Paradise had always been a safe place to live. That was changing, but I didn't want it to. I had friends here. Family. Nieces and nephews who deserved security. I hated thinking that a cold-blooded killer lived here, and I wanted him or her gone.

Oliver had been in town early the morning Felicity died. He'd seemed genuinely grief-stricken when we found her, but I'd been in a state of shock myself, so I might not have seen everything. If Ursula was telling the truth, and Oliver wasn't home on Monday night, where had he been? Setting the stage for Felicity's murder?

Back in Paradise, I passed Divinity and drove straight to the construction site. I had no idea what kind of car Oliver drove, but plenty of vehicles lined the streets, so I decided to take my chances.

In case Oliver was a murderer, I took Max with me. Max is a pussycat unless he feels a threat. Then he's all fangs. I picked my way across a concrete floor littered with nails, sawdust, boards, and other trash and, after asking around, finally found Oliver at the back of the restaurant with two crew members, inspecting the framing of a new wall.

Oliver looked surprised to see me, but not unhappy or worried. After a few minutes he finished what he was doing and left the crew members to join me. "Abby? Is there something I can do for you?"

I didn't want to leap in with questions, especially since I wasn't completely convinced he was guilty. "I've been thinking about you since Tuesday. Wondering how you're holding up."

His expression sobered, and he shook his head slowly. "I'm getting by. Can't say much more than that." Seemingly dazed, he looked around the site. "Work's been a godsend. I don't know what I would have done without the restaurant to keep me busy."

"I'm sure it's been helpful. When do you plan to open?"

"Three months. You can't believe how much work there is involved in opening a new restaurant. I don't suppose you'd be interested in the fifty-cent tour?"

I definitely wasn't interested in letting him get me alone somewhere. "Some other time, maybe," I said, trying to look regretful. "I really can only stay for a minute. I just came from talking to Ursula. It seems that someone called Felicity out the night she died. Do you have any idea who it might have been?"

He ran a hand across the back of his neck. "No, but I

wish I did. Ursula would know more about that than I would. What did she say?"

I was sure he already knew, so I didn't bother answering. "So Felicity didn't say anything to you about what she was doing or where she was going that night?"

"I didn't talk to her at all that day. We were both busy with our own things."

"So you have no idea why she went out or who she was planning to meet?"

"Just what Ursula tells me."

So far, he was being spectacularly unhelpful, but that didn't necessarily make him guilty. Crossing my fingers that he hadn't talked with Ursula while I drove back to town, I asked, "You weren't worried when she didn't come home?"

"I didn't know. I wasn't there."

"You were here pretty early the next morning. Did you stay in town?"

He gave me a look from the corner of his eye. "What are you doing, Abby? Trying to figure out whether I have an alibi?"

"Do you?"

He mopped his face with one hand, and his shoulders sagged. "As a matter of fact, I do. Not that it's any of your concern, but for most of the night I was at the bottom of Devil's Canyon, lucky to be alive. My brakes gave out while I was driving back from Aspen."

"In Devil's Canyon?" I shuddered at the thought. With its tight switchbacks and steep grade, the canyon was a nightmare under the best of circumstances. I couldn't imagine trying to negotiate it without brakes. "It's a miracle you weren't hurt."

He smiled slightly. "Just a little banged up. Nothing serious."

"Was anybody with you?"

Oliver's smile faded. "Not at the time, but if you don't believe me, check with the guy from Paradise Auto Body.

He had to come out in the middle of the night and tow me back to town. We didn't get back here until about three thirty. I grabbed a room at the High Country so I could sleep for a couple of hours before meeting with Henri." He paused, raking a slow look across my face. "I know what you're trying to do. I guess I can't blame you for trying to get yourself off the hook, but you're out of luck. There's *no way* I could have killed my wife."

Maybe if I were a more trusting person, I would have taken Oliver's alibi at face value. But I'm not, so I drove directly across town to Paradise Auto Body to make sure he was telling me the truth. Max sat in the front seat for the trip, his nose sticking out of the partially open window. His delight over the scents he finds in the air is almost guaranteed to make me smile. It's the little things, y'know?

Paradise Auto Body is located in a converted gas station on the north end of town, big enough for only two repair bays with a parking lot that might hold a dozen cars. It's small, and it's dirty, but they do quality work, and that's what counts. A tow truck listed to one side at the edge of the lot, and the door of one repair bay stood open. Tinny-sounding country music drifted into the evening from a radio somewhere inside as I pulled in, and a man in low-slung jeans and a high-riding T-shirt leaned under the hood of a Toyota Corolla.

I'd seen that hairy back before. It belonged to Orly, a guy I'd met several months earlier when he repaired my car after a fender bender. Since the accident, Orly has become a sometimes customer of Divinity, but I hadn't seen him around in a couple of months.

Max noticed him and scrambled toward the car door. Since he and Orly have made peace, I let him out. Max loped toward Orly. I followed more slowly.

When Orly realized he had company, he straightened and gave an ineffectual tug on his T-shirt. He greeted Max as if they were old friends and turned toward me. Unlike Nate Svboda, Orly hadn't abandoned his mullet when the eighties were over. What can I say? The guy's loyal.

"Well, look who's here," he said with a grin. "Don't tell me you have car trouble again."

"No, thank goodness. I heard you towed a car late Monday night, and I wanted to ask you about it."

"Sure did." He jerked his head toward the second repair bay where a dark-colored Bentley waited for attention. "Picked up that baby right there."

"What was wrong with it?"

"The brakes gave out on the poor schmuck who drives it. He was damn lucky he made it to the bottom of the canyon in one piece."

"Can you tell me who it belongs to?"

"Sure. Rich guy who lives up on the hill. Birch. The one whose wife died the other day. You know him?"

I nodded. "And he was there when you got there?"

Orly wiped grease from his hands and regarded me intently. "Yeah, he was. And Svboda's already been here asking about it. The guy was definitely stuck down there."

So Oliver had been telling the truth. At least I could cross one person off my list of suspects. I shrugged innocently and crossed to the Bentley so I could look at it more closely. "I'll bet he was pretty shaken, huh?"

Orly stuffed the greasy rag into his pocket and nodded. "Poor guy said the brakes were working fine one minute and gone the next."

"He was lucky he didn't get killed." I turned to make sure Max was still nearby when the timing of Oliver's accident finally sank in. Oliver's brakes had given out the same night Felicity was killed? What were the odds?

Orly cut into my thoughts. "Something wrong?"

"I don't know. Could you tell if someone tampered with those brakes?"

"I suppose I could."

"Will you check?"

"Now?"

I wanted desperately to say yes, but it was late, and I didn't want to impose. I might be wrong. If I was right, the killer was probably watching to see if Orly discovered a cut brake line. It would be less suspicious for him to check the car in the morning. Conscious that someone might be watching even now, I moved quickly back into the open doorway. "No, not now. Just look when you get to it. I'll check with you later."

Orly's thick brows beetled over his nose. He hawked something out of his throat and spat onto the pavement. "Fine by me. You think somebody tried to kill this dude?"

"I don't know. It's possible, so be careful."

"Always."

"I'd appreciate it if you wouldn't tell anybody about this conversation. I could be wrong, and I'd hate to stir up worry over something that didn't even happen."

He shot me a toothy grin. "You got it."

I drove away without looking back and told myself to be patient. But I was almost certain that someone had tried to commit a double murder two nights ago. The fact that they'd only been 50 percent successful didn't make me feel a whole lot better.

After I left Orly, I drove slowly through town, trying to decide what to do with what I suspected. Any other time, I would have called Jawarski, but he wasn't on the case any longer, and I wasn't about to discuss any of this with Nate unless I had concrete evidence in my hands. I was hungry but too antsy to go home and too tired to cook. Giving in to impulse, I drove to Lorena's, claimed my favorite booth, and ordered a plate full of comfort food. I dug into the smothered burrito, rice, and beans as if I hadn't eaten in weeks. If I hadn't had to drive home after dinner, I'd have washed the whole thing down with a margarita or two.

Halfway through the meal, I saw a familiar figure come through the door. I lifted my hand to wave to Meena, but dropped it again when Jacqueline came inside right behind her. The hostess led them to a table on the other side of the restaurant, and they laughed together as they studied the menu like old friends.

Until this moment, I hadn't even been aware they knew each other. But now, even a fragile connection between Jacqueline, Meena, and Felicity made my nerves tingle.

I couldn't see Meena's face from where I sat, but I had a clear view of Jacqueline's. I watched her furtively as I finished my meal, searching for signs of grief. If she was mourning her mother, she hid it well. I tried to read her lips and figure out what they were talking about but finally gave up the effort as a lost cause. I even ordered flan to buy more time and tortured myself with the soothing caramel custard in the interest of uncovering whatever secrets Meena and Jacqueline were keeping. What can I say? I can be selfless when I have to be.

For days, I'd been seesawing over Jacqueline as the possible killer. Her mother had treated her like dirt for years, but it wasn't likely that Jacqueline had suddenly snapped over some decades-old event. Her tirade the other night had sounded like she was upset about something new. But if she'd been estranged from Felicity for twenty years, what had Felicity done recently—and why? Now I had to wonder if Jacqueline was not only capable of murdering her mother in cold blood but also of crawling under Oliver's Bentley and tampering with the brakes.

After I nursed my third Diet Coke, Meena excused herself and went to the ladies' room. Deciding there was no time like the present, I followed her into the two-stall lavatory, made sure the second stall was empty, and locked the bathroom door to give us some privacy.

When Meena left her stall, she was focused on adjusting the waistband of her slacks, so she didn't see me immediately. She finally looked up, and the pleasant smile she'd been ready to offer a stranger slipped from her face. "Well, hello, Abby. I didn't realize you were here. Did you just arrive?"

I shook my head and moved away from the sink so she could wash her hands. "I've been here for a while. I didn't realize you and Jacqueline were friends."

Her eyes flicked to my face in the mirror, but she looked away quickly. "I invited her to dinner tonight. I thought she might need someone to talk to because of her mother and all."

"Did Felicity know you were a friend of Jacqueline's? Is that why the mayor took you off the committee?"

Meena laughed abruptly. "What an imagination you have. Of course not. Why would she care if we were friends?"

"If that's not it, then what did happen?"

Her smile disappeared. "I told you, I don't want to talk about it."

"I know that's what you said, but what can possibly be so bad?"

She shook water from her hands and cranked out a length of paper towel. "What part of 'I don't want to talk about it' is confusing to you, Abby? If I wanted to tell everyone my business, I'd have done it already."

"But we need you on the committee, Meena. It's not the same without you there. With the construction at my place and all the curiosity seekers coming in and out of Divinity, I can't handle the committee by myself."

"You don't have to handle it alone. Rachel's up to speed on almost everything. Delegate some of the responsibility to her." Meena tossed her towel into the trash and turned toward the door.

I stepped in front of it before she could get there. "What's going on, Meena?"

"Nothing."

"I'm not the only one who thinks you're behaving strangely. Do you really want people to start speculating? Wouldn't it be better to just tell the truth about whatever it is?"

"Are you crazy? Get away from the door, Abby. This isn't funny."

"Just a couple more questions. Do you know why Jacqueline was so upset with her mother on Monday night?"

"Jackie never sees her mother."

"She saw her Monday night. I was there when she came in."

Meena's eyes narrowed. "I don't believe you."

"Ask her. For that matter, ask Ursula. She was there. Jacqueline was furious with Felicity. In fact, she said she ought to kill Felicity for what she'd done. Do you know what it was?"

She shot an uncertain glance at the door. "No."

"Was it about Brenda? About the family? Something else?"

Her eyes glittered cold and hard as she looked at me again. "I told you, I don't know. Now, move and let me out."

"Look, Meena, I'm not trying to hurt you or Jacqueline. But somebody killed Felicity, and Ursula is trying to make it look as if I did it. I need to know what was going on between Jacqueline and her mother."

"Then ask her. I don't know anything about it." She clamped her lips together so tightly, tiny lines radiated from them in a sunburst. I knew that look. She wasn't going to tell me anything.

Reluctantly, I unlocked the door and moved out of her way. "If you need to talk, I'm here."

"I'll remember that," she snapped and shot through the door as if she couldn't get away from me fast enough.

Okay, so maybe locking her in a public restroom wasn't

the best idea I'd ever had. After working with her so closely for the past six months, I'd thought we were friends. Apparently, I was wrong.

I spent the next morning pouring so many peppermint lollipops, I wondered if I'd ever get the scent of mint out of my nostrils. I'd read somewhere that peppermint actually boosts creativity, but my thoughts remained stuck in the same old rut. When I wasn't worrying about paying off all the new debt I'd acquired, I thought about the murder.

Shortly before noon, I left Divinity and stopped by City Hall to see if I could finagle a minute with Mayor Ireland. This time, I actually saw him from a distance as he hurried to his car. I tried to get his attention, but if he saw or heard me, he did a good job of pretending he didn't.

Next stop, the festival staging area to check on delivery of the light-pole banners that hadn't arrived as of the previous afternoon. Nicolette and Rachel were already there, both looking frantic. After promising to check with the supplier again, I left and hurried to Paradise Auto Body.

The doors to the repair bays stood open, and I could see Oliver Birch's Bentley on one of the hydraulic lifts. The odors of oil and gasoline permeated everything, and Procol Harum's "Whiter Shade of Pale" blared from a portable radio on a workbench. I couldn't see signs of life anywhere.

Taking a couple of steps toward the Bentley, I called out for Orly, shifted direction, and headed for the shop's small office. "Orly? Are you here?"

This time I heard a metallic clink coming from the room ahead. I knocked on the door, waited a second, then inched it open. "Orly?"

"He ain't here," a deep voice growled. "What can I do for you?"

I jerked backwards instinctively, laughed at myself, and peered into the cramped room. A short man with a stocky build and flaming red hair sat at the desk, his attention riveted on whatever he was doing with a wrench.

"Orly isn't working today?"

Red shook his head without looking at me. "He's on lunch. You got trouble with your car?"

"No. I—I just needed to check with Orly about something. Do you know what time he'll be back?"

"Whenever he gets done, I guess." He glanced away from his task long enough to jerk his head toward the McDonald's across the street. "You can find him over there if you want to bother. I don't guess he'll mind having his Big Mac interrupted."

I tossed off a thanks and turned away.

"Hey lady?" Red called after me.

"Yes?"

"You the one wondering about that Bentley in there?"

I was just paranoid enough to hesitate before I nodded. "Has Orly had a chance to check it out?"

Red wiped his nose with the back of one grease-stained hand. "We both looked at it this morning—to be sure, y'know? I'd say them brakes were messed with, all right. That cut is as clean as a whistle."

It was what I'd been expecting, but hearing him verify my suspicions made my stomach roll over. "I see. Has Orly told anyone else yet?"

"Not yet." Red pulled a grimy rag from a pocket and used it to clean whatever he was holding. "He's planning to call the police right after lunch, though."

"Good. That's exactly what he should do."

Red cocked an eyebrow. "Oh?"

"What do you mean?"

"Nothing, really. Kinda strange, though, how you figured out them brakes had been cut without even looking at the car."

"Yeah? Well it was a wild guess."

"You got any guesses about who did it?"

I shook my head. "Not really, but I wish I did. I don't suppose there's anything else you can tell me?"

Red grinned, revealing a set of stained, uneven teeth. "Like what?"

"Anything unusual about the cut that might help the police figure out who did it?"

"Nope. Sorry. Except that it had to be somebody who knew at least a little something about cars."

With any luck, that would rule me out, but I wasn't going to hold my breath. If there's one thing I've learned in thirty-nine years, it's that we all make our own luck.

Chapter 11

Karen gave me directions to Jacqueline Asbury's house, so after work that evening I drove across town to a section known as the Flats. I pulled up in front of a tiny box of a home with blue paint peeling from the siding and weeds sprouting in the lawn. A Sentra with a sagging bumper sat in the driveway. All in all, the whole picture depressed me, and I couldn't help thinking what a difference a few million dollars can make.

I didn't know Jacqueline well, so I tethered Max to a tree on the parking strip and poured water from a bottle into the dish I keep for him in the hatch. Max settled down in the shade, and I trudged up the walk toward the front door.

Jacqueline answered the bell so quickly, I thought she must have seen me coming. To say that she didn't look happy to find me on her doorstep would be a serious understatement. She frowned so deeply, her chins sagged over each other and her round cheeks turned a mottled purple that made me wonder if she would survive the next ten minutes.

"What are *you* doing here?" she asked, piercing me with a glare.

"I'd like to talk to you for a few minutes. May I come in?"

"Why? Meena didn't tell you what you wanted to know when you locked her in the bathroom last night?"

"That was a mistake. I was worried about her, and I wanted her to talk to me."

"Interesting method. Maybe you ought to teach seminars on how to make friends."

If she hadn't been looking at me as if I'd turned into a bug, I might have laughed. "Yeah," I said with a wan smile. "It's my strong suit. I'm sorry about last night. I didn't intend to upset Meena. I just wanted to make sure she was okay."

"Why? Did you think I'd hurt her?"

"I don't know what to think," I said. "She's been acting strange lately. And when I saw you on Monday night, you were pretty upset. I had no idea the two of you were friends."

Jacqueline's cheeks burned. "My mother had a habit of making life miserable for people who tried to make life better for me. Meena loaned me some money when I needed it, and I didn't want her to suffer because of me. She didn't care, but I insisted that we keep our friendship quiet."

"But your mother found out about it anyway?"

"She must have."

When she didn't offer anything more, I dug a little deeper. "Do you know why the mayor removed Meena from the committee?"

Jacqueline tucked a limp lock of hair behind an ear. "I just told you, because of my mother."

Tiny problem: I didn't believe her. Being *that* bitchy was a stretch, even for Felicity. Besides, like I said before, Jeb Ireland may be self-centered, but he's not stupid. Yanking Meena off the committee just because Felicity didn't like her would just about guarantee he'd find himself in court.

"You can't think of anything else?"

"No. Sorry."

I didn't believe that, either. "So how about it?" I asked. "Can I come in for a few minutes?"

She shrugged and turned away. "You might as well, I guess. What do you want to know?"

Inside, the blinds were drawn, leaving the small, chaotic room in shadows. Piles of magazines leaned against the couch, empty soda bottles littered a flimsy-looking coffee table, and an ashtray overflowed onto the table's scarred surface. This was the first time since coming back to Paradise that I truly appreciated the hand-me-downs in my own apartment.

I sat on the couch and tried to ignore the clutter. "To begin with, who do you think wanted your mother dead?"

Jacqueline sank into a recliner and put her feet up. "Everybody who knew my mother hated her. It would be easier to ask who didn't want her dead."

"Was anyone in particular angry with her? Was she having trouble in her business dealings or anything?"

"I have no idea who was angry with her. She and I weren't exactly on speaking terms."

"But you were there the other night, and you were upset about something she'd done. What was that about?"

"I'd rather not talk about it."

I tried not to show my disappointment. "That's all right. You can just tell the police when they ask."

Jacqueline's gaze met mine, and her round cheeks flushed. "You think I killed my mother?"

"I didn't say that."

"You might as well have."

"Then did you?"

"Of course not."

Strangely enough, I believed her. "Did you hear anything unusual while you were at your mother's house?"

"What do you mean, unusual?"

"I'm wondering if your mother mentioned anything that might help us figure out what happened. Did she get any phone calls? Did she mention any trouble she was having?"

Jacqueline shook her head. "I couldn't tell you, even if I wanted to. She kicked me out of the house about two minutes after you left. She didn't say anything to me except to remind me how I've never been anything but trouble."

"That must have upset you."

"Of course it upset me. It would upset anyone. But it wasn't anything new or unusual. I should have been used to it. Let it roll off my back like water on a duck—that's what Brenda always tells me, anyway."

Since she'd brought her up, I jumped at the chance to ask about her daughter. "Brenda doesn't mind being estranged from her grandmother?"

Jacqueline's mouth tightened slightly. "Brenda doesn't mind at all. She grew up without a grandmother. She didn't need one as a child, and she certainly doesn't need one now."

I wondered if Brenda would tell me the same thing. "Do you think she would mind answering a few questions for me?"

"I'd rather not bother her with any of this. She didn't even know my mother."

"I realize that, but she may know something you don't. Is she home?"

Jacqueline eyed me warily. "She doesn't live here anymore, but I mean what I say, Abby. I don't want you talking to her about this. She's finally found a good job, and she's doing well. For the first time in her life, she has everything going for her. I'm not going to let my mother ruin her life now that she's dead."

I wasn't giving up on the idea of talking to Brenda, but

I couldn't see any reason to butt heads with Jacqueline about it. "What about Oliver? Do you have any idea how your mother's marriage was?"

"From what I've been told, they were blissfully in love. Oliver was in love with her money, and she was in love with the attention he gave her."

Her cynicism didn't surprise me. In fact, I'd have been shocked if she hadn't said something snarky. "I understand Oliver had car trouble the night your mother was killed."

She looked mildly interested. "What kind of car trouble?"

"His brakes gave out as he drove through Devil's Canyon."

"No kidding?" Jacqueline barked a laugh. "Well, you've got to hand it to him. It's a convenient alibi."

"You think Oliver might have killed your mother?"

"I think Oliver would have done anything to get his hands on her money."

Ursula had said the same thing, but I wasn't completely convinced. "I thought Oliver had plenty of money of his own."

"To a man like Oliver, there's no such thing as plenty of money."

"You know him then?"

"No, but I know his type. I spent the first sixteen years of my life surrounded by people like him."

"Do you think he'll inherit everything now that your mother's gone?"

Jacqueline pushed a lock of hair from her eyes. "Probably."

"What about Ursula?"

"What about her? She got her share of the money when my grandfather died. She blew it. End of story."

"You don't think your mother would have made sure that her sister was taken care of?"

Jacqueline laughed through her nose. "That's a joke, right?"

Yeah, I suppose it was. "What if Oliver were to die? Who would get the money then?"

Jacqueline's eyes narrowed into thin slits that almost disappeared in her face. "You think it comes to me, don't you? Well, you're wrong. I'm out for good. There aren't any second chances in my family. I was dead to my mother, and Brenda never existed. The money is Oliver's now. It'll go to whoever he wants it to go to."

That might be true, but I wondered what would have happened if Oliver had died the same night as Felicity. It was on the tip of my tongue to ask, but I wasn't ready to let her know what I suspected. "I understand that your mother was having trouble on one of her job sites. Do you know anything about that?"

Jacqueline tilted her head to one side and ran a slow glance across my face. "Why would I know anything about that?"

"I thought you might have heard talk."

"About the MegaMart she's building in the hollow?"

Stunned, I sat back hard in my chair. "Your mother was planning to bring a MegaMart to Paradise?" That *would* mean trouble, and not just from rabid conservationists.

"You didn't know?"

I shook my head slowly. "I had no idea. Who else knew about her plans?"

"I don't know."

"How did you find out?"

"The usual way. Aunt Ursula told me."

"There can't be many people who knew about it," I mused, "or I would have heard about it before now. Do you think that's why the people at Greentree have been sabotaging her equipment?"

Jacqueline lifted a round shoulder. "I can only assume it is, but I really don't care. My mother didn't care about anyone or anything. She would have torn down anything that got in the way of something she wanted." She struggled upright and said, "You probably think that sounds heartless, but my mother was a miserable old woman. Whoever killed her did us all a favor."

I stopped at Burger King after leaving Jacqueline's house and ordered two Whoppers (one plain for Max). Max and I settled comfortably in our seats to eat, and I ran back over the conversations I'd had that day. Max may not contribute a whole lot to the conversations, but he's a great listener.

I'd heard Ursula's story, and now I'd heard Jacqueline's. I still wondered what Brenda would say about her grandmother if I talked to her, and I was curious to find out what the foreman on the MegaMart project would say if I asked him about the sabotage.

So far, everyone I'd talked to had raised more questions than they'd answered, but they'd also opened doors to several possibilities. The problem was that each one was so completely unrelated to the others, I didn't know what to think. Had Felicity been killed because of the arts festival, for her money, or because she was planning to destroy the land? Or had she been killed simply because she was a mean, nasty woman?

I still didn't think Jacqueline had killed her, and I had a hard time envisioning her crawling under Oliver's car to tamper with his brakes, but I couldn't rule her out. I'd been wrong about people before. Ursula, however, was an entirely different story. I could imagine her doing almost anything to get what she wanted.

Then there was the MegaMart deal. If Greentree knew what Felicity was planning, would they have gone after Oliver, too, or been satisfied to get rid of Felicity?

Max wolfed down his burger and watched greedily while I finished mine. I was too hungry to toss him the last bite, so I offered a few fries instead. Not the best dog fare, I know, but I wasn't going to let him go hungry just because I wasn't home with the kibble.

After tossing the trash and swallowing most of a Diet Coke, I called Karen to find out if she knew where Brenda lived. She didn't, but she knew someone who did, and twenty minutes later, I found myself in front of a new apartment complex on the north end of Paradise.

I wound my way through a series of parking lots, around the parklike atmosphere of the rambling complex. After several minutes I found the building labeled Q and, by process of elimination, apartment 18 on the top floor of the third staircase.

From the front porch, I could hear the television blaring a reality show. I rang the bell, and the sound went quiet. A moment later, Brenda opened the door.

She was a pretty girl, with long black hair and almond-shaped eyes. An unmistakable Asian influence had also left its mark in the tone of her skin and the porcelain quality of her complexion. She squinted into the darkness, only a little relieved by the dim porch light hanging near the door.

"Yeah?"

"Brenda?"

"Yeah. Do I know you?"

"Probably not." I held out a hand. "Abby Shaw. I own the candy shop downtown."

Her eyes opened wide. "The one where—" She cut herself off as if she couldn't get the rest out.

"The one where your grandmother died. Could I come in for a minute?"

"I don't know if I should," she said uncertainly. "What do you want?"

"I'm trying to find out who killed your grandmother, and I'd like to ask you a few questions, if that's okay."

"I don't know why. I can't tell you anything. I didn't know her."

"But you knew *of* her. It's possible you know more than you think you do."

Brenda gave that some thought, then invited me inside.

She motioned me toward a small, round dining table flanked by two mismatched chairs. A small pot of tulips sat in the middle of the table, lending a little cheer to the tiny space. "So, what can I tell you?"

I liked her immediately, and I wondered how three generations of women in the same family could be so different. "Is it true that you never even met your grandmother?"

She glanced at me, then quickly away. "No, it's not true. I met her once. But my mother doesn't know, and I want to keep it that way."

"She won't hear it from me," I promised. "When did you meet her?"

"A little while ago." Brenda stood and strode to the refrigerator. "Can I get you something to drink? Or I could put water on for tea . . ."

"I'm fine, thanks. How long ago is 'a little while'?"

She jerked open the door and rummaged around inside for a few seconds. When she stood up again, she clutched a bottle of iced tea in one hand. "I don't remember, exactly. A few months, maybe."

That recently? Interesting. "How did that go?"

"How do you think?" She filled a glass with ice and poured the tea over it. "She didn't want a damn thing to do with me."

"She said that?"

"She said a whole lot more than that," Brenda said with a cool smile, "but I'd rather not repeat it all."

"I take it she didn't ask to meet you."

A bitter laugh escaped as Brenda resumed her seat. "No, she didn't ask to meet me. In fact, she threatened to kick out Mom's Aunt Ursula for letting me in."

Harsh. The more I learned about Felicity, the less I liked her, and that was saying something. "You went to see her, then. Can I ask why?"

"I wanted to meet her."

"That's all?"

"Isn't that enough?"

"Why now? I mean, you've lived here in Paradise your whole life, and she's been just ten minutes away. Why did you wait so long?"

Brenda pushed at an ice cube with one finger, seemingly fascinated with the way it bobbed up and down. "My mother wouldn't let me meet her before. I had to wait until I was old enough to legally call the shots for myself."

In her own way, I guess Jacqueline was as controlling as her mother had been. But Brenda was lying about that meeting for some reason. I was pretty sure she'd stop talking if I accused her of it so, for the moment, I pretended to believe her. "You arranged the meeting through Ursula?"

"Yes."

"How well do you know her?"

"Not well at all, but I knew who she was, and she didn't turn me away when I approached her. She was probably just trying to get back at Felicity for something, but I didn't care. It got me through the door."

Okay, so maybe she was more like the other women in her family than I thought. "The day I was at your grandmother's house, your mother was there, too. Do you know why?"

Brenda's hand faltered ever so slightly as she lifted the glass to her lips. She covered it well, but I knew I'd touched a nerve. "I don't have any idea. You'll have to ask her."

"I did. She's not talking."

She glanced at me from the corners of her almond-shaped eyes. "I'm sorry, but there's nothing *I* can tell you. I don't live with my mother anymore. I have no idea what she does most of the time."

"You don't know why she'd threaten to kill your grandmother?"

Brenda closed her eyes briefly. "My mother was always threatening to kill her mother. It didn't mean anything."

"Are you sure about that?"

"Of course I'm sure. My grandmother was an awful

woman. She turned her back on my mother when she needed her most. My mother is an emotional woman. She's ruled by her heart, not her head." She looked up at me, and a soft smile curved her lips. "I'm proof of that, I guess. But I grew up knowing that her mother's decision had devastated her. She gets upset and she lashes out, but she's never out of control or anything like that. Mom would deny this, of course, but I don't think she ever really stopped hoping that Felicity would change her mind."

I tried to imagine how I'd have felt in Jacqueline's shoes, but I couldn't even get that far. My mother wouldn't have disowned me no matter what I did. Not having that kind of emotional security had to leave scars.

"Did Felicity ever show any signs of relenting?"

Brenda smiled sadly. "I'm told she never relented on anything in her life. Selfish and bitter to the end, that was my grandmother."

That about covered it. "Have you ever met Oliver Birch? Her husband?"

"No, but I've seen him around town. I know who he is."

"Did he know who you were?"

"I couldn't say. Where are you going with all of this?"

"I don't know. I'm just trying to find all the pieces. Until I have them, I won't know where any of them fit."

She smiled, but the expression didn't quite reach her eyes. When she glanced at her watch a moment later, her smile faded. "I doubt that I told you anything useful, but I really must ask you to go. It's late, and I have to work early in the morning."

I still had unanswered questions, but I didn't want to alienate her. I thanked her and followed her to the door. "If you think of anything that might help," I said, handing her a card from Divinity, "please give me a call."

She didn't even look at the card before shoving it into her pocket. "Sure thing." And for the second time that night I found myself staring at the business end of someone's door.

Chapter 12

The weekend passed uneventfully. The steady
parade of thrill seekers slowed to a trickle, and sales
picked up. I fielded several calls from frantic artists and
two from my mother, who'd heard about the murder on the
news in Denver and lamented about what was happening
to Paradise. On Saturday afternoon, I took a chance and
drove out to the construction site in the hollow. Luckily,
Felicity's foreman was there and willing, sort of, to talk to
me. He couldn't tell me anything I didn't already know,
but he confirmed the theory that Greentree seemed to have
inside information.

By Monday, I was ready for a normal day—whatever
that was. It had been almost a week since Felicity's murder. Six days since I'd last seen Jawarski. We don't go out
all that often, but I usually see him on the street at least
once in the space of a week. His silence was becoming
deafening, but I refused to let myself wig out about it.

Luckily, I'd ordered the supplies to change the store's
display window before Bea went peppermint crazy, and I'd

put off updating the display long enough. Between preparations for the festival and working on the display window, Karen and I had plenty to keep us busy all day.

I'd planned a spring scene for the window this time, complete with a red wagon made from white chocolate sprayed red and filled with an assortment of pastel-colored candy, grass made of pieces of green apple licorice rope attached to toothpick halves, a chocolate baseball mitt holding a white chocolate baseball, and candy flowers around the perimeter.

While I cut blades of licorice grass and Karen attached them, I filled her in on my conversation with Ursula, my suspicions about Oliver's near accident, and Jacqueline's claims that Oliver had married Felicity for her money.

"So someone really tampered with Oliver's brakes?" she asked when I finished talking.

"Apparently so."

"And nobody knows who?"

"I don't know about anyone else, but I don't have a clue."

Karen whistled softly. "So somebody killed Felicity and tried to kill Oliver at the same time. Why?"

"That's the million dollar question," I said, reaching once again for my kitchen shears. "Both Ursula and Jacqueline insist that Oliver inherits everything, but I'd like to know what would have happened if he'd died the same night Felicity did."

"I can talk to Sergio," Karen offered. "I don't think his firm represented Felicity, but I'm sure he knows who did. He might be able to find out the terms of her will."

I couldn't imagine Karen's husband agreeing, but all he could do was tell us no. "If you think he'd be willing," I said, "go ahead and ask."

"Oh, honey, he gets so bored handling property disputes, he'll probably jump at the chance to do something interesting."

I still wasn't convinced, but she knew the man better than I did. I snipped a few more blades of grass and asked, "What do you know about Greentree?"

"The conservation group? Not much. Why?"

"Apparently Felicity was planning to bring a MegaMart to town, and there's been a lot of sabotage since they broke ground."

Karen's mouth fell open, and anger flashed in her eyes. "Are you serious? What was she trying to do? Ruin the town? She'd put every one of the stores around here out of business, including Divinity."

"No kidding. I'm trying to find out if someone from Greentree knew what she was planning. Or if anyone else knew, for that matter."

Frowning deeply, Karen munched on a piece of green licorice, releasing the strong scent of green apple flavoring. "The problem is, nobody admits to being a member of Greentree. They're all a little nuts, if you ask me."

"What about Kirby North? Do you think he's one of them?"

Karen chewed thoughtfully. "Probably. He's pretty rabid when it comes to protecting the environment. Plus, he has a history of violence."

She had my attention now. "He does?"

"He's been in jail for assault more than once. Always with his fists, though. Never with a weapon."

That didn't mean that his anger hadn't escalated. "Do you know what kind of assault?"

Karen polished off the licorice and got up to rinse her hands. "I know he belted Jim Isaacson in the nose over the golf course project, and he tied himself to a tractor when they were building one of the hotels on the hill. There have been a couple of other incidents, too."

"Do you think he's capable of murder?"

"Who isn't, if the motive's strong enough?"

It was a good question—one I'd have to answer if I

hoped to figure out who killed Felicity. "Would he kill someone over a MegaMart?"

Karen opened a new box of toothpicks and dumped them into a plastic container that made them easier to handle. "I think it's possible. So, do all these questions mean that you think the murderer was a member of Greentree?"

"I'm not sure of anything," I said with a frown. "That's the trouble. I'm going to have to get Kirby to tell me what he knows about Greentree and its activities."

Karen stuck the blade of "grass" in a Styrofoam block and went to work on another. "Good luck with that. If he is a member of Greentree, he'll never admit it. Why don't you ask Pine? I'm sure the police have responded to plenty of calls because of them. He might know who's connected and who's not."

I sent her a look that I hoped would put an end to that discussion. "And admit that I'm asking around about the murder? Not a chance." I gestured toward the blocks of Styrofoam already filled with our candy grass. "How many did you say was on each one of those again?"

Karen stopped working and looked at me for a long, uncomfortable minute. I had the distinct feeling she knew why I'd changed the subject, but she didn't say a word. That's one of the things I like best about her. She knows when to push, and she knows when to back off. She could have asked me about Jawarski, but I wouldn't have been able to answer her. I knew even less about what was going on between us than I knew about Felicity's murder.

Karen drove away a little after seven that evening. Ready for a quiet night, I tucked the bag holding the bank deposit under my arm and locked the front door of the shop. The sun had already disappeared behind the western mountains, and streetlamps were beginning to blink on along Prospector Street. I took a deep breath of clear mountain air, hoping it would also clear away the pressures of the day. The past few days felt like they'd lasted a year, and my neck and shoulders were so tense I'd been swallowing ibuprofen all day.

Outside on the sidewalk I could hear the rhythmic pounding coming from Wyatt and his friends. I'd been listening to it for hours already, and my head throbbed right along with it as I stood on the curb and waited for traffic to clear. I didn't have any plans for the evening, and I was suddenly grateful for my lack of a social life.

I wanted nothing more than to run a hot bath and sink into the tub with a good book. Anything to help me stop thinking about the murder, the shop, and the festival for a little while. While I stood there, pondering my options, Jawarski's truck pulled up next to me, and the passenger window slid down.

Grinning as if he hadn't been invisible for a week, Jawarski leaned across the seat. "Hey there. I was just coming to see you."

"On my way to the bank," I said, holding up the bag so he could see it. "Can it wait a few minutes?"

"Hop in, and I'll take you through the drive-through."

I wasn't sure why he was coming to see me, but if he wasn't working on the murder case, maybe this was a personal visit. Now that he was here, I wasn't sure I was ready for this. My uncertainty when it comes to men drives *me* crazy at times. I can only imagine how it affects them.

I climbed into the passenger's seat and slid a sidelong glance at his face while I buckled up. "You look like you're in a good mood."

Jawarski shrugged and merged into evening traffic. "What can I say? Life's good at the moment."

"*Life's good?* On which planet?"

Jawarski flicked on his turn signal. "What's wrong with you tonight?"

"Nothing much. A woman was killed in my parking lot

last week, and so far the only thing the police have done is warn me not to leave town. No big deal."

Jawarski cut a look at me as he shot through an opening in traffic and pulled into the bank's parking lot. "Svboda's not keeping you informed of every step he takes? What the hell is wrong with him?" Sarcasm coated his voice like a layer of thick chocolate.

"Funny. Do you know what they're doing?"

"They're doing their jobs, Abby. You're not getting any ideas about getting involved, are you?"

"Of course not," I said quickly. Admitting the truth would only cause an argument, and I wasn't in the mood. What was the point? He'd tell me to stay out of it, and I'd ignore him, so why put either of us through the hassle? I steered the conversation in a different direction. "So, can I ask who the police suspect?"

"They're looking at several persons of interest."

"Who?"

"That's not important."

"I think it is."

I could feel Jawarski tense as he pulled into line behind a couple of cars. "It's important to the police, not to anyone else."

"I don't plan to tell anyone else," I assured him. "But Ursula Drake has been telling people I called Felicity and asked her to meet me, so I'm a little concerned. Silly of me, I know, but what can I say?"

Jawarski's lips twitched. He shifted into neutral and rested one arm across the back of the seat. "C'mon Abby, you know I can't discuss the case with you. The guys in the department are doing their jobs. You'll have to be content with that."

"Easy for you to say."

He locked eyes with me. "Do you honestly think I'm going to just sit back and let someone convict you of murder? I deserve better than that."

Heat crept into my cheeks, and I felt about two inches tall, but he was forgetting one important point. "You're not on the case anymore, remember? How do I know what you're going to do?"

"It's called trust. I might not be actively working the case, but I'm still there, still paying attention. Still watching out for you. I thought you knew that."

My eyes burned, but I refused to get all weepy. "Well, fine then." I looked away so he wouldn't think he'd gotten to me. "Thanks."

"No problem."

Neither of us said anything for several minutes, but at last Jawarski broke the silence. "I heard that Mayor Ireland is thinking about canceling the arts festival."

That took care of all that unwanted sentiment. I whipped around and stared at him in disbelief. "He's *what*?"

"You didn't know?"

"Of course I didn't know. Why?"

"He's worried that the public will react badly if we haven't made an arrest in the next few days. Besides, he thinks it might be a nice tribute to Felicity."

"To Felicity? Is he nuts? She spent less than twelve hours as a member of the committee, and all she did in that time was screw everything up. Why would we cancel the festival in her memory?"

Jawarski's forehead creased as his scowl deepened. "Regardless of how some people felt about her, she was a prominent member of the community."

"And the rest of us are supposed to shut down because she met an untimely end? Even Oliver hasn't stopped working, and he was her husband. I haven't even heard about funeral plans."

Jawarski let out a heavy breath. "The family is planning a private service, and I never said that everyone should shut down because Felicity died. But all things considered, maybe canceling the festival completely isn't such a bad idea this year."

I shifted in my seat as far as the seat belt would let me. "If Jeb cancels the festival, he's going to alienate every member of the guild. Do you know what that could do to the town's economy? And let's not even talk about how unprofessional we'd look if we canceled now. It would take years to undo the damage this would do to our reputations."

"I know it wouldn't be good," Jawarski admitted, "and I know the arts festival is important to a lot of people, but this isn't just about the festival. It's about murder."

"It's about Paradise," I snapped. "Canceling at this point could hurt the entire town."

"If people think there's a murderer running around loose, they won't be coming anyway," Jawarski said, his voice so calm and reasonable it made me want to throw something.

He had a point, but I wasn't convinced. "But if Felicity's murder isn't related to the festival . . ."

"She was murdered in the middle of town—right in the center of the planned activity. It doesn't matter to festivalgoers why she was murdered. It matters where. It matters that we don't have the person responsible locked up in jail. Even then, we may lose a substantial number of people."

"If we cancel," I said, my jaw tight, "we'll lose everyone. We'll also have to pay a hefty cancellation fee to most of our vendors. Who's going to foot the bill for that? The guild can't. We won't have any money unless we make it back in ticket sales."

Jawarski groaned and leaned his head against the headrest. "Well, you'd better convince Jeb of that, because I'm under the impression he's going to make the announcement tomorrow or the next day."

I tried not to panic, but staying calm wasn't easy. There were half a dozen reasons I didn't want Jeb to cancel the festival, including the fact that I had all that peppermint to get rid of, and I didn't want to be known as the woman who left the guild with a budget deficit. "How close is Nate to solving the case?"

Jawarski rolled his head to the side so he could see me. "I'm not talking about the case, Abby."

"Neither am I. I'm talking about the festival. How soon will we be able to tell the public that Felicity's murderer is behind bars?"

"I don't know. But we'll find the killer eventually. I can promise you that, so leave it alone, okay?"

Jawarski didn't actually *say* not to worry my "pretty little head" about the murder, but that's what I heard. I'd been told that too many times during my failed marriage, and almost nothing could set me off faster. If that was going to be Jawarski's attitude, I needed to seriously reevaluate whether I wanted to continue seeing him.

"Terrific," I snarled when I trusted myself to speak. "I feel so much better now."

Jawarski shot me a look that said he wasn't amused. "Don't be funny."

"Don't be patronizing."

Luckily for both of us, it was our turn at the drive-through window. I handed Jawarski the bag, and we sat in uneasy silence while the cashier processed the transaction. After what felt like one of the longest hours of my life, she dropped my receipt and empty bag into the drawer.

"What do you say we don't talk about the murder tonight?" Jawarski asked as we pulled into traffic. "I know it's late notice, but I really came by to see if you'd be interested in grabbing dinner with me. I have something I want to talk to you about that isn't work-related."

After the conversation we'd just had, I wasn't thrilled with the idea of spending the evening with him, but he'd piqued my curiosity, and that made it hard to say no. "Fine. What did you have in mind?"

"I was thinking about the new Chinese place out on Ski Jump Way. Any objections?"

I'd heard good things about the Mandarin, so I agreed, and forty-five minutes later, after waiting for a table and engaging in enough idle chatter to last both of us a lifetime, we were seated near the windows overlooking the golf course.

We must both have been trying to make nice, because we agreed on Chicken Satay with Peanut Sauce, Nanking Chicken, and Beef with Asparagus Tips in record time. Once our server had left us alone, Jawarski sat back in his chair and laced his fingers across his tight stomach, and I grew tense all over again.

He waited until I'd filled my mouth with Nanking Chicken to break the news. "I thought dinner tonight would be a good idea," he said casually, "because I probably won't be around much for the next six weeks."

"Oh? Why not?"

"My kids are coming for a visit," he said with a casual shrug—maybe a little *too* casual. He didn't even look at me while he was speaking. "They'll be here for half the summer."

"Your kids?"

"I told you about them, remember? Ridge and Cheyenne?"

Of course I remembered, but that conversation had taken place three months earlier, and he hadn't said more than a word or two about them since. At least not around me. Which wasn't that odd, considering how long it had taken him to tell me they existed at all.

Don't get me wrong. I don't hold it against him. It doesn't even come close to the secret my ex kept from me while we were married. I tried pouring a little enthusiasm over his nonchalance. "That's great. You must be excited."

His mouth quirked into a crooked half grin. "Yeah, I am, I guess. I miss having them around, y'know?"

I didn't, but I nodded as if I did. The fact that I've never had children of my own isn't easy for me to talk about. "Do they come to see you every summer?"

"There's only been a couple since the divorce, but yeah, they have so far. But Ridge turns fifteen this year, and Cheyenne's going into eighth grade. Who knows how much longer they'll want to spend time away from their friends?"

I thought about my teenaged nieces, Dana and Danielle. I couldn't imagine either of them going away for six weeks and being happy about it. They could hardly stand to be separated from their friends long enough to eat supper. "Then you'll just have to make the most of the time you've got."

Jawarski looked up from his plate and made eye contact for the first time since he'd started speaking. "That's what I plan to do, but that means I won't have a lot of time for other things while they're here. I just thought I should explain. You know . . . before they get here."

Something in his expression set off a warning bell in the back of my head. There was something else going on here. Trying to pick up on the mood I was sensing, I set my fork aside slowly. "No problem," I assured him. "I understand completely. I'd love to meet them while they're here. Maybe you could bring them over for dinner sometime."

It was nothing more than a flash across his eyes, but I knew what was coming before he opened his mouth. "Yeah. Maybe." He forked up a mound of noodles but never lifted it to his mouth. "The thing is, Abby, the kids are confused. They haven't done all that well since the divorce."

An uncomfortable feeling settled in my stomach. "I see."

"And it's been worse since their mother moved them to Montana," he went on. "And I moved up here, so even when they come to visit, they can't see much of their old friends."

My face felt frozen, but I didn't want him to think I was hurt or disappointed, especially when I didn't know what I felt. I hadn't really been in touch with my feelings since the day I walked in on my ex-husband and his mistress rolling around on my bedroom floor. Our subsequent divorce and the news of her pregnancy had seriously rattled my cage. I'd put off having children all through my twenties and thirties because Roger kept saying he wasn't ready. It wasn't until I turned thirty-eight that I realized he just didn't want children with me.

I don't know how I feel about myself half the time, and I sure don't know how I felt about Jawarski or us as a "couple." So it's not as if he has any reason to introduce me to his kids. But that just goes to show how perverse human nature is. If he'd tried to push the kids on me, I would have decided he was asking too much too fast. Let *him* be the one to say no, and suddenly I wanted nothing quite so much as to meet them.

"Of course," I said. "It was just an idea, but with the kids here and a murder to solve, you'll be too busy for socializing. Besides, with any luck, I'll be tied up with the arts festival."

And just like that, the conversation steered away from his children. We managed to stay away from the edge for the rest of our meal. But that chasm was out there, just inches away from my feet, and I didn't like knowing that I felt more comfortable talking about the murder than about Jawarski's kids.

The trouble was, I couldn't be completely honest with him unless I could be completely honest with myself first, and I think that was the most frightening hurdle of all.

Chapter 13

I tossed and turned all night, and I was still running through questions in my mind when my alarm went off the next morning. Not even close to being awake, I levered myself onto an elbow, squinted at the digital display gleaming 4:15, and dropped back onto my pillow with a groan. What had ever possessed me to think that catching Jessie McGraw before the bakery opened would be a good idea?

Thirty minutes and four Snooze buttons later, I dragged myself out of bed and threw on some clothes. To avoid having to deal with my hair, I slapped on a baseball cap and promised myself a cup of Jessie's special brew Autumn Hearth coffee for my troubles. Finally almost presentable, I clipped on Max's leash and led him down the stairs.

Paradise isn't L.A. or even Sacramento, but old habits die hard. I feel safer walking the streets in the middle of the night with an escort—especially one that can sink his teeth into a murdering maniac's shin and not let go.

A cool breeze blew into the city from the nearby canyons, and a few sporadic clouds wisped over a sky full of stars. Other than the soft whisper of leaves stirring in the breeze, no sound disturbed the city streets.

I tried not to think about the night Felicity was killed and ignored the urge to take the Jetta. Bonner's Bakery was less than three blocks away. Nobody drove that short a distance in Paradise, even in the middle of the night. I wasn't a child, and I wasn't afraid. I had Max. We could take care of ourselves.

Even with the pep talks, I jumped at every sound and shied away from the shadows as I walked along the darkened streets. When I finally reached Forest Steet and spotted lights on in the bakery's kitchen, I breathed a sigh of relief.

Trying not to frighten Jessie, I tied Max outside the door and knocked softly. She pulled it open a crack and gazed out at me with one eye. "Who's there?"

"It's Abby Shaw, Jessie. Do you mind if I come in?"

"Abby? What are you doing here in the middle of the night?"

"I want to ask you a couple of questions, if that's okay."

The eye stared, unblinking. "What kind of questions?"

"About the night Felicity Asbury was killed."

"What? Why do you want to talk to me? I don't know anything."

"Yeah, but you're the only person who might have been up and about when the murder was taking place. Maybe you saw something on your way to work or heard something out of the ordinary?"

The door creaked open an inch. "Nothing that I can remember."

"You don't remember passing any cars on your way to work?"

"Sorry, no."

"Nothing?"

She shook her head and pulled back as if she was going to shut the door.

I jumped in with another question before she could. "Which streets did you take to get here?"

"The same ones as always. I take Motherlode to Bear Hollow and Bear Hollow to Forest."

"That means you don't pass Divinity at all, doesn't it?"

"That's right."

My spirits took a nosedive. In spite of Dooley's warnings, I'd been counting on her to know something useful. "Is there anyone else you can think of who might have been out at that time of the morning?"

Jessie's eye narrowed, and the one side of her mouth I could see turned down. "Why do you want to know?"

"Because somebody murdered a woman less than three blocks from here, and I'm trying to figure out who." I sighed in frustration and turned away, taking in the back view of nearby shops. In spite of overwhelming evidence to the contrary, I didn't want to believe that I'd run into a dead end. "Did you know Felicity?"

Jessie shook her head. "Not really, but Oliver is a regular customer. Comes in for a bear claw and coffee every morning and then goes across the street to work on that new restaurant of his."

I remembered running into him the morning Felicity died and nodded slowly. "Has he been in since Felicity died?"

"Every day, why?"

"His wife's murder didn't interrupt his routine, even for a day?"

With her face puckered in suspicion, Jesse inched the door open a little further. "Everyone grieves differently. That poor man is grief-stricken. He's practically buried himself in his work since his wife died. He's over there all hours of the day and night, driving himself like there's no tomorrow. It wouldn't be my way, necessarily, but if it's what he needs to do, who am I to judge?"

Under normal circumstances, I wouldn't judge him either. Under present conditions, I'd be smart to question everyone and everything—even if he did have an alibi. "Has he said anything to you about the murder?"

"Not a word. He can barely make himself talk about it. Not that I blame him. Felicity always came across as such a bitch, but she wasn't really. Not once you got to know her."

Not in my opinion, but I refrained from contradicting her.

"Felicity was a regular, too—in her own way. She didn't often come into the bakery herself until recently, but Ursula would call and place an order for her two or three times a week."

"But Felicity *did* come in sometimes?"

"Once or twice." Jessie frowned suddenly and motioned me inside. "You look half-frozen out there. I just put on a pot of coffee. I guess you might as well come in and have some."

I followed her inside gratefully and took a seat at a small, round table near the back window. While she grabbed mugs, spoons, sugar, and cream, I grasped at straws. "You said that she came into the bakery a couple of times lately. Can you remember when?"

Jessie gave a matter-of-fact nod. "The first time was about three months ago. The last time was two days before she died."

"Did she say why she decided to come in after such a long time?"

"I didn't ask." Jessie set a full mug in front of me. "I didn't really have to. She'd been across the street with Oliver. They must have had some kind of trouble between them, because she came in with Henri."

"The chef?"

Jessie nodded and sipped. Pleasure lightened her features, and she briefly closed her eyes in appreciation before she answered me. "Yes, but it's not what you're think-ing. She looked very upset, and Henri calmed her down."

That was interesting. I couldn't picture Felicity seeking solace from her husband's employee, but what did I know? "Did she and Oliver have an argument?"

"I don't know. All I *do* know is that she was fit to be tied when she came in here. She and Henri had their heads to-gether for a little while, and by the time she left, she seemed all right again." She glanced at the clock and let out a little squeal of surprise. "Goodness, where has the time gone? If I don't get the bread started, it won't be done in time. Stay, finish your coffee. Just lock the door behind you after you leave. I'm feeling just a little paranoid since the murder."

She wasn't the only one.

Shortly after nine o'clock, I climbed the steps to City Hall and tugged open the heavy glass door. City Hall sits about two blocks from Divinity, at the apex of Prospector Circle, giving city workers a broad view of downtown and almost everything that goes on there. Jeb Ireland seemed so out of touch with his constituents, I wondered if he ever bothered to look. Jeb's not stupid; it's just that he's so wrapped up in himself, I'm not sure he pays much atten-tion to the rest of us.

Maybe I was on a fool's mission, but I had to try to rea-son with him, not only about putting Meena back to work, but even more crucially, about not canceling the festival. Too many people had worked too hard to get us this far. Of everyone in Paradise, Jeb Ireland would probably be least affected by his decision. But that's how it had always been with Jeb.

Steeling myself for a confrontation, I climbed the steps to the second floor and headed toward the mayor's suite of offices at the end of a broad marble corridor. His assistant, Tamara, sat behind her desk, framed by an old-fashioned arched window that was part of the original, historical structure.

I'd guess Tamara's age at around forty. She's a pretty brunette who stands no more than five two and probably doesn't weigh a hundred pounds soaking wet. With her long, curly hair, tiny frame, and flawless complexion, she looks more like a china doll than a pit bull, but we all know that appearances can be deceiving.

She glanced up as I walked into her office, her delicate face illuminated by an equally delicate smile. "Well, Abby. What a surprise." She turned away from her computer screen and linked her manicured hands together on her desk. "I hope you're not here to see the mayor. He has a horrendous schedule today, so he won't be able to take any walk-in appointments."

I tossed off an equally friendly smile and dropped into a chair, grabbing a magazine on my way down. "That's okay," I said, flipping open the pages and feigning interest in a hair color advertisement. "I don't mind waiting."

Tamara didn't bat an eye, but I thought her smile grew a trifle less friendly. "I'll be glad to make an appointment for you on a day when he's not so busy. I'm sure I could work you in sometime later in the week."

"I'm afraid this can't wait. But I only need a few minutes. I promise I won't throw him off schedule."

This time I didn't have to wonder if I'd annoyed her. Tamara's dark eyes shadowed, and her smile dimmed noticeably. "I really can't let you disturb him at all. Mayor Ireland relies on me to keep his schedule running smoothly. I can't do that if people interrupt him whenever they feel the need."

I marked my place in the magazine with one finger, as if I had every intention of going back to it. "I wouldn't need to interrupt if the mayor would simply return the messages I've left for him."

"I've given him your messages," Tamara said, her voice

growing more cool by the moment. "I'm sure he'll call when he has time."

I shrugged and let the magazine fall open again. "It'll be quicker to just answer my question while I'm here."

Tamara's lips narrowed. "Your calls aren't the only ones the mayor has to think about. One of Paradise's most prominent citizens was found murdered last week. Since then, the mayor has been on the phone almost constantly with the police, the media, and the Asbury family. He's working his way down the list in order of priority. I'm sure you'll be hearing from him soon."

I set aside the magazine and stood. "Okay. But first, tell me where the arts festival falls on his list of priorities."

"I don't know."

"Will he call me back today?"

"I'm sure I don't know."

"Do you know what he's planning to do about the festival?"

Annoyance flashed through Tamara's eyes. "I have no idea. Now, if you don't mind, I have work to do."

I held up both hands, still trying to at least *appear* agreeable. "I don't mean to be a bother," I said which, if not entirely true, at least sounded good. "But I've heard a rumor that the mayor is thinking about canceling the festival. If that's true, then this *is* a priority. I need to see him before he makes any decisions."

Tamara rested both fists on top of her appointment book and glared at me. "I understand that this is important to you, Abby, but you don't decide the mayor's priorities. Not even I do that."

"Canceling the festival now would have a negative financial impact on the majority of businesses in town. It would make the entire town appear unprofessional. If he hasn't thought about that, he needs to. Give me two minutes with him this afternoon. That's all."

Her tiny face puckered into a deep scowl that almost

looked painful. "Impossible. Now, I really must ask you to leave. If you won't, I'll have to call security."

I had my mouth open, ready to say something else, but the threat she'd just uttered wiped everything right out of my mind. "Security? You have to be joking."

Tamara placed one delicate hand on the telephone. "I'm absolutely serious."

In hindsight, I can say that leaving would probably have been the smartest thing to do under the circumstances. But she'd blown me right out of the water, and I was struggling just to convince myself I'd heard her right. "There's no need to get weird," I began.

She shot me a look that could have petrified cotton candy and lifted the receiver.

Holding out one hand to show how harmless I was, I motioned with the other for her to hang up. "Hey, I'm not trying to cause trouble."

Tamara's mouth puckered as if she'd just swallowed a handful of sour balls. She stopped dialing, but she didn't replace the receiver. "You're in here demanding to see the mayor and refusing to take no for an answer. You may not be trying to cause trouble, but you're doing a bang-up job of it anyway. Not to mention the fact that I don't know if you're dangerous or not."

"Me? Dangerous? You have to be kidding."

"How do I know you didn't do something to Mrs. Asbury?"

My mouth fell open in shock. "For one thing, I had no reason to want her dead. For another, I'm not a killer. And if you really thought I was, you wouldn't say so to my face while we're alone in a room together."

Tamara lifted her chin. "She was found in your parking lot."

"A parking lot I share with at least one other business."

"You're the one who threatened her."

"With a lawsuit, not murder."

Tamara gestured toward the door with the receiver. "Fine. Whatever. But I'm responsible for keeping the mayor safe, and I have work to do. I don't have time to argue with you. Leave now, or I *will* call."

She looked as if she'd enjoy doing just that, and I decided not to test her. I didn't have time to spend even a few hours in a jail cell. "All right," I said, "I'm going. But would you at least ask the mayor to call me before he makes any decisions about the festival?"

"I'll tell him you'd like to hear from him."

Like that was going to do any good. Annoyed, I strode from the room and hurried down the steps to the main floor. My heels echoed on the marble foyer as I crossed to the glass doors and pushed outside into the warm, spring sunshine.

Usually, being outside on a nice day could lift my spirits like nothing else. Today, even the clear blue sky and the scent of lilac didn't make me feel better. I kept going round and round the issues but getting no closer to finding answers to my questions.

I still had a few minutes before I needed to open the shop, so I detoured up Forest Street on my way back. I wondered if Oliver had considered the possibility that someone had tried to kill him. Would he be able to name a suspect if he knew that his brakes had been cut, or would he be as lost and confused as I was?

As usual, half a dozen pickup trucks clustered around the restaurant. I looked them over, but none of them was an old gray Ford with a blue door. That would have been too easy. For the second time in a week, I slipped past the scaffolding and through the open door into the cavernous room with its roughly framed walls. On the far side of the room a piece of plywood rested on two wooden sawhorses, and a short, round man with a balding head used it as a table while he gave serious consideration to the contents of a white paper bag.

"Excuse me?"

He glanced up at the sound of my voice and palmed his thinning gray hair. "*Pardonez moi*. I didn't hear you come in. How may I help you?"

We don't have a lot of Frenchmen running around Paradise, so I took a guess at his identity. "Henri Guischard?"

He nodded and set the bag aside. "*Oui*. And you are?"

"Abby Shaw. I own a candy shop on Prospector Street." I moved closer and offered a hand. "I've heard a lot about you."

Henri responded with a limp handshake. "Good things I 'ope?"

"Very good. Oliver seems excited that you're here. He's expecting a lot of success for the restaurant."

"Ah, poor man. Then he shall have it."

Henri glanced into his bag again, and I checked out the construction crew swarming over the building. I couldn't see Oliver among them. "Is Oliver here this morning?"

"Oliver? No." Henri pulled out an eclair and beamed with pleasure.

"Do you know when he'll be here?"

Scowling at me for keeping him from his pastry, Henri shook his head. "He does not answer to me. You know his wife 'as been killed, *oui*?"

"Yes, I heard. It's terrible."

"*Oui*. Terrible." He sent a longing glance at the eclair. "A . . . how you say? . . . tragedy. Someone else can help you, no?"

"I don't think so." I could have turned around and walked out the door, but I wondered if Henri could give me some insight into Oliver's friends and enemies or the argument Felicity and Oliver had shortly before her death. It wouldn't hurt anything to ask. "I haven't seen Oliver for a couple of days," I said. "How is he holding up?"

"He is sad, of course. Heartbroken, poor man."

"Yes, of course." Unless he'd killed Felicity for the money. "Did you know his wife well?"

"Mrs. Asbury? No, she never came in here."

My internal lie detector let out a buzz. "Never? That's surprising. I thought Felicity kept one finger in all of her business dealings."

"Ah, but you see, the restaurant isn't hers. It is Oliver's project only."

"Really? Hmm," I said, pretending to be confused. "I could have sworn somebody told me they saw Felicity here shortly before she died." I let that sink in for a few seconds, then shook it off and smiled. "Oh well, they must have been mistaken. Does Oliver have any business partners or investors in the restaurant?"

Henri eyed me skeptically. "Why do you want to know that?"

"I'm just curious." I wagged a hand aimlessly, hoping I looked vague and unfocused. "It's just that a restaurant like this must take a huge amount of money. I didn't realize Oliver was wealthy enough to finance it all on his own."

"Per'aps he is, per'aps he is not," Henri said. He dug around for a clean piece of paper and put the eclair on it. "I don't know the details of his finances, you understand. But I can tell you that Mrs. Asbury was not involved in the restaurant."

"Right." I let a silence fall for a few seconds, then asked, "Has Oliver said how the police investigation is going? Do they have any idea who wanted her dead?"

Henri shrugged. "Another issue on which I am not informed."

"What about you? Who do you think killed her?"

He tensed but managed to keep a smile in place. "I don't know. As I said before, I barely knew her."

"Oh. Right." I turned away, then back again, Columbo-like. "See, that's where I'm confused. I heard you and Felicity had coffee together at Bonner's the other day—right after she and Oliver had an argument. So I was under the impression that you *did* know her."

Henri's pleasant expression vanished. "Who told you that?"

"I don't remember. Someone who saw the two of you together."

"Well, it's not true."

"No? How odd." Lie number two. But who was counting? And why was he so determined to create such a distance between himself and the dead woman? "Has Oliver said anything else about Felicity?"

"To me? No. We talked of food, nothing else."

Hoping my face wouldn't betray what I was thinking, I offered an apologetic smile. "I've taken up enough of your time. I'll just try to catch Oliver at home."

Henri looked up in surprise. "You would disturb the family in their grief?"

What grief? But if the guy believed that, why burst his bubble? Let him think sorrow had knocked over the whole clan. "I'm sure Oliver would like to find out who killed his wife."

"And you are going to tell him?"

"No, but he might be able to tell me." Waving a hand toward the eclair, I turned away. "Enjoy your breakfast."

"Ms. Shaw?"

I stopped at the door and looked back at him. "Yes?"

"The killer . . . he has nothing to lose now. You really shouldn't go around asking questions like this."

His words chilled me. I searched his eyes for signs of malice, but I couldn't find any. I couldn't find concern, either. I turned away without responding and hurried out into the sunshine. And I wondered as I strode toward Divinity whether I'd just been warned . . . or threatened.

Chapter 14

That conversation with Henri made me antsy all day. I made another three dozen peppermint lollipops, and by the time I'd finished overheating the kitchen, I forced myself to sit still and finish snipping umpteen pounds of licorice into blades of grass.

By the time Wyatt and the guys showed up that afternoon, I was ready to think about something else, even if it meant facing reality about the building repairs. I covered my mound of licorice grass and climbed the steps to the second floor.

After swimming through layers of Visqueen, I glanced around to see what had been done, but if the guys had made any progress since I was up there last, I couldn't see it. Swallowing disappointment, I tried not to think about how long this project was going to take or how much it was going to cost.

Charlie and Toby huddled together in front of the window, studying a piece of paper that looked like their version of a floor plan. On the other side of the room Wyatt squatted next to his toolbox, a deep scowl tugging at the tips of his mustache. His hair was shaggy and unkempt, and even the parts of his face he usually shaved were stubbled with whiskers. That's my brother's idea of a vacation.

Wyatt doesn't intimidate me—much. But the look on his face did make me think twice about talking to him. I hesitated for a minute, trying to decide which would be worse: braving Wyatt's temper or attaching the rest of the licorice grass to the remaining toothpicks.

Turns out the decision was a no-brainer. I'm usually even-tempered and easy to get along with—at least, I think I am. But at my current level of frustration, anything would be better than sitting in the candy kitchen, thinking, and contracting a raging case of restless leg syndrome.

I tapped Wyatt's shin lightly with the toe of my shoe. "Something wrong?"

Irritation flashed through his eyes as he glanced up at me. "Not funny, Abby. You can bring everything back now."

Have I mentioned that my brother can be an insufferable jerk sometimes? "What stuff?"

"Whatever you took out of here. You've made your point, okay?"

He was seriously starting to bug me. "*What* point?"

"Knock it off." Wyatt stood so he could glare down at me and gain the advantage. "I know you took stuff out of here. You were all over my ass the other day about leaving my tools out."

An uneasy feeling crept up my spine, but I tried to ignore it. "That doesn't mean I made off with your tools when you weren't looking."

"Well, someone did."

I almost didn't want to ask. "What stuff is missing?"

"I don't know." He scowled at the toolbox and gave it a jiggle with his boot. "A wrench. My new hammer—"

"An awl?"

His head shot up, and I watched him reach the same conclusion I had. "Holy shit."

"You're missing one, aren't you?"

My big, strong brother actually looked shaky. "Somebody stole *my* tools to kill that old bat with?"

"It sure looks like it. And I'll bet any amount of money that the awl was one of the tools I picked up from your truck bed. Which means my fingerprints are probably all over the stupid thing."

Wyatt wagged his shaggy head. "So? Nobody can seriously suspect you of doing the old lady in."

"Yeah? Well, they're sure giving a good imitation of it." My eyes burned, and that made me angry. I don't like crying, and I sure didn't want to do it in front of Wyatt. "Do you have any idea when the tools disappeared?"

"Not a clue." Swearing, Wyatt kicked the toolbox shut. "What in the hell's going on around here?"

"I wish I knew." I turned over a bucket and sat. "Half the town probably wanted Felicity dead. That's the easy part. What I don't understand is why anybody would want to frame me for her murder."

One of Wyatt's thick eyebrows rose toward the sweaty old cap he wore. "You been pissing people off?"

"Not that I know of, but thanks for the vote of confidence."

Wyatt dug into a sack and pulled out a handful of nails. He stuffed them into a pocket and picked up a hammer. "Don't get upset. I didn't mean anything by it. But if somebody's trying to set you up, they must have a reason."

"And that reason is automatically something I've done wrong?"

"I didn't say that, either." With an old-man groan, Wyatt tugged a two-by-four from a pile of lumber. Neither of us was a kid any longer, but sometimes I'm shocked by the realization that we're turning into our parents. "All I meant was that somebody's got it in for you. Either that, or putting the blame on you is just convenient. It's got to be one or the other."

Somewhat mollified, I dragged the toe of my shoe through the sawdust. "I don't think I've crossed anybody, but I probably wouldn't know, would I?"

Wyatt slid a glance at me. "You don't know if somebody's been pissed off at you?"

"Well, yeah. Bea. But I don't think she'd kill someone and try to frame me for it."

"Cousin Bea?" Wyatt laughed through his nose. "I'm not even going to ask. What about the folks down at the whoosit guild?"

"The artists' guild?" I thought back over the past few months, but nothing came to mind. "I don't remember arguing with anyone there."

"What about customers?"

I shook my head slowly. "No."

"You been messing around with somebody's husband?"

Wyatt knew how I felt about infidelity, so I didn't dignify the question with a response. "Maybe I'm just convenient. But that means the killer has to be somebody who knew I was going to visit Felicity that night. Either someone at the guild or someone who was at her house while I was there."

"That narrows it down, doesn't it?"

"Not really. The guild was packed with people last Monday night." As I had a hundred times, I ran back over the list of people I remembered seeing that night. "What do you know about Greentree?"

"The tree huggers? They're nothing but trouble. Why?"

"Have you ever heard anything about trouble between them and Felicity?"

"There's always trouble between them and Felicity." Wyatt fit the two-by-four in place and pounded in a nail. He knelt to place another nail but paused before hammering. "Matter of fact, I heard down at Sid's the other day that there'd been some real trouble down in the hollow. Some people are saying they must have an inside source at Drake, because either somebody's cluing them in to when it'll be okay to strike, or they're awful damn lucky."

"Are you talking about the sabotage?"

"Yeah. Dirt in the gas tanks and air filters of the equipment. Set an expensive backhoe on fire a few weeks back, among other things. They've done some real damage, from what I hear. Enough to shut down work for a while."

"Do you know why?"

Wyatt shrugged. "Does it matter?"

"It might. I'm pretty sure Felicity was planning to bring in a MegaMart."

Wyatt almost dropped his hammer. *"Here?"*

"That's what I've been told. But wouldn't the city have to give her zoning clearance? Do you think they would?"

Wyatt shook his head. "The hollow isn't in city limits. It's county. She'd have to talk to the County Commission, and those doughheads are only interested in money."

"So she could have been given the zoning she needed. And if Greentree found out—"

Wyatt brushed dirt off the knee of his jeans. "There'd be hell to pay."

"How well do you know Kirby North?"

"Kirby? He's a nutcase. He'd do anything to make a point. And Sandy Welch is almost as bad. Why?"

"I don't know Sandy, but I think it's past time for me to talk to Kirby."

Wyatt turned away from the wall and locked eyes with me. "Are you nuts?"

"Look, Wyatt, I appreciate the concern, but don't worry about it, okay?"

"Somebody has to. You sure as hell don't. It's like you think you're immortal or something."

"I don't think I'm immortal."

"Could'a fooled me. You damn near got us both killed

last time you started messing around in a police investigation, remember?"

I'd come closer to breathing my last than he had, but this didn't seem like the time to clarify the details. I tossed him a grin and pushed to my feet. "'Damn near' only counts in horseshoes."

Color flooded Wyatt's cheeks. "If you're not careful, one of these times it won't be damn near."

"Then I'll be careful."

"Dammit, Abby—"

He reached for my arm, but I sidestepped him easily. "Back off, Wyatt. If I'm right about the murder weapon, I'm going to be in real trouble soon. I can't just sit here counting lollipops while my life falls apart."

Giving me a look that was pure Grandpa Shaw, Wyatt ran a hand across his face and shifted his weight a couple of times. "Look, I understand how you feel, but you start messing around with those Greentree freaks, you're asking for trouble. They're not normal."

"I'll be careful," I said again. "I just want to ask Kirby a few questions. He won't even know I'm there to ask about the building site. I'll tell him I'm there to talk about the arts festival."

"He won't believe you."

"Yes he will." He *had* to. I wasn't going to stand around arguing about it all day, so I turned away. "I'm a big girl, Wyatt. I know what I'm doing."

"Yeah?" His voice was gravelly. Angry. "Well, if you get yourself in trouble again, don't call me to rescue you."

"Don't worry," I tossed over my shoulder as I strode away. I indulged in a few unkind thoughts about Wyatt in particular and men in general, but only because I didn't want to think about what lay in store for me. I didn't think Kirby was dangerous, but what if I was wrong?

Chapter 15

Kirby North lived in an old cabin built about fifty years earlier in the middle of a small clearing halfway up Black Ridge. It had originally been a trapper's cabin, but I'd heard that Kirby had added a couple of rooms and put in large windows to let in the sunlight and the view. In recent years, large summer homes had started scrambling up the hillside, each new builder jockeying for a better position than the last. But even with all the new construction, it would take a long time for the summer people to reach Kirby.

With Wyatt's warning still ringing in my ears, I drove onto the Ridge that evening after work. Max hung out the back window while I ran through my story half a hundred times, trying to find an explanation for my visit that sounded realistic. I still hadn't found one when I reached the turnoff to Kirby's place, buried so deep in the trees I almost missed it.

As I left the main highway, trees shrouded the road, casting deep shadows along the rutted dirt path. The Jetta bounced hard over a couple of deep ruts and tilted precariously when I swerved to avoid a deep hole. I kept one eye on Max in the rearview mirror, alert for any change in his mood that might signal trouble.

Approaching Kirby's cabin in broad daylight would have been nerve-racking enough, but driving through the silent forest at dusk made all my nerve endings hum. Even the birds, audible along the highway, grew silent as I drove deep into the woods.

After about a mile and a half I drove past a rickety shed, the first sign of civilization since leaving the main road. A hundred feet later, the road ended in front of a small cabin, barely large enough for two rooms. Smoke drifted sluggishly from the chimney, and Kirby's Pathfinder was parked in front of an old barn a few feet away.

I swallowed my nerves and parked the Jetta so I could get away easily if I needed to. *Show time.*

Hooking Max to his leash, I climbed the two short steps to the cabin and raised my hand to knock. The door flew open before I could make contact, and Kirby loomed large in the doorway.

"Abby? What are you doing way out here?"

It was too late to turn back now, and I didn't want him to smell my fear, so I tossed off a grin. "I was in the neighborhood. Thought I'd drop by."

"Yeah?" His expression was inscrutable.

"Yeah. Do you mind if I come in?"

Kirby didn't move for an uncomfortably long time. Just when I thought he'd send me away, he stepped away from the door. "I guess it won't hurt anything, but you're going to have to leave the dog outside."

That pretty much defeated the purpose of bringing along protection.

Kirby must have noticed my frown. "I'm allergic," he said. "Come on inside and tell me what I can do for you."

Reluctantly, I tied Max to a post and stepped into the

cabin's cool interior. Kirby hadn't turned on any lights, so I couldn't see him. My heart shot straight into my throat. The stale scent of cigarette smoke hung over everything.

"Well, come on. You might as well get what you came for." His voice sounded from the other side of the room, and I finally located him in a large leather chair hidden deep in the shadows. "So? What do you want?"

I opted for the sofa because of its proximity to the door. "I came to talk to you about putting up the bleachers. I need someone to take charge of the work crew. Are you interested?"

"You drove all the way out here to ask me that?" Even in the dim lighting, I could see Kirby smirk. "You could have called."

"I prefer talking about important things in person."

Kirby leaned forward, resting his massive forearms on his thighs. "All right. What's involved?"

"Mainly just making sure everyone shows up and keeping them on task. Supervising to make sure they've followed all the safety regulations."

"Okay. Sure. Anything else?"

"I understand that Felicity insisted on approving all the pieces you wanted to sell at the festival. I've heard that you were upset about that. Do you still have concerns?"

He sat back in his chair and dismissed the idea with one wag of a jumbo paw. "I never had concerns. I didn't take her seriously, and neither did anyone else. She couldn't have followed through without bringing a lawsuit down on the city."

Not concerned? He'd given a good imitation of "concern" that night at the guild. "I understand she was worried that you might exhibit something politically inflammatory."

He grinned. "Yeah? Well, I'm not worried about it. It's not an issue anymore. So why are you really here?"

So much for subtlety. My face burned, and I prayed

silently that it wasn't as red as it felt. "I told you. The bleachers. But you're right. I do have another reason for being here."

"I thought so." His brows jutted up toward his hairline. "Are you going to tell me what it is?"

"I'd like to ask you a few questions about Greentree."

He pulled back a fraction of an inch, and a mask dropped over his face. "What about it?"

"How much do you know about it?"

"Same as anybody else, just what I read in the papers."

"That's too bad. How much do you know about Felicity Asbury's most recent project?"

His eyebrows snaked slowly downward. "I don't know anything about it. Felicity was keeping it top secret."

"Is there anyone in Greentree who might know what she was planning?"

Kirby shook his head. "I wouldn't know. I don't know who's a member and who isn't."

It was a predictable answer, but I didn't believe him. "I've heard there's been some trouble at the job site—dirt in the gas tanks. Equipment set on fire. That sort of thing."

"Yeah, I've heard that, too. I take it you think Greentree is responsible."

"It's possible."

Kirby reached for a pack of cigarettes on the table. "I don't think anyone's claimed responsibility yet," he said, holding up the pack to offer me one.

I shook my head. "Look, Kirby, I know that membership in Greentree is top secret. Nobody who is a member would ever admit it aloud. But I also know that putting up a MegaMart on the edge of town would upset a lot of people."

Kirby reared up in his seat. "Where did you hear that?"

I wasn't going to give names unless he did. "From a reliable source. You didn't know?"

"Hell no." He got up and paced the small room. Anger

radiated from him, but I suspected that he'd already heard about the MegaMart deal. His reaction was way too subdued for Kirby.

"I'm trying to figure out if someone from Greentree killed Felicity to stop her."

"And you think I know the answer to that?" Kirby laughed softly and flicked his lighter. He inhaled so deeply his cheeks caved in, then let out a rush of smoke in my direction. "You give me too much credit. I take it you're playing detective again?"

The smoke made my throat constrict. I resisted the urge to cough. "I think someone is trying to frame me for the murder, and I'm trying to make sure they don't. So who would know about Felicity's plans?"

"I don't know."

"Who's in charge of Greentree?"

"I don't know."

"Do you know who dumped the dirt on the gas tanks and set the backhoe on fire?"

His gaze narrowed slightly. "No. I don't. Is that all you came for, or do you have questions that I might actually be able to answer?"

I didn't want him to know how frustrated I was, so I offered a smile. "Sure. When does Greentree hold its meetings, and where?"

"Are you interested in joining?"

"I'm interested in talking to anyone who won't stonewall me the way you are."

"You'd just be wasting your time." Kirby's voice took on a cold note. "The members of Greentree care about the environment. They might occasionally indulge in a bit of sabotage, but they don't believe in violence against people."

"Yeah?" Too agitated to stay in one spot, I stood and glared at him. "Well, neither do I. If you won't tell me what I want to know, I'll find some other way to get the answers."

I made it halfway to the door before Kirby spoke again. "You're taking an awfully big chance poking around in things that aren't any of your business, Abby. I'd be careful if I were you."

A chill slithered down my spine. That was the second time in as many days that I'd been told that. "Is that a threat?"

"Not from me. But if you didn't kill Felicity, then someone else did. I have a feeling that whoever did it won't be happy about you asking questions. Like I said, I'd be careful if I were you."

Yeah. Thanks.

I found Max standing at attention on the porch, glad to see me but not growling or baring his teeth or doing any of the other canine protective type things I'd expect him to do under the circumstances. Maybe Kirby wasn't threatening me, but I still wanted nothing more than to get away from that cabin and back to civilization.

It was nearly dark by the time I got home, but not dark enough to hide Jawarski's truck hulking on the edge of the street. I slowed as I drove past, and my heart skittered around in my chest when I saw his shadow behind the wheel. I told myself to calm down. This was probably a professional visit. After all, he'd made it pretty clear that he wasn't going to be around on a personal level.

By the time I parked and let Max out of the car, Jawarski came around the corner of the building. He wore his usual jeans and a light-colored shirt under a dark sport jacket. The sound of his boots striking the pavement as he walked echoed in the near silence.

"Abby."

"Jawarski. This is a surprise. What are you doing here?"

He came close enough for me to see his face in the dim lighting. "I've been hearing rumors. I thought I'd better check them out."

"Oh? What rumors?"

"I think you know. You promised that you'd stay out of this investigation, and you broke your word. You want to tell me why?"

"Do I really have to explain it? Felicity was found a few feet from my front door. There's a very good chance my fingerprints are on the murder weapon, since it probably came out of Wyatt's toolbox. I think I ought to be able to clear my name."

Jawarski groaned and rubbed his face. "Why are your fingerprints on the murder weapon?"

"Because the tools were scattered all over Wyatt's truck, and I picked them up."

"Abby—"

I held up a hand to stop the lecture I felt coming. "You don't have to say it. If I'd known what was going to happen, I would have been more careful. But what's done is done, Jawarski. I can't turn back the clock."

"Maybe you ought to think about hiring an attorney. Don't try to do this yourself."

"I will, if it comes to that. Call me crazy, but I'd rather it didn't."

Jawarski shifted his weight impatiently. "Why do you have to be so damn stubborn?"

"Why do you have to be so unreasonable? If you were considered a 'person of interest' in a murder investigation, would you sit on your hands and wait for somebody else to clear you?"

"Yeah, I would."

"I'll just bet you would." Fuming, I led Max toward the stairs.

Jawarski followed me. "You're not doing yourself any favors, Abby. The chief heard about your visit to Ursula Drake, and he's livid."

"Is that supposed to frighten me?"

"It's *supposed* to knock some common sense into you. You don't want to turn the guys on the force against you."

I stopped at the top of the stairs and turned to face him. "Why? Because they'd just let me take the blame for a murder I didn't commit?"

He gripped the handrails tightly, and I could see the muscles in his jaw working as he struggled for patience. "If you're trying to be funny, it's not working. We don't have dirty cops in the department. All I'm asking is for you to be reasonable. We don't have any idea who killed Felicity. We don't have any idea *why* she was killed. If you keep asking questions, there's no telling who you'll cross or what they'll do."

"Then maybe it will bring them out of the woodwork." I turned away so I could fumble with my key and the lock. And so I could process the concern on Jawarski's face without having to look him in the eye.

He stepped onto the landing behind me and put one hand on my shoulder. Gently, he turned me around to face him. One part of me wanted to resist, to stay focused on unlocking the door. The other wanted to see what else I could read in his expression. I gave in to the latter and forced myself to look.

"I don't want you to get hurt," he said, his voice low and intimate.

In spite of the warm evening, I shivered, but the sensation wasn't unpleasant. "I don't intend to get hurt."

"I'm sure Felicity didn't, either."

I took a deep breath and let it out again slowly, trying to organize the emotions jumping around inside me. Stop looking at his profile. Stop breathing the faded scent of aftershave. Stop looking into his eyes and remembering how his lips felt the last time he kissed me. "That," I said, hating that my voice caught, "was different. Felicity's murder. It was different."

"You're sure about that? Whoever killed her isn't going to want to get caught, Abby. If you get too close—"

He was making me nervous, and I hated that, too. Like

I always do when there's a choice between anger and some other emotion, I defaulted to anger. "I'm not going to get too close, Jawarski. You don't need to save me from myself, okay?"

"Dammit, Abby, stop being so prickly."

"I'm not prickly."

He let go of me and took the key from my hand. "Call it whatever you want, but it's about time you let somebody care about you."

"That's *so* unfair. I let people care about me all the time."

"Really?" He unlocked the door easily and pushed it open. "Who? And when? You don't even let your own brother get close."

I pushed past him into the apartment and flipped on a light. "I don't need you to rescue me, and I don't need you to psychoanalyze me. Wyatt and I are just fine."

He tossed my keys onto the coffee table and made himself at home on the couch. "Have it your way. Who have you been talking to about the Asbury case?"

"What? You mean your sources didn't fill you in on all the details?"

"Can the cute stuff, Shaw. Just tell me what you've been doing."

Relieved that we were back on more comfortable footing, I dropped into a chair and kicked my feet onto the coffee table. Max sensed the release of tension and curled up on a throw rug. "I haven't found out anything, really. Just that Felicity was planning to build a MegaMart in the hollow, and somebody's been sabotaging the equipment."

"Who told you that?"

"Her daughter, Jacqueline. Haven't your guys talked to her?"

He nodded. "Yeah, we've talked to her. She must have forgotten to mention it."

"This may come as a surprise, Jawarski, but some people don't like talking to cops. If you think about it that way, I'm actually helping by getting information you can't."

"Yeah, except we're not thinking about it that way. What else?"

"I talked to Kirby North. I'm pretty sure he's a member of Greentree, and I'm pretty sure they're the ones sabotaging Felicity's equipment, but Kirby won't admit anything, and he won't say who's calling the shots."

"That's not surprising. Anything else?"

"Did you know that Oliver Birch was nearly killed the same night Felicity died?"

"That I did know. Got a call from your man Orly about the brakes."

"Which pretty much takes the suspicion off anybody connected with the arts festival," I said. "Nobody's going to kill Oliver over Felicity wanting to pull a painting or change a booth assignment."

"You're probably right." Jawarski ran a hand over his chin. I could hear the stubble scratching his fingers. "But with your fingerprints on the murder weapon, we have a problem. Not to mention the fact that you threatened Felicity just hours before she died."

"I *didn't* threaten her."

He held up both hands. "I believe you. I also know you didn't commit murder. But the department is working up the case, and they'll present it to the DA. Whether he'll believe you is anybody's guess."

"Which is exactly why I'm trying to find some way to *prove* I'm innocent before it comes to that."

"I've already told you that I'm not going to let you take the fall for this. I promise you, so trust me, okay?"

"Trust me." His promise sounded good . . . in theory. But I'd learned a few hard lessons about trust, and I'd spent so long taking care of myself, I wasn't even sure I remembered how.

Chapter 16

With less than two weeks until the festival, I spent the next morning in the town square, checking on the delivery of poles and tarp for the booths we'd be providing, light-pole banners for the downtown area, and barricades and extra parking cones for traffic control. There was still no word from the mayor's office, so I just kept moving forward with our plans. Karen had promised to call someone for help in the shop if she needed it, so I was able to put the store out of my mind and focus on the festival.

I put Rachel to work phoning the soft drink vendor we'd contracted to make sure everything was on track. I took Nicolette with me to help move half of the tarp and poles from one side of the square to the other. It meant a lot of hard work today, but it would make putting up the booths easier when the time came.

By eleven, the sun had climbed high overhead, and I'd worked up a sweat. Even perky Nicolette was starting to drag. I bent to lift one end of the poles and waited for Nico-

lette to grab the other. She finally got there, but the gri-
mace on her face made it clear that she wasn't happy. "I
don't know why we have to do this. These things are
heavy."

"Somebody has to move them," I reminded her. "It
might as well be us."

"If I ruin my manicure, the committee is going to pay
for a new set of nails."

"I'll be sure to pass that along. I'm sure it will be top
priority." I jerked my head, indicating that she should turn
the corner. Sweat trickled down my back, and I began to
regret coming outside without sun block.

"So how's the murder investigation coming?" Nicolette
called back over her shoulder.

A welcome breeze stirred the air around my face.
"Slow. At first, I thought someone from Greentree might
have killed her, but I haven't been able to make any head-
way in proving that. It looks as if the only person in her
family who would have gained from her death was Oliver,
but he has an alibi for the time of the murder."

Nicolette reached the end of the row and stopped walking. We lowered the pipes onto the growing stack and took
a minute to stretch the kinks out of our backs. "So Oliver
inherits all that money?"

"According to Ursula and Jacqueline."

"Any idea how much?"

I shook my head. "Enough, I'm sure."

"Well, I'll bet he's happy." Nicolette studied the nails
on one hand carefully. "Then again, maybe money wasn't
the motive. Maybe she was killed because of something
else."

"I've wondered the same thing, but even though everybody hated her, nobody seemed passionate enough to do
anything about it. They all just accepted that she was miserable and obnoxious, and they adjusted around her."

"Maybe somebody wanted revenge for an old hurt. You

know how mean she was. Maybe she said something that just pushed one of them over the edge, and they wanted to shut her up."

I noticed a grease smudge on my arm and tried to wipe it off, but I only succeeded in smearing it around. "How well do you know Felicity's family?" I asked as we started walking again.

"Not well at all, really. Jacqueline and I belong to the same church group, but neither of us goes very often. I've met Brenda a few times, though. She doesn't even seem to fit with the rest of them, you know? She's like the normal cousin on *The Munsters*."

Laughing, I stepped over a puddle left by the sprinklers. "I know what you mean. I met her the other night. I liked her, but I got the feeling she was hiding something from me."

"She probably was. It was her grandmother who got killed, after all."

"And her mother who threatened to do the job. I just wish I could find out why Jacqueline was so upset that night."

Nicolette swiped a bead from her cheek with the back of her hand. "Somebody has to know. You just haven't asked the right person yet."

I laughed. "Thanks." We walked in silence for a few feet. "Brenda seems awfully calm about her family situation. Do you think she's really okay with it?"

"That depends on how you define 'okay.' She doesn't know anything about her father or his family, and I know that bugs her."

"She told you that?"

"Not in so many words, but a few months ago she was asking Quincy Fox about using the Internet to find something. And she spends an awful lot of time at the library."

"Looking for her father?"

Nicolette shrugged. "That would be my guess."

"Interesting. I wonder if Jacqueline knows what she's doing."

"I don't know, but can you imagine the fireworks if Felicity had found out?"

I slowed my step. "Are we sure she didn't?"

"No. But she wouldn't have been happy, that's for sure."

I thought that idea over once more, but it didn't feel right. In that scenario, Felicity would have been the angry one. Of course, the mysterious female caller, *if* she even existed, could have been Jacqueline or Brenda. I wasn't entirely convinced Ursula hadn't made that up to divert suspicion from herself. But this news made me more certain that Brenda hadn't asked to meet Felicity out of mere curiosity. She'd wanted something. I would have bet on it. I couldn't answer those questions now, so I changed the subject. "Has Meena told you why the mayor took her off the committee?"

Nicolette shook her head. "She's still not talking."

"I wish she'd tell someone what's going on. The closer we get to D-day, the more I wish she were here." We rounded a corner, and a truck on the edge of the lawn caught my eye. Old. Beat-up. Gunmetal gray with one blue door. I stopped abruptly and lowered my voice to make sure I wouldn't be overheard. "Don't look now," I said, "but do you know whose truck that is? The one with the blue door?"

I should have known better. It's human nature, I guess, to look immediately whenever someone says *not* to. "The Ford?"

"Yeah. Do you know who it belongs to?"

"Sure. It's the truck Kirby uses to haul his sculptures around."

"Are you sure?"

"Positive. I've seen it a thousand times."

So it was Kirby who went to see Felicity the night she died? I have to admit, I'd never thought of him. Was it possible he'd made it from the guild to the Drake Mansion before I had? He hadn't said a word about it when I talked to him, but neither had Felicity or Ursula.

"What do you know about Kirby and Felicity?" I asked Nicolette.

Her end of the poles jostled. "They hated each other. Why?"

"Then why would he rush up to see her right after the meeting at the guild the night she was put in charge?"

"He wouldn't."

"And yet he did."

Nicolette almost dropped her end of the poles. "You're kidding."

I scrambled to hang on, so we wouldn't lose the whole bunch in the mud. "That's the truck I saw leaving when I arrived. I can't say absolutely that he was behind the wheel."

"But that doesn't make any sense. He hated Felicity. Why would he go up there?"

"That's what I'd like to know. Is it possible they weren't really enemies like everyone thought?"

Nicolette readjusted her grip, and we started moving once more. "If they weren't enemies, they sure put on a great act. Do you think Felicity actually talked to him when he went up there?"

"Maybe." I thought about Felicity as she'd been that night and realized I might be making an assumption that wasn't true. "Maybe she didn't," I said. "Maybe Ursula turned him away. She sure tried hard enough to get rid of me. But that still doesn't explain why he went up there in the first place. Do you think he would have told somebody at the guild what he had in mind?"

"Kirby? I doubt it. You know what a loner he is. Maybe Ursula knows."

"Maybe. But I don't think she'd tell me."

Nicolette blew a breath into her bangs and brushed a

lock of pale hair off her shoulder. "Look, it's not as if you have to solve the case, you know. That's what the police are for. What are they saying? Where are they with their investigation?"

"They're not saying anything to me."

"Not even Jawarski?"

"Not even him."

"Are you two on the outs or something?"

"We're not on the outs. We're not on the ins, either. We're just friends."

"Oh, puh-lease." The poles in my hand shifted dangerously, and I had to work fast to maintain a grip on them. "Everybody knows the two of you are dating. I don't know why neither of you can admit it."

Using my shoulder, I wiped a trickle of sweat from near my eye. "We've gone out a couple of times. That doesn't qualify as *dating*."

I couldn't see her, but I heard the huff of exasperation. "You're wrong," she said. "Everybody knows he's crazy about you. Everybody but *you*."

"Then you're all delusional." I rounded the last corner between us and the end of the line and had to dance to one side to avoid plowing into Shellee Marshall.

"*There* you are," she said when she saw me. "I've been looking everywhere for you. I need your help."

"That's what I'm here for. What's wrong?"

"Kirby's supposed to be helping put up the bleachers. Dave Shapiro sent me to find him, but nobody's seen him anywhere. I'm *not* going to spend all day looking for him."

We'd reached the end of the line, so I lowered my end of the pipes to the ground. "He's here somewhere. I just saw his truck."

"Great. If you see him, tell him to get his ass over to the east field, where he was supposed to be an hour ago." She flounced away, apparently believing that telling me her troubles relieved her of the obligation to keep searching.

This was why we needed Meena to come back. She's much better at handling people than I am. I met Nicolette's amused glance with a roll of my eyes. "If you want something done right . . ." I said. "You want to see if you can find Kirby? I don't want Shellee complaining to people because he's not where he's supposed to be."

Nicolette wiped a smudge from her cheek and nodded. "Sure. I'll see what I can do."

Grateful there were at least one or two people I could count on, I walked to the parking lot where Gavin Trotter and Duncan Farmer had their heads together over a clipboard. A few feet away, Tej Lakshman chugged water from a bottle while Tommy Jerrick dug through the toolbox in the bed of his truck. If only everyone on site was working so well together.

All around me I could hear raised voices and evidence of increasingly frazzled tempers, and if the festival wasn't canceled, it was only going to get worse over the next few weeks. Thankfully, nobody seemed to be paying any attention to me, so I took the opportunity to take a closer look at Kirby's truck. I doubted there'd be evidence sitting out in plain sight, but you never can tell.

Just as I reached the truck bed, a scream pierced the air. Time stood still for a second, then everyone burst into action. Straining to hear another scream over the shouts of concerned people, I raced toward the south end of the square half a step behind Gavin Trotter.

Wild-eyed and sobbing, Nicolette burst around the corner. I'd never seen her that upset before, and I don't mind admitting that it worried me. While Gavin shot past her to see what had upset her, I ground to a stop to make sure she was all right.

"What is it?" I demanded. "What's wrong?"

Nicolette gulped air and made a visible effort to pull herself together. "He's . . . he's *dead*."

"What are you talking about? Who's dead?"

"B-back there." She shuddered convulsively and covered her face with her hands.

"Are you sure? Who is it?"

"K-Kirby. I think. It looked like him anyway."

My heart plummeted, and bile rose in my throat. Another death? What was going on in Paradise? I tried to escape Nicolette's clutches so I could see for myself, but she held too tightly.

"It was so awful," she said, darting a glance over her shoulder. "I've never seen a dead body before."

"Are you sure he's dead? Maybe he's just hurt."

"No. I'm sure. He's—he's—" Her voice caught, and she broke off, unable to go on. She clutched my hand and held on tightly. "Don't go back there, Abby. You don't need to see it. I wish to God I hadn't."

It wouldn't be my first dead body, but I didn't point that out. I was still having flashbacks of seeing Felicity's body at odd moments during the day, and I didn't want to add another image I couldn't forget. But I was having a tough time accepting the idea of Kirby dead. I guess maybe I needed to see for myself.

Working carefully so I didn't alarm her, I withdrew from Nicolette's grip. "How did he die?"

"I don't know! He's just lying there with his face all bluish gray."

"Then he must have been there for a little while. I wonder how long he's been AWOL." Surely, this would be enough to convince the police that I wasn't the killer. I'd been with Nicolette since eight o'clock this morning, and we'd never come near this spot until now. Did this mean that the killer *was* someone involved in the festival?

Nicolette grabbed me by the shoulders and shook me—hard. "Abby! Stop! I just saw a *dead body*. Maybe that's no big deal to you, but I'm freaking out, and I could use a little emotional support."

I snapped out of my reverie with a jerk. She had a point.

I wasn't being a very good friend. "I'm sorry, Nicolette. Believe me, finding someone dead is no picnic for me, either."

She shivered and wrapped her arms around herself as if she needed warmth in the eighty degree weather. "Has anyone called the police?"

"I don't think so." I pulled my cell phone from my pocket. "I should call right now."

Nicolette shook her head and held out her hand. "Let me do it. You don't need to be tied to this murder."

The offer surprised and touched me. "You're sure?"

"Of course I'm sure." She wiggled her fingers impatiently. "I'm the one who found him. I should be the one to call."

It had been a long time since I'd had close friends and even longer since I'd felt a part of something. The reaction of people around town since Felicity's death had almost convinced me that I never would.

I resisted my normal impulse to do it all myself and handed her the cell phone. And I wondered if she had any idea how difficult it was for me to do it.

"Let's go over this again," Nate Svboda said, his eyes cold, his expression harsh. "You went to see Kirby North yesterday in his cabin. Why?"

My head was pounding, the muscles in my neck and shoulders were tense, and the skin on my cheeks and nose burned from spending too long in the sun. Nate had been doing his Barney Fife imitation for more than an hour already, and my patience was wearing thin.

I hunched over the table in the police station's interrogation room and ran my fingers through my hair. "I went to see him because I wanted to ask if he'd be in charge of putting up the bleachers for the festival. We ended up talking about the sabotage out at the construction site in the hollow."

"He just happened to bring it up, I suppose?"

"No, I asked."

"What made you think he'd know anything about it?"

"I heard he was a member of Greentree."

"And was he?"

"I don't know. He didn't admit it, but he didn't deny it, either."

"That upset you?"

"No, it didn't upset me. Come on, Nate. What's wrong with you? I went out there to talk to him, and that was the last time I saw him."

"You didn't see him this morning at the square?"

"No, but I saw his truck."

"The one you say you saw leaving the Asbury house on the fourteenth. Did Kirby tell you what he was doing there?"

The overhead light glared in the room, making my eyes tired. "I didn't get a chance to ask him. I didn't realize it was his truck until this morning. How did he die, anyway?"

"We're not ready to release that information yet. Now tell me again why you went to see Kirby at his cabin."

"Are you kidding? We've gone over this three times already, and I need to get back to work. Karen's been there on her own all morning."

"You can leave when I'm through here."

I tried to hang on to my rapidly unraveling patience, but I was too tired and too frustrated. "Would you mind telling me just why you're so hostile toward me? What did I ever do to you?"

"I'm not hostile."

"You could have fooled me. You've been pissed off at me since I came back to town, and I want to know why."

"Don't try to make this personal, Abby. I'm just doing my job."

"The hell you are." I'd been doing my best to appear cooperative. I'd tried not to annoy people by flaunting my legal education. But the attorney I'd been in my previous life had finally had enough. "There's no evidence against me," I said. "Nothing to indicate that I murdered Felicity or Kirby. Not even anything that would make a rational person think I might have. But you're acting as if you caught me with a smoking gun in my hand, and you're enjoying every minute of it."

Nate leaned back in his chair and crossed his arms across his chest. "You want to file a formal complaint?"

I was seriously tempted to say yes, but there was a gleam in his eye, daring me to do it. Is that what he wanted? *What was his problem?* I was irritated but not irrational. I wouldn't give him the satisfaction.

"Not today," I said, reserving the right to leave my options open. "For the record, I did not kill Felicity Asbury. I did not kill Kirby North, and I have no idea who killed either one. So unless you have something up your sleeve more compelling than some very weak circumstantial evidence, this interrogation is over." Shaking with anger, I stood and glared at him, daring him to push me.

He got to his feet more slowly and spent a minute adjusting the belt around his waist. "Murder's a serious business, Abby. This isn't something a girl like you ought to be playing around with."

A *girl*? Was he purposely trying to push my buttons? I could have set him straight, but I've learned not to go into a battle of wits with the unarmed. "Open the door so I can get out of here," I snarled, barely resisting the urge to wipe the smirk off his face.

Nate ambled around the table and turned the knob. He dragged open the door and bowed mockingly as I strode through. I'd been wrong about Nate, I realized as I bore down on the front door of the police station. He wasn't just a harmless idiot. He was a dangerous one.

Chapter 17

"The secret is in the lime juice," Rachel said that evening. She stood behind the counter of her gleaming kitchen and worked a knife through the bits of avocado in the bowl in front of her. "Most people don't add enough. And the garlic. It has to be fresh, not powdered. If you use powdered, you'll regret it."

I doubted that, but the chances that I'd ever make my own guacamole were so slim, it probably wasn't an issue I'd ever encounter.

Rachel nodded toward a mound of greens on the counter. "How do you feel about cilantro? People either love it or hate it."

"I have no strong feelings either way. If you like it, put it in."

"I *love* it." She held the bunched sprigs of leaves to my nose. "Smell that. Is that not the best smell in the world?"

I inhaled dutifully, surprised by the clean, earthy scent that, for a moment, eclipsed the spicy scent of chicken enchiladas in the oven. "It's . . . unusual."

"It's distinctive." Rachel pulled a couple of sprigs from the bunch and attacked them with her knife. She whacked at it for a few minutes, then stopped and stared at her knife. "I'm having the hardest time believing that Kirby's dead. It's surreal, you know?"

I nodded. "I know."

"I'm starting to think the arts festival has been cursed or something." She started to work on the cilantro again, scooping it into the bowl when she'd finished. "Isn't that color gorgeous?"

I glanced at the avocado mush and nodded. "Green."

"It's not green. It's *green*."

"Sorry." I grinned and opened the wine cooler she'd put in front of me a few minutes earlier. I'd hesitated over accepting her dinner invitation when she extended it that afternoon, but now I was glad I'd come. "You like cooking?"

"I love it. It relaxes me. Don't you?"

I shook my head. "I enjoy making candy, but the rest of the kitchen is beyond me. I cook when I have to, but it's not something I'd do by choice."

Rachel sighed dreamily. "It's not a chore to me. It's a creative outlet. I get excited over little things." She held up the bowl so I could see inside better. "Like the contrast of the two greens. It's pretty, and it's satisfying."

I grinned and swallowed a mouthful of margarita cooler. "And it's *green*."

Laughing, Rachel rinsed a couple of tomatoes under the faucet. "Yeah. But not for long. So what did Nate ask you down at the station?"

I made a face. "That toad? He's determined to make me miserable. I just can't figure out why."

"He's a weird one, all right. I never could figure out how he passed the police academy."

"He probably cheated," I groused. I took another swig, propped my elbows on the counter and my chin in my hands. "You know, Kirby warned me to be careful yesterday. He knew something, but I didn't realize it. I thought he might've been threatening me."

"He was pretty intense," Rachel agreed. "What do you think he knew?"

"I have no idea." I could feel tension slipping from my shoulders. Enough to help me remember things I'd forgotten in the heat of the moment. I sat up stiffly and swore under my breath. "I left the registration information at the staging area. In all the chaos, I forgot all about it."

Rachel waved a hand at me. "You can swing by and pick it up when you leave here. It's not going anywhere."

She was probably right, so I allowed myself to relax again. "Where were you when Nicolette found Kirby?"

Rachel ran her knife through one of the tomatoes. "I was on the other side of the square, trying to figure out what to do with a hundred light-pole banners."

"They came?"

"Yeah. About ten minutes before Nicolette screamed."

"Did you see anybody who looked suspicious?"

Rachel glanced up from her work. "Like a murderous stranger walking around with deadly construction tools in his hand? No. Sorry."

"How about somebody who wasn't a stranger? Maybe walking quickly to get away, or looking unconcerned when he heard the scream?"

"Sorry."

"You didn't see *anything*?"

Rachel stirred the tomatoes into the guacamole and conducted a taste test. Nodding satisfaction, she spooned the guacamole into a serving dish and set it on a tray surrounded by tortilla chips. "I'm sorry, Abby. I was busy. I didn't even know Kirby was there."

I rubbed my temples with my fingertips. "Whoever killed Felicity must have killed Kirby. He must have known something the killer didn't want anyone else to know."

Rachel scooped up a generous mound of guacamole and

munched thoughtfully. "Do you think Kirby left a note or something?"

"I doubt it, and after today I'm not going to be able to get close to his cabin to find out. Or his truck." I stopped rubbing and reached for the wine cooler again. "What could Kirby have known?"

"Maybe he saw Felicity's murder."

"Then why didn't he come forward?"

"He could have been blackmailing the killer."

I nodded slowly. "I suppose that's possible, but it doesn't seem like Kirby's style. He's a lot more straightforward than that."

Rachel's sleeve draped dangerously close to the guacamole. She caught it with her free hand and held it out of the way. "Apparently not, or he wouldn't be dead now. You know . . . if he knew something that got him killed."

I groaned and leaned my forehead on the counter. "This case is making my head hurt," I mumbled into the granite countertop. "Nothing makes sense."

"Sure it does. You're just not looking at it the right way, that's all. I'll bet you know everything you need to know, but you're making an assumption about something that isn't actually true."

I rolled my head to one side so I could look at her. "Like what?"

"I don't know. That's what we have to figure out. But something isn't as it seems." She scooped again and held the chip out to me. "Come on. Eat. It'll help."

"You sound like my mother," I complained, taking the chip and lifting my head so I could put it in my mouth.

"It's just common sense. If you don't eat, you'll get light-headed. Who can think then?"

She had a point. Plus, the guacamole was the best I'd ever tasted. I told her so and sat up a little straighter. "Do you remember who was working on the south end of the square this morning?"

"Just the group who was putting up the bleachers."

"Shellee, Dave Shapiro. Who else?"

"Eddie Long. Pete Gallegos." Rachel thought some more, but shook her head. "Sorry, I don't remember anyone else."

"That's okay. Shellee will probably remember. Unless she was too angry with Kirby to pay attention."

Rachel leaned onto the counter. "You don't think Shellee did it, do you?"

"She'd be an easy solution, but I doubt she'd commit a double murder over the neckline of her tank tops."

Rachel laughed. "Can you imagine? Although, I have heard some pretty weird stories. I heard on the news about some guy who killed his roommate over Toaster Strudels."

"If these murders were committed over something like that," I said with a groan, "I'm going to fling myself off the table."

The timer buzzed, and Rachel slipped her hand into an oven mitt. "Eat first," she warned. "You'll recover faster."

Maybe she was right. I needed to talk to Shellee and a few of the others about what they saw that morning, and I wouldn't be able to read between the lines on an empty stomach. At least, that's the excuse I gave myself for putting two enchiladas on my plate and taking a second spoonful of guacamole.

Halfway through dinner, I heard a distant rumble. A few seconds later, light flashed in the sky. Rachel and I made eye contact briefly, then launched from our chairs as if we'd been shot from a cannon. The weather had been warm and dry for weeks. Tonight, with the square filled with supplies and equipment, we were going to get rain.

By the time Rachel and I made it into our cars, the wind had picked up. Bits of dirt, grass, garbage, and leaves flew across the road in front of me, and wind buffeted the Jetta. With each clap of thunder, Max turned another circle on the seat, searching desperately for a safe place to hide from the noise.

I punched numbers into my cell phone as I drove, calling anyone I could think of to ask for help. Rachel was doing the same from her car, each of us promising to pick up anyone who had transportation issues.

The light-pole banners would be all right in the rain. They'd been designed to hold up in our Rocky Mountain weather. So would the tarp for the booths. But nothing was secure enough to withstand the driving wind. After waiting for weeks for the banners to be delivered, we could lose them all in less than twenty-four hours. And without the registration information I'd accidentally left behind, we'd be in a world of trouble.

Just thinking about the bedlam such a loss would create made me hit the gas a little harder. Splotches of rain pelted my windshield, slowly at first, then more rapidly. By the time I reached the town square, I'd rounded up half a dozen volunteers. Two cars were there when I arrived, and three more showed up less than two minutes later. With a silent prayer that Max wouldn't decide to chew up the Jetta in his distress, I let myself out into the stinging rain.

I sent Shellee and Dave to secure the banners and dispatched the rest to make sure everything else was secure. I picked up the first box of registration information and started toward my car, but the rain came down so hard, I couldn't see more than a few inches in front of me.

Bending my head to protect my face from the rain's bite, I stumbled over a rock and nearly lost my footing. As I struggled to keep both my balance and my grip on the box, a shadow loomed out of the rain directly in front of me. A dozen disasters flew through my head in less than three seconds, and my heart, already racing with adrenaline, threatened to fly right out of my chest. I heard a small scream and realized with surprise that it had come from me.

The shadow gripped my arm tightly, and Henri Guischard materialized out of the storm. "Be careful, *cherie*. You could fall and hurt yourself."

I gulped air and nodded. "Thank you. I thought I was a goner. What are you doing here?"

Henri reached for the box, and in gratitude I let him take it. "I was walking back to the restaurant when the storm began. Then I see all of you rushing about, so I help. What can I do?"

"I have three of these boxes that I need to get into my car," I said, turning carefully. "It's the Jetta right over there. The hatch is unlocked."

"*Oui.* And the rest?"

"I'll get them. With your help we can relay them and save time. Do you understand what I mean by relay?"

He nodded quickly. "*Oui.* I know the word. Off you go, then. I will see you back here in a minute or two, no?"

"Yes." I slipped on the mud and grass as I hurried back across the lawn, but in just a few minutes Henri and I had the registration information safely locked in my car.

"Now what?" he asked as he shut the hatch for the final time. "Where do you need me?"

"You've done more than enough," I said, feeling guilty for taking advantage of his generosity. "Go home. Get out of the rain."

"And leave the rest of you here? No." He sketched a mock salute and wiped rain from his face. "Put me to work, mademoiselle. I implore you."

I grinned as rain snaked down my back. "Who could ignore a request like that? All right. We have to check the whole area. Anything that the rain can destroy needs to be moved into a car. Anything the wind can blow away should be secured with something heavy. Leave whenever you've had enough, okay?"

"*Absolument.*"

I stood in the rain for a minute, watching him run away from me. His kindness touched me, and I wondered if

Jawarski was right. Maybe I did hold myself too aloof from people. Maybe it wouldn't hurt to let my guard down just a little.

In less than an hour we had everything secure, and the waterlogged, mud-splattered group of us stood under the roof of a bowery, shivering in the cold wind. I offered to buy everyone coffee so we could all warm up, but only Shellee and Rachel took me up on the offer.

After a little discussion, we found ourselves at Sid's, an old-fashioned family restaurant that is Wyatt's hangout of choice. It was the only place in town a trio of waterlogged, mud-spattered, and windblown women wouldn't look out of place.

We settled into a booth, shivering in our wet clothes, and laughing a little at the experience we'd just been through. I was relieved to find that Wyatt wasn't there. It was better for his marriage if he were home and not parked on a stool at Sid's counter.

Shellee fed quarters into the jukebox on our table and punched in the numbers for a few eighties songs that had us laughing and reliving memories of outrageous clothes and haircuts of days gone by. But our levity didn't last long. Exhaustion hit by the time the third song began to play, and with it came the memory of Kirby's murder. I didn't want to end the evening on a bad note, but I needed to know if Shellee had seen anything unusual that afternoon.

After signaling our waitress for a warm-up and pouring in the proper amounts of sugar and creamer, I waited for an opening in the conversation. "I hate to change the subject," I said when the other two paused for a breath, "but I need to ask you a couple of questions about this afternoon. Is that okay?"

Shellee nodded uncertainly. "What about it?"

"I need to know what happened when you were looking

for Kirby. Where did you look? Who did you see? Did you notice anything unusual?"

"Unusual?"

"Something you wouldn't expect to see at the staging area. Someone who shouldn't have been there."

Shellee stirred her coffee for a long minute before she spoke. "I don't think so. Dave was pissed because Kirby wasn't there when he was supposed to be. We waited for a while, and then he sent me to look for him. I have to confess, I wasn't really paying attention to much while I was walking around. I was pissed off, myself, for having to do it."

"Did you see Kirby at all today?"

She shook her head. "No, and I didn't talk to anyone who did, either. I didn't even know he was there until you told me you'd seen his truck."

"So Kirby must have run into his killer shortly after he got there," I mused. "Otherwise, you'd think somebody would have seen him."

Rachel tore open a packet of sugar and emptied half of it into her cup. "You're probably right. Maybe he got there early. Maybe he was already dead before the rest of us got there."

"You're probably right," I said with an exasperated sigh. "And if that's the case, the killer was probably just as careful this time as he was last time."

Rachel propped her chin in one hand. "No evidence, no witnesses."

Shellee looked from me to Rachel and back again. "I'm sorry. If I remember anything later, I'll tell the police . . . and you."

"I know you will," I said, making a real effort not to look disappointed. "It was a long shot, but I had to ask. I wish I knew if Kirby was killed for some reason, or if he was just in the wrong place at the wrong time."

"Kirby wasn't a little guy," Shellee pointed out. "It

would have taken somebody pretty strong to get the best of him."

"Someone from Greentree?" Rachel suggested.

I nodded. "Maybe, but why?"

Nobody had an answer to that, but I hadn't expected one. The door opened, and a young couple ducked inside out of the rain. I shivered in the gust of wind that came in with them and felt my spirits droop. "What did Felicity, Oliver, and Kirby have in common? Why would someone want all three of them dead?"

"Oliver?" Shellee signaled the waitress for a warm-up. "He's dead, too?"

"No, he's the lucky one. Somebody cut his brake line, and he was nearly killed in Devil's Canyon."

"Seriously?" Shellee slid down in her seat, her face scrunched with worry. "This is getting really creepy. Kirby was a jerk sometimes, but he didn't deserve to die."

"None of them did," I said. "Not this way. There's some connection I'm missing. Some reason Kirby went to the Drake Mansion the night of the murder. I'm beginning to wonder if we'll ever know what happened."

Rachel dabbed her mouth with a napkin. "There are unsolved cases all over."

Looking lost, Shellee put her cup down. "Kirby went to Felicity's? Who told you that?"

"Nobody. I saw his truck there."

"Kirby's?" Clearly confused, Shellee chewed a fingernail. "You think he went there to see Felicity, or to cut Oliver's brakes?"

"Oliver wasn't home that night," I said. "And Kirby knew I was on my way to see Felicity. Why would he rush to get there before me?"

"Maybe he wasn't there to see Felicity," Rachel said. "Maybe he went out there to see someone else. One of the household staff."

"Or Ursula." It was my suggestion, but it didn't make

any sense unless Kirby was secretly working against Green-tree . . . or Ursula was secretly working against Felicity.

The jukebox changed to a George Michael song, and we all fell silent in tribute. When George stopped singing, Shellee checked her watch and made a face. "I'd better go. I still have a few pieces to finish before the festival."

"If we even have one after this." I dredged up a grateful smile. "Thanks for your help tonight. I think we'll get through the storm without a loss."

"Not a problem. I feel kind of bad, you know? I was so pissed at Kirby today, and the whole time, he was already dead."

"You didn't know," Rachel said gently.

"Yeah, I guess." Shellee stood and slung a large leather pouch over her shoulder. "So who is that guy who was there tonight? I don't think I've met him."

Rachel wasn't ready to leave yet. She dug into her pocket and came up with another handful of quarters. "Which guy?"

"The guy with the accent. Is he new at the guild?"

"Henri's not a member of the guild," I explained. "In fact, he's not involved with the festival at all. He's the chef at Oliver's new restaurant. He saw us having trouble and came to help."

"That's weird, don't you think? All these people who are members of the guild won't lift a finger to help, and then you've got somebody who isn't even connected out there working his tail off. I guess he's fascinated by art or something, huh?"

"I don't know. What makes you say that?"

"Just that this isn't the first time I've seen him."

Rachel dropped change into the jukebox and punched in her selections. "I'm sure it isn't. I think he's been in town for a couple of weeks."

"No, I mean this isn't the first time I've seen him there—at the staging area."

Rachel's hand froze, and I almost choked on my coffee. "Henri has been there before? When?"

"He was there this afternoon," Shellee said, her face pinched in confusion once more. "I thought you knew."

Chapter 18

Rain ran down my neck in rivulets as I pounded on the door for the third time. "Come on, Jawarski," I muttered into the howling wind, "open the damn door." To make sure he knew I was there, I pressed the doorbell again, too. Twice.

A gust of wind tossed wet hair into my eyes. I pushed it off my forehead impatiently, but it didn't do any good. Between the rain, the wind, and the mud, I was a lost cause.

I waited to the count of ten and pounded again, this time using both fists. "Jawarski. Open up. This is important." Ten more beats, and I rang the bell. Before I could begin all over again, the porch light came on, and the door opened to reveal a very unhappy Jawarski wearing boxers and a T-shirt.

"What in the hell—?"

Movement on the stairs caught my eye, and I realized his kids were huddled there, watching to see what kind of maniac had disturbed their sleep. Score one for Abby.

I didn't waste time on preliminaries, but I lowered my

voice so the kids wouldn't overhear. "It's Henri. The killer. It's Henri."

"How do you know that?"

"He was there tonight at the staging area. Helping us move supplies out of the rain."

"O-kay."

"And Shellee saw him there this afternoon, around the time Nicolette found Kirby."

"And from that you've decided he's guilty of murder? Twice?"

Lightning zagged through the sky, and he seemed to realize for the first time that I was out in the elements. He pulled me inside, where I immediately created a puddle on the hardwood floor. "Do you have a towel or something? I don't want to ruin the wood."

He muttered something under his breath and disappeared. He came back a few seconds later holding two towels. Man-sized. I put one on the floor under my feet and toweled my hair dry with the other before wrapping it around me for what little warmth it could offer.

Jawarski watched me, his expression unforgiving. "You do realize it's the middle of the night."

"I know, and I'm sorry." I smiled up at the kids, telegraphing an apology to them. They stared back at me, as stiff and unsmiling as their father. I shifted uncomfortably under the weight of their combined gazes and forced myself to remember why I'd disturbed them in the first place. "I wouldn't have come for any other reason. But if I'm right, and Henri is the murderer—"

"What if you're wrong?"

"I don't think I am."

Jawarski laughed, but he didn't sound amused. "Of course you don't. But you have no proof, Abby. You don't have a single shred of evidence against the man, and I'm not going to race off into the night to arrest him just because he was seen walking around town in the middle of the day."

"He wasn't just walking around town," I argued. "He was at the staging area."

"In the middle of the town square."

"He was there," I said again, "at the same time Kirby was killed." When his expression didn't change, I shrugged out of the towel in frustration. "Are you even listening to me?"

"I've heard every word. Now it's your turn. *You have no proof.*"

"So send somebody to question him. Ask him what he was doing there."

"Will that make you happy?"

The question hit me like ice water in the face. "Don't patronize me, Jawarski. It's not like I haven't ever brought you good information on one of your cases."

He dipped his head just once. "I'll tell Svboda about it in the morning."

"If you do that, don't tell him the tip came from me. If you do, he'll ignore it."

Jawarski let out a breath loaded with frustration. "Nate's a good cop, Abby. Maybe you don't like him, but that doesn't change the facts. I'll tell him about all of this tomorrow. If he chooses not to follow up on it, it's probably because he doesn't think there's any reason to be concerned."

A couple of responses rose to my lips, but I bit them back. There were kids present. I handed the towel back to him and turned away. This was a new side to Jawarski, and I didn't like it very much.

"I guess I can't ask for more than that," I said. "Thanks for the use of your towels." I let myself outside before he could respond. Apparently, it wasn't enough to ignore me as a friend while his kids were here. I wasn't even supposed to exist.

Jerk!

This was why I didn't want to rush things. This was

why I held back, put up walls, constructed protective barriers. At that moment, I was merely pissed. Imagine what I would have felt if I'd let myself really care.

I slid behind the wheel of the Jetta and, because my suspicions about Henri had me spooked, locked myself in. Once I felt safe, I scratched Max between the ears to let him know everything was all right. Just as I slipped the key into the ignition, a hulking shadow appeared by my window, and Jawarski knocked on the glass. "We need to talk," he shouted.

He'd put a ski jacket over his T-shirt, but his legs were still bare, and I wasn't sure he'd taken the time to find shoes.

Shaking my head, I cranked the ignition. "Don't worry about it," I shouted back. "Go back inside. Your kids will be worried."

He tried the door. I felt a little jolt of triumph when it didn't open, and an even bigger one when he became agitated. "Dammit, Abby. Open the door."

I could have played with his head a bit longer, but that would have been childish. And mean. And eventually I'd probably regret it. I unlocked the door and told Max to get in the backseat so Jawarski could drench my passenger's seat.

As soon as he shut himself inside, the car felt small and crowded, and the smells of wet dog and wet man filled my senses.

"I didn't mean to sound rude in there," Jawarski said while I was still sifting through the various aromas. "The kids and I were in the middle of something when you came. It wasn't a good time."

That made me feel *so* much better. I didn't trust myself to look at him. It might make me soft. So I stared straight ahead at the rain running down the windshield. "I shouldn't have come. You told me not to, but I thought it would be okay to tell you about the case. I didn't realize even that would be stepping over the line."

"That's not it." He stopped talking, and from the corner of my eye I saw him run a hand across his face in frustration. He sat facing straight ahead, the mirror image of my own posture. "I've made a mess of things, and I know it. I just didn't know what to tell the kids. I didn't know what I *wanted* to tell them. What you and I have is . . . it's new. It's—"

"Untested? Untried? Uncertain?"

"All of that and then some. The kids have been through a lot," he said to the windshield wipers. "I just want to make sure how things are first."

"Yeah. I know. I understand all of that, but I also really, really hate feeling like I'm your dirty little secret. I don't know why, but it bugs me. A lot."

"Fair enough." I thought I saw him glance at me, but I couldn't be sure. "For what it's worth, I don't consider you my dirty little secret, and that's not how I meant to come across."

"Okay."

"So, are we good?"

I nodded. "I think so."

"Okay then. I'll call you."

"I'll answer."

He let himself out into the storm, and I watched him splash up the walk in his ski jacket, boxers, and bare feet. And I wondered if the two of us would ever figure out what we were doing, or if we'd just keep tripping over each other until one of us grew tired of it.

The next day brought a cloudless blue sky and a warm breeze. Last night's storm was nothing but a memory . . . and a few scattered puddles that would dry up by noon. By the clear light of day, my panic of the night before seemed foolish. Henri hadn't done anything to make me suspect him except show up in the wrong place at the wrong time. And he *had* been helpful. Jawarski was probably right. I didn't have a shred of evidence against him, and much as

I hated to admit it, accusing him on circumstantial evidence was no more justified than accusing me.

I walked Max for a long time, working through a few things in my head, so that by the time I got back to Divinity I was ready to put the murder behind me and the festival on hold for a day. With two unsolved murders hanging over our heads, I was convinced I'd be hearing from Jeb very soon. And anyway, I still hadn't finished the display window. The most difficult tasks—molding the baseball glove and creating the wagon—still lay ahead of me.

Determined not to let anything distract me, I gathered the supplies I needed and got right to work. Within minutes, I had chocolate melting slowly over a double boiler, and I was reacquainting myself with the airbrush I'd use to paint the wagon red. Other than the sheer size of them, creating the pieces of the wagon bed wouldn't be difficult, so I'd decided to make two of each piece. That way, I'd have plenty of molded pieces to practice on until I could trust myself to use the brush on the final product.

I worked slowly, focusing on what I was doing each step along the way. When I was a kid, Aunt Grace had scolded me more than once for letting outside influences distract me. It was still a problem, but I wasn't a kid anymore. I didn't have to give in to curiosity every time I heard people walking by or caught snatches of conversation through my open window.

I'd poured two of the four wagon sides when I heard the bell over the front door jingle to announce a customer. I kept my vow to stay focused on my work until I heard Karen hiss at me from the doorway.

"*Pssst.* Abby. There's a guy here to see you."

I didn't even look up, that's how focused I was. "Can you help him, Karen? I really want to finish this now that I've started."

"He doesn't want to talk to me. He specifically asked for you."

Grudgingly, I looked away from the mold I was filling. "Who is it?"

"I think he's that chef Oliver Birch hired. He sounds like a French guy, anyway."

I leaned up to look into the shop and realized that Henri Guischard was watching me. Between one breath and the next, last night's suspicions came rushing back. Since he could see me, I couldn't avoid talking to him, so I turned off the burner and removed the chocolate from the heat so it wouldn't become grainy.

Grabbing a towel from the rack, I carried it with me into the store and pasted on a smile as if I was glad to see him. "I wasn't expecting to see you this morning."

He smiled as if we were old friends and leaned on the counter. "Oliver has other obligations, so once again I find myself at loose ends. I thought a tour of your shop might be a pleasant diversion."

"I wish I'd known. Today's not a good day. I'm right in the middle of molding some chocolate pieces, and I can't leave them."

"Ah." He straightened, lips pursed. "I am sad, but I understand. The work, it must always come first, no?"

"Usually." I tried not to notice the fingerprints he'd left on the freshly cleaned glass, but the smudges glared at me. Two years ago, I wouldn't even have seen them, but I've grown fussy since keeping this much glass clean had become my responsibility. "Thank you again for your help last night," I said, dragging my gaze away from the display case. "It was kind of you to stop."

"It was nothing. I was glad to be of service." He helped himself to a piece of peppermint bark from the sample dish. "Very good. You made this?"

"Yes, but it's really not difficult. It's only melted chocolate and crushed pieces of peppermint. It doesn't take a lot of skill."

"You denigrate yourself. Why?"

I didn't know what to say to that, so I changed the subject. "One of the artists mentioned that she saw you at the staging area yesterday afternoon. I didn't realize you were there."

"It is okay, yes?"

"Yes. Did you find what you needed?"

He waved the question away with one hand and helped himself to more bark with the other. "I was there as I am here today. At loose ends and much too curious."

"So you were just there looking around?"

"*Oui*. And, of course, I saw Oliver's stepdaughter, Jacqueline, and I wanted to offer my condolences. Did I disturb something?"

I shook my head, but I was focused on the other part of his explanation. "You saw Jacqueline? Where?"

"At the town square, of course."

"What was she doing there?"

"I don't know. She was gone before I could reach her, and so was the man she was talking to."

"What man?"

"I don't know. A big man. With a beard."

"Kirby?" My stomach knotted painfully. "You saw Jacqueline talking to Kirby?"

"Did I? I suppose if you say so, then I did."

None of it made any sense to me. Why would Jacqueline kill Kirby? For that matter, why would Henri kill Kirby? I had suspects galore, but I was short motives. "I didn't realize you knew Jacqueline."

"I didn't know her. I saw her only when she came to talk to Oliver at the restaurant. He told me who she was."

I scrambled to add that to what I already knew. "When did she talk to Oliver? Before or after Felicity died?"

"Why, a few days before."

"Do you know what they talked about?"

He lowered his eyes, and I half expected him to scuff a toe on the floor. "I happened to overhear part of their conversation," he admitted. "She was angry with Oliver because of something Felicity did."

"Do you know what it was?"

He shook his head slowly. "I don't think—I didn't hear much, mind you, but she did say something about her daughter. *Quel est son nom?* Brenda?"

"Yes. Brenda. You didn't hear what it was that Felicity did to Brenda?"

"*Non.* I'm sorry."

"That's all right. I'm sure Brenda can fill in the blanks for me." My imagination was already running wild, but I tried to rein it in. "Do you mind if I give you a rain check on that tour of the shop? I really shouldn't leave the chocolate cooling much longer."

"Of course." He wagged a hand toward the kitchen. "Back to work with you. I shall entertain myself today."

Dismissed, I went back to the kitchen and tried to regain my earlier focus, but I couldn't even begin to concentrate until I heard the bell tinkle again, signaling that Henri had gone. He seemed so harmless, but was he? Could I really write off as coincidence the fact that he'd been at the staging area when Kirby was murdered? And what about Jacqueline? I'd have understood her being there if Meena was still working on the festival, but she wasn't.

"So what did he want?" Karen asked, pulling me back to the moment again.

"I'm not sure." I tapped both filled molds lightly on the countertop to dislodge air bubbles. "I really don't know what to make of him."

"Oh? Why?"

"Because he's . . ." I shook my head and sighed heavily. "Shellee saw him at the staging area yesterday around the time that we found Kirby, but there's no other reason to suspect him of doing anything wrong. He seems like a nice enough guy—although he did lie to me about one thing." I turned on the burner and put the double boiler over the flame again. "But, then, doesn't everybody lie when they're being questioned about a murder? I mean, we all have our secrets—don't we?"

Karen laughed and held up both hands to ward off the barrage. "If you really wonder about him, look hiim up on Google."

"Google?"

"On the computer. Put his name into the search engine, and see what you get back."

"I know what Google is, but isn't that kind of sneaky?"

Karen rolled her eyes at me. "Not at all. Everybody does it. It's an easy way to check people out without spending a fortune on a private detective. You can turn up some interesting stuff that way."

"And you think I can find something on Henri?"

"Probably. If he's ever been involved with anything that's online, his name will turn up." She checked behind her, saw that the shop was empty, and said, "Do you want me to look now? I'm not busy."

I hesitated, but only for a heartbeat. "Do it."

"You're sure."

"Do it. If he checks out, there's no harm done. If he doesn't, I need to know."

Chapter 19

Karen was back in less than fifteen minutes, her brows knit in consternation, and a look in her eye that made my heart slow with dread.

"You found something bad, didn't you?"

"Nope. Just the opposite in fact."

"He checked out?" I didn't even try to hide my surprise. "I was so certain he wouldn't."

"I didn't say that, either." Karen dug in the fridge and brought out two cans of Pepsi. She filled two glasses with ice and set one within my reach. "Actually, I didn't find anything about him."

"Nothing?"

"Nothing."

"Did you spell his name right?"

She made a face at me. "Yes, and also as many wrong ways as I could think of."

"So either he's never been involved in anything that's on the computer, or he doesn't exist, is that what you're saying?"

"Something like that. I think you're going to have to ask Jawarski to check him out."

After my visit last night, I dreaded going to him. We'd parted on good terms, but I didn't want him to think I was some hysterical female whose imagination went nuts every other day. "Yeah. Maybe."

"Don't you want to know?"

"Of course. I just don't want to use Jawarski to find out. But what choice do I have? The only other person I could ask would be Nate, and the chances that he'll run a background check if I ask are slim to none."

Karen nodded sympathetically. "You'd think Oliver Birch would have run a check on him, wouldn't you?"

"Maybe he did," I said. "In fact, I'd be surprised if he hadn't."

"Well, then, ask him about it. If he did, and Henri checked out, it will set your mind at ease."

I didn't want to talk to Oliver at the restaurant where Henri might overhear our conversation, and I didn't want to talk to him at home, either. I still wasn't sure where Ursula figured in all of this, and I didn't want her to overhear us.

Remembering what Jessie McGraw had told me about Oliver's habits, I arrived at Bonner's Bakery early the next morning and claimed a table with a clear view of the restaurant.

Now that I was here, I started second-guessing my plans. How would Oliver react? Would he resent me asking about Henri? Would he tell me what I wanted to know?

I nursed a cup of coffee until seven o'clock, when Oliver pulled up in front of the site in a silver Mercedes. My heart began beating faster in anticipation, but before he could get out of the car, Henri came out of the restaurant to meet him.

Until that moment, it hadn't occurred to me that they might come in for coffee and bear claws together. But even if they did, I didn't have to worry. I had as much right to coffee and pastry in the mornings as anyone else. My being here didn't automatically make it look as if I was up to something.

Oliver got out of the Mercedes and joined Henri on the sidewalk, and from Henri's gestures and the expression on his face, I realized he was upset about something. Oliver listened to him for a moment, then put an arm around his shoulder and led him toward the restaurant.

Just my luck, today would be the one day Oliver didn't come in for coffee and a bear claw.

I stood, intending to warm up my coffee from the thermos on the counter, when Henri jerked away from Oliver and took a couple of steps back. I'd have given anything to hear what they were saying, but if I tried to get closer, they'd see me, and I doubted they'd continue arguing in front of an audience.

Intrigued, I sat again and watched their argument play out. Clearly agitated, Oliver paced back and forth over the same five steps, pausing occasionally to jab at Henri with a finger. Oliver always seemed so unflappable, his anger surprised me.

"Abby? Good grief, you're a million miles away. Are you all right?"

I jerked my head around at the sound of my name, and my heart sank when I realized Paisley Pringle had come up behind me. Paisley owns Curl Up and Dye, a hair salon just up the street from Divinity. She's always trying to talk me into a makeover, but if her own hair and makeup are any indication of the work she does, I'll pass.

Last time I saw her, she'd been blond—her natural color, or at least it was once. Today, her hair was an unnatural shade of burgundy that made her skin tone pasty. She'd pulled her hair up loosely, and pieces of hair stuck out at various angles that I think she intended to look random, but which I'm sure had been carefully orchestrated.

"Are you all right?" she asked again.

I forced my attention away from the window and managed a weak smile. "I'm fine. Just preoccupied, I guess."

"Mind if I join you?" She plunked herself into a chair before I could give her an answer and picked a bite-sized piece from a croissant with pink-taloned fingers. "I've been thinking about you a lot lately. How are you holding up?"

"Me? I'm fine. Why?"

She leaned closer and dropped her voice to a stage whisper. "Well *you* know . . . the m-u-r-d-e-r. This whole thing must have been just awful for you."

I couldn't deny that the past week or so had been a challenge, but it wasn't one I wanted to share with Paisley. "I'm sure it's been much worse for the family," I said, craning to see what Oliver and Henri were doing now, but they'd disappeared inside the restaurant.

Paisley followed the direction of my gaze and bobbed her head in agreement. "That poor, poor man. He must be just devastated."

"Yes, I think he is."

"And don't you think it's a shame that Felicity died before Brenda had a chance to make peace with her?"

Surprised by the question, I nodded slowly. "Yeah. I do." I shifted in my seat so I could get a better look at Paisley's face. "Do you know Brenda?"

"Oh sure. She's a regular customer of mine. I know I shouldn't speak ill of the dead, but that grandmother of hers was a mean, nasty woman."

"That seems to be the general consensus," I said. "Has Brenda ever talked to you about Felicity?"

"All the time. At least recently. They never even met each other until two weeks ago. Did you know that? Brenda's twenty-one, and I don't think her grandmother even set eyes on her close up until she went over there."

"You're probably right. So it was only two weeks ago that Brenda met her grandmother?"

"About." Paisley absently fingered a lock of hair. "I don't remember exactly, but it was a few days before the old lady turned up dead."

Interesting. Brenda had made it sound as if her encounter with Felicity had been months before her death. Oliver came outside again, alone this time, but for the first time in history, I wanted to hear what Paisley had to say. "Did Brenda tell you why she wanted to meet her grandmother after all this time?"

Paisley ripped open a packet of sugar substitute and poured it into her coffee. "Oh sure. It was about her dad." Her eyes widened, and she touched two pink-tipped fingers to her lips. "Oh, but don't tell her mother. Brenda didn't want her to know."

"Brenda was trying to find her father?"

"She *did* find him. Her mother didn't want her to look, but she did anyway." Paisley sipped noisily and tilted her head to one side while she conducted a taste test.

I watched Oliver from the corner of my eye. He stood on the sidewalk for a moment, then started across the street toward the bakery. Great. Henri wasn't around, but I still couldn't ask Oliver what I wanted to know. My question wouldn't remain a secret for two seconds if Paisley overheard me asking, and the information she'd been sharing was too good to walk away from. "Did Brenda tell Felicity she'd found her father?"

"Yep. And Felicity got really nasty about it. You know how she was."

I was finding out a little more every day. "Surely Brenda knew, or had at least heard, what Felicity was like, too. Why would she tell her?"

Obviously enjoying herself, Paisley leaned close and lowered her voice. "Because he claims Felicity paid him to leave town. Or paid his parents, anyway, to make him disappear. *And* she tried to force Jacqueline to have an abortion after he left."

I wish I could say I was surprised, but Felicity had lost her ability to shock me. "So Brenda confronted her grandmother."

"Yeah, and Felicity admitted the whole thing. Said she'd done what had to be done. Really cold, you know? Brenda was crushed, poor thing, and who can blame her? She'd spent her whole life so far wishing for a dad, and then to find out that Felicity not only drove him away but wanted to get rid of her, too."

Just when I thought it was safe to rule out the family as suspects . . .

Paisley tore off another bite of croissant as Oliver strode through the bakery door. She lowered her voice to a near whisper, apparently reluctant to let Oliver hear her. "I don't think Brenda believed that her grandmother was that bad, you know? She thought her mother was exaggerating or contributing to the rift between them somehow. I think she really thought that if she could meet Felicity face-to-face, everything would be different."

"But it wasn't."

"No, it was worse. Much worse." Paisley popped the bite into her mouth and caught a glimpse of her watch as she did. "Oh goodness! Will you look at the time? Mom's going to be wondering where I am." She stood and gathered her things, struggling a little to fit the plastic lid on her paper cup. "You won't say anything about what I told you, will you? I really should have kept my big mouth shut."

"Don't worry about it," I said with a reassuring smile. "I won't say a thing unless it's a matter of life and death."

A relieved grin stretched across her face. "Thanks Abby, I owe you one. Stop by one of these days, and I'll do your hair—on the house. A few highlights would take *years* off your face."

"Don't shoot that!" I lunged at Karen just as her finger tightened on the spray bottle trigger. Lemony-fresh glass cleaner misted my cheek, but I didn't care. I'd managed to divert the spray, and that's all that mattered.

Karen stared at me as if I'd sprouted licorice whips from my head. "Have you lost your mind? That glass looks awful. Now move and let me finish."

I refused to budge. "Do you know what that is?"

"Yes. It's somebody's greasy fingerprints."

"It's *Henri's* greasy fingerprints," I clarified. "And I don't want to get rid of them until we know if he checks out."

Karen's outrage faded, but she still looked skeptical. "And how are we going to find that out?"

"I'm hoping I can convince Jawarski to run him through the police department computer."

"He'll know what you've been doing."

"Yeah, I know, but I think he's figured it out already. Did you ever ask Sergio if he could find out about Felicity's will?"

Karen turned away, grabbing the broom and attacking the floors. "Yeah, but I don't think it's going to help much. If both Felicity and Oliver had died that night, the money would have gone into a trust fund that would have been used to keep Drake Development running. The only person who would have directly benefitted financially from Felicity's death is Oliver."

"Then the motive wasn't money." I tucked the glass cleaner and rag in the cupboard beneath the sink. "Not unless Oliver killed her and tried to make it *look* as if he'd been attacked."

"By cutting his own brakes and then driving through Devil's Canyon? He'd have to be crazy."

"Yeah? Well—?"

Karen laughed and shook her head. "It would have been too risky, Abby. You've been through that canyon. There's no way he could be sure he'd survive. Then there's the little matter of his alibi. Orly towed him back to town, remember? He couldn't have been in two places at once."

"No, but he was back in Paradise by three thirty that morning. That left three hours—"

"Which he would have needed to walk here from the High Country Inn, murder Felicity, and walk back."

"He could have had a second car stashed at the motel," I reasoned.

"Just in case he made it down the canyon in one piece and managed to get a tow truck out there in time?" Karen shook her head. "The whole thing is off, Abby. What if Orly hadn't been able to come right away? What if it took longer than he expected to get the car back here? What if he couldn't get a room at the High Country? There would have been too much he couldn't control. And I thought Felicity left home around midnight. There's no way she would have waited three or four hours for anybody."

"You're probably right," I agreed grudgingly. "So where does that leave us? Felicity could have been killed over the MegaMart deal, but probably not by Kirby North—which leaves us missing a suspect. Or she could have been killed by Jacqueline or Brenda over what she did to Brenda's father."

"Or Ursula," Karen said.

"Or Ursula—although she has no motive that I know of."

"I don't know," Karen said, moving on to another display case. "She arranged the meeting between Brenda and Felicity, which seems kind of underhanded to me. She knew how Felicity felt, but she didn't hesitate to blindside her."

I thought again about seeing Kirby at the Drake Mansion and the suspicions that someone had been leaking information to Greentree. Could Ursula have done it? Without question. But had she?

"If you want my advice," Karen said without looking at me, "you should leave it alone and let the police figure it out."

Any reasonable person might have agreed with her, but I'd started this, and I wanted to finish it. Before I could say so, the bell over the door tinkled, and Jawarski came inside. He'd promised to call, but I hadn't expected to hear from him for a while. Seeing him walk through the door left me speechless.

He looked good, too. Long. Tall. Broad-shouldered. Tight jeans and a white shirt under a black jacket. Black cowboy hat tilted low over one eye.

"Abby. Karen." He touched the brim of his hat in greeting, and my heart gave that little flip it does whenever he's around.

"Jawarski. What can I do for you?"

"For one thing, you can package up a pound of those Louisiana pralines. And give me some of your caramel corn while you're at it. Enough for a couple of hungry kids."

"You got it." I set to work filling his order. "I'm glad you came in this morning. I was going to call you."

"Oh? Why? What's up?"

"I need to ask you for a favor," I said, scooping pralines into a bag bearing Divinity's distinctive gold label. "And don't get angry, okay? It's important."

"Let me guess. Something about the Asbury murder."

He sounded so sure of himself, I shook my head. "No. As a matter of fact, this is about Kirby North's murder."

"Semantics, Abby."

I stopped working and looked at him, letting silence do the talking for me.

"Fine. What do you want?"

"I want you to run a background check on Henri Guischard."

"Is that all?"

"That's all."

"Do you mind telling me why?"

"Because there's something wrong there. I can't put my

finger on it, and no, I don't have any proof. It's just a feeling I have."

"I see."

"I've searched for him on Google, and I can't find any mention of him." I left out Karen's involvement. She didn't need Jawarski giving her a rough time, too.

"And Google is an authority on finding people?"

"I didn't say that. I know Google's not a definitive authority, but don't you think it's odd that he's supposed to be a world-class chef, but there's not a single mention of him anywhere? He's supposed to have trained in France, and Oliver says that he spent ten years at a top New York restaurant, but there's no sign out there that Henri existed before he came to Paradise."

"Not one you can find."

"True. That's why I'm asking you to check." I put the bag on the scales, pleased to see that I was learning to feel the weight of a pound in my hand. "If he's legitimate, you'll be able to find him, and then you can tell me, so I can stop suspecting him."

Jawarski chuckled softly. "You're one exasperating woman. You know that, don't you?"

I grinned and added an extra scoop of pralines to his bag. "Is that supposed to be a compliment?"

"Nope. Just the truth." He let out a breath weighted with long suffering. "All right. I'll see what I can find. But if he checks out, you have to promise that you'll stay out of this from now on."

I sketched an *X* across my chest. And set to work on the caramel corn. "Absolutely."

A slow grin curved his lips. "Man, I wish I could believe that."

I looked up in mock outrage. "You wound me, Jawarski."

"I'm sure I do." He leaned on the counter and watched me work. "So you're still making Henri Guischard as the killer?"

I shook my head. "I'm not sure yet. Henri was there that afternoon, but apparently so was Jacqueline Asbury. Either one of them could have done it."

"Anybody have a motive?"

"Just the obvious one. Kirby must have known something the killer didn't want anyone else to know."

Jawarski shook his head and glanced at Karen. "Are you encouraging this?"

"Me?" One hand flew to her chest, and she looked remarkably innocent—for a woman who was guilty as charged. "Honestly, Detective. How could you think that?" She emptied the dustpan into the trash and put the broom away. "But if you need his fingerprints, we're saving them for you."

Chapter 20

"There's nothing better than peppermint tea to soothe the digestion," I said to a trio of middle-aged women who'd wandered into Divinity. I hadn't heard from Jawarski for a couple of days, but the convention of quilters staying in one of Paradise's new hotels had kept us so busy I hadn't had much time to worry about the murders. The mayor had called a meeting of the city council to discuss the arts festival, and with two unsolved murders, I couldn't argue with him anymore. Whatever decision he made, Paradise would suffer some losses.

One of the customers, a short, stubby woman with uneven teeth, nodded soberly. "That's what my grandmother always gave me when I had an upset tummy: peppermint tea."

I heard the phone ring, but Karen was closer, so I let her worry about it. "Did you know it's also good for asthma and allergies? According to Greek mythology," I said as I showed the women a peppermint gift basket I'd thrown together earlier that morning, "mint actually began as a nymph named Minthe. Persephone grew jealous of Minthe when Pluto, Persephone's husband, began to show too much affection toward Minthe. Persephone changed Minthe into a plant—a skill that I'm sure some women today wish they had."

The third member of the group laughed softly. "I'd eat that whole basket by myself if it would give me the ability to turn my ex's new little wife into a weed."

"If I'd been Persephone," I said with a grin, "I'd have turned Pluto into the plant, but that's just me. Pluto couldn't reverse the spell, but he did give Minthe a sweet smell, so that when people walked on her in the garden, her aroma would be a delight to the senses." I grinned and added, "I'm not sure that would have made me feel a whole lot better if I were in Minthe's place, but what's a girl to do?"

"You have a call, Abby," Karen called to me as she approached a new group of customers. Apparently, she could tell that I wasn't planning to abandon live customers for a phone call, so she added, "You might want to take it. It's Mayor Ireland."

That convinced me. Excusing myself from the quilters, I hurried to the kitchen where I could talk more freely. "Good morning, Mayor. Thanks for returning my calls," I said, trying hard not to sound sarcastic. After all, it had only taken him two weeks.

"Actually, I'm not returning your calls." Count on Jeb to ruin a perfectly good delusion. "Before I get started, Abby, I want you to know that I've given this a great deal of thought. I've spoken with advisors and members of the city council, and we're all in agreement."

"Why do I get the feeling I'm not going to like this?"

"You probably won't. We've had two murders here in the past two weeks, and the police are no closer to an arrest than they were in the beginning. I can't in good conscience allow members of the public to come to Paradise when we have no idea who's doing this or why. We simply don't have enough manpower to provide adequate security."

I couldn't argue with anything he said, but I felt compelled to point out a few things. "This is going to devastate a number of our local businesses, you know. People have spent money getting ready for this, and now they'll have no way to recoup their losses."

"I'm aware of that, and I wish I had a solution."

At least that was an honest answer. "The guild is going to take a heavy loss on this. It's going to take a long time to recover."

"I realize that, too. I'm sorry, Abby. I don't want to hurt anyone, but I simply don't see an alternative. Do you?"

"No, I don't," I admitted.

"Thank you. I know you're disappointed."

"Not as disappointed as I'd be if some innocent person got hurt."

"We're considering rescheduling later in the year. I'll get back to you tomorrow or the next day. Meanwhile, you'll have a lot of work on your hands getting the word out to vendors and exhibitors. We'll take care of notifying the general public from my office. Let me know if you need any volunteer help to make phone calls."

"I will."

"It's been a rough couple of weeks," he said. "I need you to know that I appreciate the work you've done trying to hold this thing together."

That was about the last thing I'd expected to hear from him, but it pleased me anyway. "Meena Driggs did the real work," I reminded him.

"Yes. Meena. That was an unfortunate situation."

That was one way of putting it, I guess. "Can you tell me why you removed her?"

"I'm afraid not. I can tell you that some information came to light that made me question her judgment. I acted in what I felt was the best interest of the city."

Clear as mud. Maybe I'd never know, but not knowing would bug me for a long time. That's the curse of the curious.

"If we do reschedule, is there any chance you'd be interested in chairing the committee?"

Would I? It was a lot of work, and I wasn't a natural at organization like Meena. Dealing with the artists was like herding cats, and I wasn't a natural cat herder, either. "I appreciate the offer, and I've survived the past couple of weeks, but I don't know how I feel about handling the whole thing. Can I think about it?"

"Sure. Take a few days or even a few weeks. We don't have to get started tomorrow."

"Maybe not, but whoever takes the job will need to get started soon. If I'm going to seriously consider saying yes, I need some answers to a few questions. I need to know I'm not going to pour my heart and soul into the festival, only to be removed three weeks before the event."

"Then we're at a stalemate, aren't we? Because I can't tell you what you want to know, Abby. There's only one person who can."

The lights were on in Meena's house when I pulled into the driveway that evening. I knew she'd be unhappy to see me, but I had to ask the questions one more time. If she wouldn't tell me why the mayor took her off the committee, at least I'd know what my answer to him would have to be.

She scowled when she opened the door and found me standing there, but she invited me inside right away, which I found surprising. Maybe she'd cooled off since I locked her in the ladies' room at Lorena's.

She led me into the kitchen, a large room with a black and white checked floor, chrome appliances, and retro decor. Chairs upholstered in red vinyl flanked a table that looked suspiciously like the one my mother had when I was a kid—only without the scorch marks on top where Wyatt used his wood burning set.

"What do you want?" Meena asked when we'd both taken a seat at the table.

Okay, so we were going to skip the small-talk portion of our conversation. I shifted into gear and launched right in. "The mayor called this afternoon. He's canceling the festival for now."

Meena sighed. "Well, I'm not surprised. Ever since I heard about Kirby, I've been expecting it."

"Me, too," I admitted. "They may be rescheduling later in the year. He asked if I'd be interested in chairing the committee."

She looked up quickly, and I could see the surprise in her eyes. Maybe a little disappointment, too. "Good choice. You'll do a great job."

"Thanks, but I haven't given him an answer yet. I asked for a few days to think about it."

"Well, it's a lot of work, but you know that." Meena stood abruptly and turned toward a long counter. "I was just about to make some tea. Would you like some?"

Despite pushing peppermint tea on my customers, I'm not a big tea lover. Give me coffee or a Pepsi anytime. But I didn't want to offend her. "That sounds great. Thanks."

I waited to go on while she filled a kettle with water and turned on the burner, selected tea bags, and put them carefully into china cups. When she had everything under control, I told her what I really wanted to know. "I asked Jeb for time to think because I don't want to put all the work into the festival you did and end up getting kicked out at the last minute. What he did was unfair to you, and I don't want to leave myself vulnerable to the same thing."

Meena's spine stiffened. "So you want to know what happened."

"Look, I know it's probably difficult to talk about, and I know you really don't want to tell me. I'd much rather see you chairing the committee next year than me, but if that's not an option, I need to feel reasonably sure history isn't going to repeat itself before I say yes."

Sighing heavily, Meena came back to the table. "It's not hard to talk about, I just didn't want everyone to know. I didn't want Jackie to find out before I was ready to tell her."

I couldn't hide my surprise. "This is about Jacqueline?"

"I'm afraid so. And you really don't have to worry about history repeating itself, since Felicity isn't around anymore."

"So it's about Jacqueline and Felicity."

"And Brenda." Meena's nerves got the best of her, and she got up again. "Mostly about Brenda. You know that Jackie and I have been friends for a while." She waited for my nod, then pulled a tray from a cupboard and settled the cups on it. "I've known Brenda since she was a teenager, and sometimes, when her mom is busy, she and I have talked. She's had a rough childhood, you know."

I nodded again. "She seems pretty well-adjusted, considering."

"I think she is, but there are things that bother her. It's tough on a girl that age knowing that her grandmother wants nothing to do with her. Having no idea where her father is . . ." Meena pulled spoons from a drawer and lined up a sugar bowl and honey in a crystal dish. "Somewhere along the way, I got the bright idea of helping her find her father. It was foolish, I know. Jacqueline hasn't ever forgiven him for leaving the way he did. But Brenda's not a child any longer, and not knowing Galen has left a huge hole in her life."

"So you helped Brenda look for him."

"Yes, but quietly. I planned to tell Jacqueline, but in my own time, in my own way. I had no idea if I'd find him, and I didn't want to upset her needlessly."

"Makes sense to me," I said. "But what does all of this have to do with the festival?"

Meena gave a thin laugh and leaned against the counter. "I didn't expect Brenda to confront Felicity, but she did."

"And Felicity was angry because she didn't want Jacqueline to know that she'd paid Galen's family to leave town?"

Meena's eyes grew round. "You know about that?"

"Yeah, but it doesn't make sense. Felicity didn't give a rip what Jacqueline and Brenda thought of her, so why would she care if they knew about that?"

"I don't think she did. She was hard as nails in every area of her life but one. I don't think she wanted Oliver to know what she was capable of."

I blurted a disbelieving laugh. "Are you saying she was afraid of losing him?"

Meena smiled gently. "Did you ever see them together?"

I shook my head. "Only from a distance. I never spent time around them as a couple."

"Well, she was a completely different woman when she was with him. She'd run off everyone else in her life, and I think Oliver became extremely important to her. He was all she had, and she would have done almost anything to keep him."

I couldn't reconcile that image of Felicity with the one in my own head. "So she was trying to keep him from finding out that she was cold and heartless."

"It makes sense if you really think about it. Why else would she have poured so much money into his restaurant?"

"Wait a minute," I said, holding up a hand to stop her. "What makes you think she was doing that?"

"My sister works at the bank."

"And she gave you that kind of information? That's illegal."

"If you ever tell anybody else, I'll deny it."

That was the least of my worries. I waved away her concerns. "What kind of money are we talking about?"

"Over two hundred thousand at last count."

I let out a soft whistle. "Are you sure about that?"

"As sure as I can be without seeing the checks myself. They're all made out to restaurant supply outfits or contractors."

"Oliver told me that they never got involved in each other's business concerns."

Meena looked at me as if I'd just asked if the tooth fairy would come that night. "Oliver is lying."

Apparently. "So Felicity found out that you were helping Brenda find her father, and she told the mayor to kick you off the committee? I don't get it. Why did he agree?"

"I'm sure she hammered at him until he couldn't take it anymore. By that time, she'd convinced him that my actions were evidence of a serious lack of judgment."

"And that's the excuse he gave you?"

She nodded, and a self-deprecating smile curled her lips. "What can I say? She brought my character into question, and Jeb caved. You know how he is. You can't really be surprised."

"Surprised, no. Disappointed. But if that's why he removed you, why didn't you just tell me that from the beginning? Jeb might have believed Felicity, but the rest of us can think for ourselves."

The kettle whistled. Meena poured hot water over the tea bags and carried the tray to the table. "I told you, I didn't want Jackie to know. She's a friend. A good friend. I didn't want to hurt her. I didn't want her to be angry with me. I understood why she felt the way she did, but I ached for Brenda, too. Jackie had to find out someday, but I didn't want her to hear it from somebody else first."

I could understand that, I guess. I might have done the same thing in her shoes. "Is Jacqueline okay with it now?"

"I think she'll get there eventually."

"I hope so," I said, and I was surprised to realize how much I meant it. I felt a pang of sympathy for Jacqueline and Brenda, and another wave of anger for Felicity. Life's tough enough without someone intentionally trying to make it worse. Maybe she genuinely thought she was doing the right thing by paying Galen and his family to disappear. Anything's possible, I guess. But it was hard for me to believe that she'd had anyone's interest at heart but her own.

Chapter 21

"You got lucky," Wyatt said as he led me through the second-floor construction site a couple of days later. Early morning sunlight spilled into the room through new windows, making everything look fresh and new. The missing wall had been reframed, Sheetrock covered most of the other walls, and someone had started patching at the far end of the room. "Charlie was able to save that outer wall after all."

I looked around slowly, taking in all the work they'd done and wondering when all the changes had come about. "Thank heaven for small favors. What about the wiring?"

"Toby's got a cousin who's a licensed electrician. He's gonna call in a favor or two, get the job done for nothing."

I glanced up at him in surprise. "Are you serious?"

"Do I look like I'm kidding?"

"Charlie and Toby are doing that for me?"

I must have shown a bit too much emotion, because Wyatt shrugged and looked away. "What can I say? They're a couple of soft touches."

I had the strangest urge to hug him, but I knew it would make us both uncomfortable. I stuffed my hands in my pockets and looked down at my shoe instead. "They're all right, you know?"

"Good guys."

"Yeah." I liked knowing that they had Wyatt's back—and, apparently, mine. "So how are things going at home? You and Elizabeth doing okay?"

Wyatt shrugged again. "So far, so good. We spend a fair amount of time trying not to do or say the wrong thing, but it could be worse. I could still be sleeping on that lumpy bed at the motel."

I grinned. "I hope Elizabeth doesn't know you only came home for the mattress."

"Not a chance. I've hidden my true agenda behind a lot of mushy talk and shit. She's completely fooled."

Funny, I didn't remember Wyatt having a sense of humor. Maybe I'd just missed it. "Well, I'm glad," I said with a laugh. "No sense gumming everything up with the truth."

"That's what I've been saying. I even let her think she's the boss half the time. Keeps her happy."

The sound of Visqueen rustling brought us both around just in time to see Jawarski fighting through the last layer of plastic. He stopped just inside and looked around the room, nodding approval as he saw the work the guys had done.

"Your boyfriend's here," Wyatt muttered under his breath. "Want me to leave you alone?"

"Yeah. Would ya? I want to roll around naked in the sawdust for a little while."

Chuckling, Wyatt turned back to his work. I picked my way across the floor, stepping over the nails, odd pieces of wood, and garbage. "What brings you here?" I said when I got closer to Jawarski.

"I came to eat a little crow. Thought you might appreciate watching."

"Oh?"

"Henri Guischard. You were right. There's no record of him anywhere until he came to Paradise."

I don't know what I expected, but the mix of disappointment and relief I felt surprised me. "Do you have any idea who he really is?"

"Not yet. I don't suppose you still have those fingerprints Karen was saving for me?"

"Yeah. We covered them with a piece of paper. I hope we didn't ruin them."

"There's only one way to find out. I'll send one of the guys over this afternoon to lift them."

I couldn't resist taking a jab at him. "Wow. Who could have guessed I'd be right?"

He rolled his eyes, and I laughed. I had to give Wyatt credit; he was doing a great job of pretending to be engrossed in his work.

"So, what now?" I asked. "How do you find out who Henri really is?"

"We'll talk to him. See if we can learn anything that way."

"And if not?"

"We'll move on to plan B."

"And what's plan B?"

"Can't tell you. It's classified information. On a need-to-know basis only."

"Yeah. You could tell me, but then you'd have to kill me, is that it?"

"You got it." He looked into my eyes and held my gaze for a long moment.

My breath caught, and everything inside turned to jelly. I could feel Wyatt watching us from the corner of his eye, but I didn't let myself look away first.

Right before he broke, the smile slid from Jawarski's eyes. "Seriously, Abby, I want you to be careful. I don't know if Henri's our guy or not, but he has some reason for pretending to be someone he's not, and he's not going to be happy that we've figured him out."

"I know."

"If he is the killer, he could come after someone else."

"Like the person who figured him out?"

Jawarski nodded. "We won't tell him we got the tip from you, but he may deduce it on his own. This is where it gets serious. You have to stay away from both murder cases from here on out."

"Absolutely." I meant it this time, and I could tell by the look in his eyes that Jawarski sensed that.

"I hate to encourage you," he said, "but you done good, kid. Just don't do it again, okay?"

"I'll try."

"That's it? You can't give me more than that?"

I tried to look sorry, but I probably failed miserably. "Not if you want the truth."

To my surprise, he pulled me into a brief hug that ended almost as quickly as it began. Before I had time to recover, he was working back through the Visqueen on his way out.

I glanced at Wyatt, who'd given up pretending not to listen. "You didn't see that."

"Relax, Sis. This one's a good guy."

"Yeah? How can you tell?"

"A man can always tell. We can tell a player the minute he walks into the room."

The same way one woman could size up another at a glance, I guess. "And you think Jawarski's on the up-and-up?"

"I'd say so."

I didn't say anything to that, but I agreed with him. Trouble was, I didn't know if that made me feel better . . . or worse.

Steak. One. Rib eye. One potato, a small container of sour cream, and a packaged Caesar salad from the deli section. One package rawhide bones, basted. One box bone-shaped dog biscuits. I took mental inventory of the items in my shopping cart, decided Max and I didn't need anything else to eat, and turned toward the cooler for a four-pack of wine coolers.

Like I said before, I don't like to cook, but I desperately wanted a quiet night in, and grilling a steak and baking a potato didn't require much effort on my part.

Now that the festival had been canceled, at least for the time being, I'd have to get the guild members to help me pack away the supplies and equipment we'd left at the staging area, but that could wait at least one night. I wasn't even sure I wanted to expend the energy necessary to read a good book. An hour or two of channel surfing might be my limit.

I spent a few minutes vacillating between the margarita coolers and fuzzy navels, finally forced myself to choose, and aimed my cart toward the checkout stands. I would have made it, too, if I hadn't noticed Jacqueline Asbury sitting at one of the tables in the store's deli section and if she hadn't looked up while I stood there trying to decide whether to say hello or not.

I couldn't very well pretend I hadn't seen her, so I wheeled my cart closer, and we spent a few minutes on that inane small talk people suffer through when they run into someone they don't really know. She observed that I was shopping. I asked if the doughnuts from the bakery were fresh. She said I'd probably have one happy dog when I got home. I tried to think of a good exit line until I realized I hadn't talked to her since Henri had mentioned seeing her at the festival staging area the day of Kirby's murder.

What the heck. We were in public, surrounded by people. What could she do to me here?

She'd already turned her attention to a powdered doughnut, fully expecting me to walk away.

I didn't. "Can I ask one question, Jacqueline? Why were you at the festival staging area the day Kirby was killed?"

The question caught her midbite. She looked up at me as if I'd lost my mind, and powdered sugar puffed into the air in front of her as she exhaled sharply. "What are you talking about?"

"The staging area in the town square. You were there the day Kirby was killed. Someone saw the two of you talking."

She grabbed a paper napkin from the dispenser on the table and tried to clean away the sugar that had landed everywhere. "Well, someone is mistaken. I wasn't anywhere near the town square the day Kirby North was killed, and I certainly wasn't talking to him. I barely knew the man."

"Can you prove that?"

"That I wasn't there? Yes, I can. And I will, if the police ask me about it." She wadded the napkin into a tight ball, dropped it on the table, and pulled out two more. "Who told you I was there?"

I shook my head and offered a tight smile. Instinct told me she was telling the truth, but I wasn't going to offer Henri up on a platter. I didn't want anyone saying anything to him that might make him decide to leave town before Jawarski had a chance to talk to him.

"Sorry. I can't say. If my information was wrong, I apologize. It's just that Kirby's death makes no sense. Why would someone want him dead? What connection, if any, did he have with your mother?"

"I'm sure *I* don't know."

"He was at your mother's house the night before she died. I saw him leaving as I arrived. Do you have any idea what he might have been doing there?"

Jacqueline turned a sympathetic smile on me. "Now, how would I know that? I'd hardly spoken to my mother in years before that night."

"That doesn't mean you didn't know a few things about her life. It's not as if you were living on opposite sides of the world." I hesitated for a moment, uncertain whether to ask my next question. But nothing ventured, nothing gained, right? "Do you think it's possible that Ursula was providing Kirby information about the construction at the MegaMart site?"

Jacqueline's unplucked brows disappeared beneath her bangs. "Ursula? Sure, I guess. Anything's possible."

"Do you think it's probable?"

Jacqueline swept the crumbs she'd dropped into the empty white bag. "Let's just say I wouldn't be surprised. There wasn't any love lost between my mother and her sister. But even if she was, what would that have to do with his death?"

"I'm still working on that part," I admitted. "One step at a time. Right now, I'm just trying to establish some connection between your mother and Kirby."

Jacqueline tossed the paper bag into the trash. "Maybe Kirby was getting information from Aunt Ursula, but my mother was already dead by the time he was killed. And I seriously doubt anyone would have murdered him over that information. Besides, Aunt Ursula would have been the one to betray the company."

She had a point. But then why *was* Kirby killed? He must have seen or heard something that could incriminate somebody, but how would we ever know for sure?

Chapter 22

It took an entire evening flicking between reality TV shows and *CSI* reruns to argue myself into calling Oliver Birch to warn him. On the one hand, I'd promised Jawarski that I'd stay out of the case from now on. On the other, Oliver could be in danger. By morning, I'd decided the decision was a no-brainer. I just hoped Jawarski would see it that way.

About thirty minutes before I needed to open the store, I went downstairs and put on a pot of coffee. When it had brewed, I carried a cup into the office and dialed the number for the Drake Mansion.

The phone rang several times before someone answered, and I was relieved to hear a deep voice on the other end saying, "Oliver Birch."

"Oliver, it's Abby Shaw. Do you have a minute?"

"I wish I did. I'm just running out the door for a meeting."

"It's important, Oliver. It will just take a few moments."

I could hear impatient footsteps through the telephone.

"I'm really sorry, but I'm already late. Can I call you later?"

"It's about Henri," I said. "I've learned something about him, and you need to know."

A lengthy pause filled the air before Oliver said, "All right. I'll be at the restaurant in an hour. Meet me there. If I'm late, wait for me. I'll do my best to cut this meeting short, but I may not be able to get away as quickly as I'd like."

"What about Henri? I don't want to have this conversation with him around."

"He won't be," Oliver promised. "He's going in to Denver today to check out a produce supplier. He should be gone all day."

Good news for me, bad news for Jawarski—and all the more reason for me to tell Oliver what I knew, since Jawarski wouldn't be able to question Henri right away. "I'll be there," I promised.

"Be where?" Karen asked as I hung up.

I turned to find her standing in the office doorway, a deep frown dragging at the corners of her mouth. "Oliver's restaurant. I need to tell him about Henri."

"Why?"

"Because I don't feel right leaving him in the dark, especially since I'm pretty sure Henri has already tried to kill him once."

Karen came into the office and sat across from me. "There's something that doesn't feel right about that. What reason would Henri have for killing *anybody*?"

Trust Karen to mess up a perfectly good theory with logic. "I don't know. But he's not who he claims to be, we know that for sure."

"That doesn't make him a murderer."

"I don't plan to accuse him of being one. I just want to make sure Oliver knows that Henri's been lying to him."

Karen threw her hands into the air in frustration. "Okay. Fine. So Oliver needs to know. But why not let Jawarski take care of that? Isn't protecting and serving what he gets paid to do?"

"It's no big deal," I insisted. "I'm just going to warn him, that's all. I'll be there five minutes at the most. But I won't be able to live with myself if I don't tell him what's going on, and then something happens to him."

Karen got that look on her face I swear only mothers can pull off. "Don't do it."

"It'll be fine. Henri isn't even in town today. He's going to Denver to check out a supplier. And I won't go alone. I'll take Max with me. Will that make you stop worrying?"

That seemed to mollify her somewhat, but she still looked skeptical. "No, but it's better than nothing." She moved away from the door to let me out, but she trailed behind me, scolding like a mother hen. "You really should take Wyatt. That would be even safer."

"Wyatt's teeth aren't as sharp as Max's."

"I'm serious, Abby." She hurried to get in front of me. "I don't like this at all. I have a bad feeling about it."

Her concern touched me, but I was more worried about Oliver. "It'll be fine," I said again. "At the very least, Oliver deserves to know that he's been lied to. If Henri is dangerous, Oliver deserves a chance to protect himself. Now please, stop fussing. I wouldn't go if Henri was anywhere around, but he's not, and I'll be all right—okay?"

"You'd better be. If you're not back here in half an hour, I'm calling the police."

"Make it forty-five minutes," I said, "in case Oliver's running late."

He was waiting for me when I got there, and to my surprise he was alone. Completely alone. The construction crews that had been swarming all over the property last time I was there were conspicuously absent, and Oliver's voice as he greeted me echoed through the cavernous space.

He scratched Max's head and smiled at me. "You can tie him out back if you want to. There's a little grass and some trees. I'm sure the dog would like that better than being in here with all this mess."

Max spends so little time outside, I decided to take advantage of the offer. I secured him outside, made sure his collar was tight enough to keep him from slipping out of it, but loose enough to allow for escape in an emergency. Then I went back inside and walked from room to room, looking for Oliver. I finally found him in what looked like it would eventually become the kitchen.

Oliver stared out the window, eyes straight ahead, obviously lost in thought. I wondered if he was thinking about Felicity. If he missed her. Or was he as glad to see her gone as everyone else seemed to be?

He turned when he heard my footsteps and offered a sheepish smile. "Sorry. I do that sometimes—stand here and look outside, imagining what this place will be like in another few months." He shrugged, obviously embarrassed at having been observed. "Now, what is this about Henri?"

"He's not who he claims to be."

Oliver shook his head in confusion. "What do you mean?"

"I mean he's been lying to you. I don't know who he *is*, but he's not Henri Guischard."

"You must be mistaken. I had him checked out."

"I don't know who did the background check, but the police have run one, and they can't find him. He's an imposter, and I have reason to think he may have tried to hurt you."

"Me? How?"

"The night your brakes went out. The mechanic verified that someone tampered with them. I think it may have been Henri." Yeah, I know, I'd promised Karen. But *technically*, I'd kept that promise. I hadn't said one word about murder.

Oliver looked shaky. "Henri? But why?"

"I don't know yet."

Oliver's head drooped. He kneaded his forehead with one hand and shook his head repeatedly as he tried to process what I'd told him. "Are you saying that you also think he killed Felicity?"

"It's possible. And Kirby North, as well."

"But that's—"

I heard Max growl a split second before a different voice sounded in my ear, low and ominous. "That's brilliant, Abby. *Brava*."

I turned quickly and found myself looking into the hard eyes of Henri Guischard—or whatever his name was. The first thought that went through my head was, *Run*! The next was that Karen would kill me for this. I pulled back slightly and caught sight of something black and bulky in his hand.

He saw where I was looking and lifted the handgun so I could get a better look. "Don't be stupid."

Great advice. I wish I'd paid attention earlier when I heard it from Karen. My throat grew tight and dry, my hands clammy. Since my body blocked Oliver's view of Henri, I forced myself to say something. "Get out of here, Oliver. Now!"

He didn't move. I shot a glance over my shoulder, hoping I could convince him that the situation was desperate before it was too late. Oliver stood frozen in place. Facing your wife's killer would probably do that to a person.

"Oliver," I said, my voice harsh. "He's got a gun. Get out of here."

He looked at me then, and I realized my mistake.

"If you don't mind," he said with a slow smile, "I think I'll stay." His gaze shifted to Henri. "Did you take care of everything?"

"Thanks to the magic of the Internet. Now don't just stand there, tie her hands and feet, and for God's sake, put something in her mouth."

My mind grew sluggish, and it seemed to take forever to process each thought. They knew each other. They were in this together. "You killed Felicity," I said, but my voice sounded thick and rough.

Henri flashed a toothy grin. "A mind like a steel trap, that's what you've got."

Oliver came up behind me and jerked my hands together behind my back. Pain shot through my shoulder, and my wrists burned as he lashed them together tightly.

I bit my lip to distract me from the pain. "Why did you do it? For the money?"

"Her *mouth*," Henri snapped before Oliver could answer. "Where's the damned tape?"

I had two choices: shut up or keep talking. I had to trust my instincts on this one, and they were screaming at me that turning quiet and passive wouldn't save me. "And what about Kirby?" I demanded. "Why did you kill him?"

Henri lunged toward me and held the barrel of the gun beneath my chin. "You really want to know? Okay then. He saw something he shouldn't have seen, and he decided to talk about it. He just chose the wrong person to talk to. Now you've seen what happens to people who can't keep their mouths shut. Maybe you'll shut yours."

How could I have been so slow? How could I *not* have seen the connection between these two? It seemed so obvious now, but I guess everything's easier to spot when there's a gun pointing at your head.

"You killed Felicity for the money?"

"Shut up."

I looked beyond Henri to Oliver. "What about your accident? Did you cut your own brakes?"

He smiled, and my heart grew cold. "I was particularly proud of that touch. It threw everybody off track, didn't it?" He dug around in a box and came up with a rag and a roll of duct tape.

I tried to judge my chances of escape if I made a run for

it, but both men stood between me and freedom. I'd prob-ably never make it, but I had to try. Counting on the ele-ment of surprise to give me some small advantage, I watched Henri slide his gaze from me to the roll of tape in Oliver's hand, then I bolted for the door. I'd heard enough advice over the years to know that going quietly wasn't an option, so I screamed for help as I ran. Most stores on the block weren't open yet, but people would be arriving for work, and the bakery was open. I had to believe that some-one would hear me.

Heavy footsteps pounded on the wooden floor behind me, and before I could get even halfway to the door, one of the men circled my waist with his arm. He pulled me off my feet and clamped a hand over my mouth.

I kicked furiously, trying to inflict enough pain to make him loosen his grip, even for a moment. Over the years, I'd taken a few classes on self-defense for women, but I hadn't practiced what I'd learned enough to remember what I was supposed to do.

While Henri held me, Oliver stuffed the rag into my mouth and covered it with duct tape. I gagged, wondering oddly whether the rag was clean and wishing I'd have the chance to tell Karen that she'd been right.

Think! I told myself sternly. I could grow maudlin later. There had to be some way out of this, I just had to figure out what it was.

Satisfied that I wouldn't be making any more noise, Oliver forced me to sit on the floor, then bound my feet with a length of rope so thick I knew I'd never be able to saw through it—assuming I could get away and find a sharp object to use on it.

Unable to move my hands or feet, I felt panic setting in. My breath came faster and grew more shallow, my lungs felt pinched and tight, and with the tape over my mouth, I grew frightened that I wouldn't be able to get enough air into my lungs to keep me alive.

While Oliver disappeared into another section of the restaurant, Henri hunkered down in front of me. "I have to admit, you're one smart cookie. We've never been caught before. Almost, but not quite." He shook his head and grinned. "Too bad you weren't smart enough to know when to back the hell off, huh?"

He laughed softly and stood again. "You want to know the whole story, don't you? Every sordid detail. But I think some things are best left to the imagination. Besides, you won't be alive long enough to share the story with anyone else, so why bother?"

I tried to console myself with the thought that if they wanted to shoot me, they would have done it already. I managed to hang on to that thought for almost two solid minutes, but when Oliver came back into the room carrying two five-gallon cans of gasoline, I knew I couldn't have been more wrong.

They weren't going to shoot me. They had something far worse in mind.

Chapter 23

The sharp scent of sawdust mixed with gasoline sent me into a panic again as I watched Oliver sprinkle the accelerant across the dry, exposed wood all around me. I tried to fight the heightened sense of terror, but I couldn't move, couldn't shout, couldn't do a thing to save myself. I'd never felt so helpless, and somewhere beneath my fear, I raged at the feeling of powerlessness.

I could hear Henri and Oliver talking. They kept their voices low, but if I could control my breathing and stop the screaming inside my head, I might be able to hear them. I could see them—at least the backs of their heads and their shoulders, as they worked at something on the ground. I couldn't see what they were doing, but I knew I had very little time left to find a way to save myself.

"You took care of the last wire transfer?" Henri asked.

"I told you, yes. Everything's done. The supply companies we set up have disappeared. Their accounts have been closed. This isn't my first time, you know." Oliver sounded irritated, and strangely enough, that lifted my spirits a little.

"What the hell's wrong with you?" Henri snapped.

Oliver shot a glance at me over his shoulder. "I don't like this. It's not right."

"You want to leave her alive so she can blow the whistle on us?" Henri reached across the space between them and smacked Oliver behind the head. "You're too involved. *Again.* One of these days that damn bleeding heart of yours is going to get *us* killed."

Oliver knocked Henri's hand away and pulled back sharply. "Do that again, and you'll lose that hand."

Laughing, Henri got to his feet. "What about that mutt of hers?"

"I'm *not* killing the dog. Leave him chained up out back. I tightened his collar. He won't be able to get away."

Henri's smile evaporated, and his face contorted with anger. "You're such a fucking wimp. I swear to God, you're getting softer all the time."

"Think whatever you want, I'm not killing the dog."

On one level, I was grateful that Max would escape this alive. On another, it seemed odd to me that Oliver would morally object to hurting Max, but I rated little more than a token objection. I looked at my immediate surroundings, hoping I'd find something the construction crew had forgotten—something I could use to cut the ropes that held me. It might take a while, but at least it would give me a chance at survival. But Henri and Oliver had been thorough. They'd cleaned the area around me so that only the bare concrete floor and walls roughed in with Sheetrock remained.

My mind screamed at me to *do* something. I couldn't die like this. But if there was a way out, I couldn't find it. The only hope I had was for Karen to decide I'd been gone too long and call for help. I prayed silently that she'd do exactly that, but the minutes ticked past, each second feeling like an hour, so that I lost track of time and had no idea whether I'd been tied up for two minutes or two hours.

Oliver finished whatever he was doing and turned around, holding a bottle of water. "If you insist on doing this, get the pills."

The pills? A protest tumbled out of my mouth automatically, but the duct tape muffled it so that I managed only a few audible grunts.

Henri crossed the room and tore the tape from my mouth. Pressing the gun against my temple, he removed the handkerchief and grinned down at me as if he were having the time of his life. "Don't look so worried. It's just a little sleep aid. Something to help you get through the fire."

I couldn't let him force those pills on me. I met his gaze steadily. "I'm not taking them."

"Sure you are." He grabbed my face and squeezed my cheeks until my face burned. I pulled back sharply, but I was no match for his strength. He forced my mouth open and dropped a couple of pills inside.

Gagging, I tried to force them out of my mouth with my tongue, but Oliver uncapped the bottle of water and poured it into my mouth before I could. I combated the urge to swallow for as long as I could, but again I was no match for the two men. Henri held my face still until the sheer volume of water forced me to swallow.

I couldn't swallow all of the water; there was too much of it. Choking, I gasped for air, and felt my lungs burn where I had inhaled liquid. Filled with a sudden, intense hatred, I tried to expel the water, but I couldn't do anything but cough and sputter harmlessly.

Henri watched me, keeping the gun to my head the whole time, while Oliver loaded boxes into a vehicle in the back. "So how did he convince Felicity to leave all her money to him?" I asked after several minutes.

Henri grinned. "It wasn't as difficult as you might imagine. Owen's good at what he does."

Owen, not Oliver. The whole thing had been a scam two

years in the making. "Felicity wasn't stupid," I said. "She must have figured out what you were doing."

"Not entirely, but she came close. She found out that the companies she'd been writing checks to were phony, and she confronted Owen about it. Told him it had to stop, but we hadn't skimmed off anywhere near what we wanted at that point. Unfortunately for her, I was right there to offer comfort in her time of distress."

"And that's when you decided to kill her."

He lifted his arms in a gesture of helplessness. "What else could we do? She was a vindictive bitch. Do you know she actually asked me to help her get rid of her husband?"

"She wanted you to kill him?" There was irony in that. I just hoped I lived long enough to appreciate it. "So instead, you killed Felicity. But why did you choose my parking lot for the murder?"

He gave me a look filled with malice. "It was her suggestion, actually. It's that simple. I called her that night, pretending that I was all set to kill her poor, unsuspecting husband. She suggested meeting at your place. Who was I to say no?"

"So *you* made the phone call?"

"You got it."

And Felicity had lied to Ursula about the caller being a woman. "And this is what you do? How you make your living? The two of you travel around living off women until you finally kill them?"

Henri's smile slipped. "The bitch wouldn't have had to die if she hadn't started checking up on the books. She could have left well enough alone, trusted her husband, and we'd have disappeared once the money was ours. It's not *that* hard to vanish when you know what you're doing. Trust me, nobody would have found us."

He was probably right. And they probably wouldn't find them after I was gone, either. I had the answers to some of my questions now, but they wouldn't do me any good if I couldn't get away.

While I was still debating my options, I heard a sound like the song of angels: Karen's voice shouting, "Abby? Are you in here?"

Without moving the gun from my head, Henri shot to his feet and stuffed the handkerchief into my mouth before I could react. The cloth had picked up a coating of sawdust as it lay there, and I retched at the feel of it in my throat.

Oliver appeared in the doorway. I couldn't see Karen from where I sat, but I could see Oliver's smooth face and unruffled expression. "You're looking for Abby?"

"Is she here?"

"She was. She left about fifteen minutes ago."

"Are you sure? I thought she'd be back by now." I could hear the distrust in her voice, but Henri's eyes had taken on a hunted animal look, and I didn't know whether to hope Karen would find me or pray she didn't.

"I'm sure. She had the dog with her. Maybe she decided to take him for a walk."

"Maybe." Karen's voice sounded closer now.

Look in the back, I pleaded silently. *Max is back there. Don't believe him.* I tried to spit out the handkerchief, but Henri had forced my mouth open too wide. I couldn't do anything but push harmlessly at it with my tongue when I wasn't gagging.

Oliver moved toward her stealthily, his face still a mask of culture and breeding, his voice smooth as melted chocolate. "Did she tell you why she came to see me?"

"About Henri? Yes."

The room swam in front of my eyes, and I realized the pills they'd fed me were taking effect. *Run, Karen! Get out of here while you can!* I closed my eyes, frustrated by the futility of it all, and a groan rolled around in the back of my throat.

"I don't mind telling you, I was shocked." Oliver disappeared from view, but I heard footsteps moving away from me, and I breathed a little easier. "You don't know how much I appreciate the warning. I hope the police find him soon."

"I'm sure they will. And if Abby comes back here, will you tell her to call me? I'm worried sick."

"I can only imagine. Yes, I'll tell her, but try not to worry. Henri isn't anywhere around here today. I'm sure she's just fine."

My hands and arms tingled, my feet were already numb. Was it because of the pills or merely the lack of circulation? My head was growing heavy, and my eyes refused to stay open. Karen's voice faded, and Henri's face floated in and out.

I could hear voices now, both male, but I could no longer make out what they were saying. The last thing I saw was the gleam in Henri's eyes as he lit the match that would end my life.

I woke to the smell of smoke and the crackle of burning wood. Something wet swept across my face, and I could hear a high-pitched sound pulsing near my ear. My lungs ached, and I lurched upright, coughing so hard the muscles in my stomach cramped. It took me a few seconds to realize that my hands were no longer tied. I guess Oliver and Henri thought it would look suspicious if my body was found with my hands and mouth bound—thank God. A moment later, I realized that the moisture on my face came from a dog's tongue. The high-pitched sound, Max's whine as he tried to wake me from my drugged sleep.

My wrists stung where the ropes had been, but I reached for Max, pulling his massive head into a quick embrace as I registered that the building around me was fully engulfed in flame. Considering how much gasoline they'd used, it wouldn't take long for the whole building to burn.

"Come on, Max," I said, but my throat was already so

raw from breathing in the smoke, it came out hoarse and barely audible.

Glancing around quickly, I tried to get my bearings. Which way was the back door? Which way to the front? Every angle looked the same to me. Drugs fogged my brain, but I was alert enough to remember that I needed to stay low to the ground. On all fours, I picked a direction and started crawling.

Flames scorched my face. The heat was excruciating. Max followed me for a foot or two, then lunged off in another direction. He stopped and looked back at me, his eyes pleading with me to follow.

Who was I to argue?

Splinters dug into my hands as I crawled. Ash and sparks flew into my face and landed on my back and hair. The heat grew more oppressive as we moved, inch by inch, through a wall of flames that threatened to engulf us at any moment.

I placed my faith in Max and added a quick and silent prayer for a little help from above. Smoke pressed down on me, too heavy to breathe, too dense to see through. I lost sight of Max once, but he quickly realized that I wasn't with him, and he came back to find me.

He pulled on my shirt, tugging me with his teeth toward whatever exit he sensed. My strength was gone, but I tried to drag up enough to help propel myself.

Overhead, boards crackled, and something crashed to the ground behind us. It hit, and flames roared to life, higher, hotter, and stronger than they'd been before. The second floor was giving way, I realized. We probably had only a few seconds to escape before we were trapped beneath it.

Once or twice, I thought I heard voices. I had no idea how long I'd been out, but surely people had seen the fire. There had to be help outside.

My lungs ached from the effort of breathing. My arms

and legs shook from the effort of holding myself up. I urged myself forward, one step at a time, but I didn't know how much longer I could go on. My head buzzed, and I could feel myself on the edge of consciousness from the lack of oxygen.

Max led me around a smoldering, blackened pile of wood, and suddenly I saw daylight. Almost weeping with relief, I plunged ahead and finally pushed out into the fresh air. I saw faces over me just before I blacked out, but I was too far gone to know whose faces they were. Greedily, I sucked air into my lungs, but the air burned as it went in, and I buckled over, coughing and choking as I let it out again.

And then it was over. Blackness fell, and I finally felt the blessed relief from pain.

Chapter 24

"I'd kill for a breeze," Karen mumbled, just loud enough for me to hear over the constant rumble of conversation and music all around us. Red-faced from the mid-July heat, she leaned against the plastic display case that held mounds of peppermint Ant Sticks, fudge, fondant, and petits fours.

A generator-operated cooler blew a weak supply of refrigerated air into the display case, doing its best to keep the chocolate from melting. Unfortunately, Karen and I didn't get the same consideration.

In each corner of the sweltering booth, small artificial Christmas trees sparkled with clear lights and peppermint candy decorations. Temporary shelving held displays of candy made from Aunt Grace's recipes and, dotted here and there among the displays, painted baskets held bouquets of massive red and white striped lollipops, each one tied with a festive green bow.

I picked up a large black teddy bear that had toppled from his position, adjusted the bow around his neck, and lodged him against an open trunk spilling over with boxes we'd filled with homemade peppermint sticks and wrapped with holiday paper and bows.

Bing Crosby crooned "Please have snow and mistletoe" from the CD player behind me, but the sun beat relentlessly on the canvas booth. Even minor exertion put beads of perspiration on my forehead, so I created my own breeze by waving a mistletoe-and-wreath-adorned price list in front of my face. My cousin and I might both be miserable in the summer heat, but Karen's idea for a Christmas booth had turned out even better than I'd expected, and business had been brisk all day.

"The sun will go down in a couple of hours," I said, trying to sound optimistic. "Just hang on until then."

Karen looked skeptical, but her mood shifted abruptly when a group of women veered out of foot traffic and swarmed into the booth, exclaiming with delight over the Christmas decorations. It did my heart good to see her idea getting such an enthusiastic reception. After all, I owed her my life. If not for her, I might have died in that fire, and Oliver and Henri would probably have escaped.

I strolled toward the front of the booth and dug a wad of dollar bills from my pocket. "You haven't had a break in a while," I told Karen. "Why don't you go now? If you don't mind, bring something cold to drink when you come back."

She grinned and held out her hand for the money. "You've got yourself a deal. Any preferences?"

I shook my head. "Just something that will stay cold for a few minutes."

She wandered off, and I turned back to see if my customers had questions. We'd managed to hold the shop together for the past few months, thanks mostly to a cash infusion provided by Wyatt and Elizabeth. I'd protested for a few days, but with the festival postponed and a kitchen full of peppermint, I'd been between a rock and a hard place. Eventually, I'd caved, and I had to admit my brother and his wife had saved us.

As I turned, a woman with long, dark hair looking through the watercolor prints at the next booth caught my attention. I hadn't seen Brenda since I talked to her before the fire two months earlier, but I'd thought about her a few times and wondered how she was doing.

She stopped looking at the prints and glanced up and around, as if she could feel someone watching her. When she saw me, she offered a shy smile and strolled over. "Hey, Abby. I've been meaning to stop by and see you."

"Really? Any special reason?"

She looked out over the milling crowd as if she was having trouble making eye contact. "I heard you were hurt in the fire at Oliver's restaurant. Are you doing okay now?"

"I had a couple of bruised ribs," I said. "I had to stay in the hospital for a few days because of smoke inhalation, but I'm fine now."

She turned her head slowly and looked at me. "I heard you're testifying at the trials? Is that true?"

Within a few days of their arrest, police had identified Oliver and Henri as Owen and Ethan Nye, brothers who'd made careers out of executing elaborate scams with wealthy women as their targets. To the best of our knowledge, Felicity and Kirby were the only actual murders they'd committed, but I had a feeling the authorities had just begun to uncover the whole story.

Two months later, I still had nightmares about being trapped in that fire, and each one made me angrier than the one before it. At this point, it would take some earthshaking event to keep me from testifying.

"Yeah," I said, "but it will be a while before that happens. I'm sure the attorneys will drag out the pretrial stage as long as they possibly can."

"As long as they put the two of them away for the rest

of their lives, I don't care how long it takes." Brenda fell silent and watched the passing throngs for another few minutes. I kept one eye on the customers drifting in and out of the booth, but I could tell that Brenda wasn't finished yet, so I waited for her to go on.

"I've tried to keep up with all the news," she said after a minute or two, "but I haven't heard if they found out why that sculptor was killed."

"Kirby?" A wave of sadness surprised me when I thought about him. Maybe because his had been such a senseless murder. Or maybe because thinking about him made me realize how close I'd come to being number three. "As far as the police can tell at this point, Kirby was getting inside information about the MegaMart project from Ursula. While he was at your grandmother's house talking to Ursula, he overheard Felicity talking to Henri about killing Oliver and made the mistake of taking that information to Oliver instead of going to the police."

Brenda shivered and stepped aside to let a couple of teenage girls into the booth. "I suppose you've heard the other news."

"I heard about the money, if that's what you mean." Thanks to the intricacies of the legal system and the complexity of old Andrew Drake's will, everything had reverted to Ursula, after all.

"Yeah," Brenda said. "I think she'll do okay."

Too many people were already speculating that Ursula would lose what was left, as she'd done with her own inheritance. I wasn't so sure, and Brenda looked so hopeful, I couldn't do anything but agree with her. "I'm sure she will."

"And did you hear that Ursula hired my mom?"

"Really?" That was news to me. "What will she be doing?"

"Working at Drake Development. Ursula tried to get out of the MegaMart deal, but she can't without incurring a major lawsuit, so she and Mom are trying to figure how to minimize the impact MegaMart will have on the town."

If they could do that, they just might turn the tide of public sentiment against the Drake-Asbury clan. "What about you?" I asked. "Are you working for Drake, too?"

She shook her head. "Not yet. But Ursula offered me a job, and I might take it when I get back."

"You're going somewhere?"

Her smile returned, and her gaze fluttered to her hands. "Yeah, I'm going to Oregon for a month to spend some time with my dad."

"That's great! But how does your mom feel? Is she okay with you going?"

"She doesn't like it," Brenda said with a shrug, "but she's adjusting to the idea. I guess I can't really ask for more than that."

"It sounds promising," I told her. "And your mom has had a lot to deal with. After all, she spent most of her life thinking your dad abandoned her when she needed him most. It must be hard to shift gears all of a sudden."

Brenda slid a glance at me. "I know. Sometimes I worry, you know? I wonder if Felicity's nastiness is genetic."

She looked so young and vulnerable, I gave in to instinct and squeezed her shoulders briefly. "It's not genetic," I assured her. "I don't know what happened in Felicity's life to harden her heart so completely, but I'm pretty sure she wasn't born that way. You don't *have* to be like her."

Brenda's lips curved into a hopeful smile. "Promise?"

I laughed and released her before either of us could start to feel uncomfortable. "Absolutely. It's all about choices, you know. Besides, if you were like Felicity, you wouldn't be willing to give Ursula a second chance, and you wouldn't have spent the past year or so trying to find your father."

"Yeah, I guess." She slipped her hands into her pockets and rocked up onto her toes. "I'm a little nervous."

"That's understandable," I said. "I would be, too, but even if things don't work out the way you'd like them to, you'll be glad you went ahead with this."

"I guess you're right. He seems nice enough, and he's told his wife and kids about Mom and me, so it'll probably be okay."

"I'm sure it will be," I said, smiling encouragement. "Just try not to be disappointed if this meeting doesn't match up to your expectations. He's your dad, not some kind of superhero. He's going to make mistakes, and he's going to occasionally say the wrong thing, and he's going to make you crazy. It's all part of being human. That doesn't mean he doesn't love you."

Brenda laughed and settled back on her heels. A few feet away, the crowd parted, and I saw Jawarski coming toward me holding a paper cone filled with crushed ice. We'd been so busy with last-minute festival preparations, this was the first time I'd seen him since his kids went home to their mother, and the sudden drumming of my heart drowned out whatever Brenda said next.

He looked good enough to eat in a pair of tight jeans, a crisp white shirt, and a cowboy hat. With a nod at Brenda, he stopped in front of me and offered the cone. "It's hotter than hell today. Thought maybe you could use this."

The advice I'd just given Brenda echoed in my ears, and I felt the brittle pieces of my heart soften. I couldn't keep shutting myself off from Jawarski just because I was afraid of the future. Oh sure, he might occasionally disappoint me or make a mistake. There would inevitably be times when he would hurt me or make me angry. He was only human, after all. But he was honest and reliable, and I knew that every once in a while he'd do something truly heroic, like bringing ice chips on a hellishly hot day. What woman in her right mind would ask for anything more?

Candy Recipes

Chocolate Ant Sticks

Makes 24 pieces

> 12 ounces chocolate chips or white chocolate chips
> 24 (8-inch size) pretzel rods
> chocolate or colored sprinkles, crushed candy, or nuts

In a heat-proof bowl, melt the chocolate over a pot of simmering water or in a double boiler. Dunk the pretzel rods halfway into the chocolate.

Immediately roll chocolate-coated pretzel rods in sprinkles, candy, or nuts.

Transfer to a waxed paper–lined sheet pan, and allow to cool until hardened.

Almond Roca

Serves 10

   1 *cup granulated white sugar*
   ¼ *cup water*
   1 *tablespoon light corn syrup*
   ½ *pound butter (do not use margarine)*
   2½ *pounds almonds, blanched & slivered*
   1½ *cups milk chocolate chips*

In a heavy skillet combine sugar, water, syrup, butter and almonds. Stirring constantly, cook to hard crack stage, or until the almonds are toasted a light brown.

Pour into a greased baking pan. While still warm, sprinkle the milk chocolate chips over the mixture and spread when softened.

Let cool. Remove from pan and break into pieces.

Peppermint Fondant

Number of candies varies, depending on size

> 5 tablespoons butter (not *margarine*)
> food colors
> 1 teaspoon peppermint (or spearmint, if desired)
> 1 pound powdered sugar
> 2 tablespoons cold water

Melt the butter over a low heat. Add coloring and flavoring. Stir in powdered sugar and water.

Knead in the pan (or in a dish). Roll out in balls by hand and press with a fork or meat tenderizer. (Should be rolled out quite small, like a party mint.)

Place on waxed paper or cake rack for several hours to dry.

Peppermint Petits Fours

Makes 16 pieces

1   pack frozen pound cake
⅓   cup strawberry preserves
3   cups granulated sugar
1½   cups hot water
1   teaspoon cream of tartar
1¼   cups powdered sugar
½   teaspoon peppermint extract
2   drops red food coloring

OPTIONAL
    crushed peppermint candies
    colored sugar
    fresh strawberry slices

Trim the crusts from the pound cake and cut the cake lengthwise into 4 layers. Spread 1 layer with half the preserves.

Top with second layer of cake and repeat to make 2 double layers.

Cut each layer into eight 2" squares (16 squares total). Set aside.

Combine granulated sugar, water, and cream of tartar in 3-quart casserole. Microwave on high for 5 to 7 minutes, or until the mixture boils.

Stir, and insert a microwave candy thermometer.

Microwave at high for 7 to 11 minutes, or until the mixture reaches 226°F.

Let cool on counter for an hour (slightly longer if necessary) or until the mixture is cooled to 110°F.

Add powdered sugar, peppermint extract, and food coloring. Beat on medium speed of an electric mixer until smooth. Use 2 forks to dip each layered pound cake square into the frosting, making sure to coat all sides. Let excess frosting drip off, then place on a wire rack over waxed paper.

Repeat, dipping each square twice. Decorate with crushed peppermint or other candies, colored sugar, or strawberry slices.

Let stand until set.